SAVAGERY OF THE
MOUNTAIN MAN

SAVAGERY OF THE MOUNTAIN MAN

William W. Johnstone
with J. A. Johnstone

PINNACLE BOOKS
Kensington Publishing Corp.
www.kensingtonbooks.com

PINNACLE BOOKS are published by

Kensington Publishing Corp.
119 West 40th Street
New York, NY 10018

PUBLISHER'S NOTE
Following the death of William W. Johnstone, the Johnstone family
is working with a carefully selected writer to organize and complete
Mr. Johnstone's outlines and many unfinished manuscripts to create addi-
tional novels in all of his series like The Last Gunfighter, Mountain Man,
and Eagles, among others. This novel was inspired by Mr. Johnstone's
superb storytelling.

All Kensington titles, imprints, and distributed lines are available at
special quantity discounts for bulk purchases for sales promotions,
premiums, fund-raising, educational, or institutional use. Special book
excerpts or customized printings can also be created to fit specific needs.
For details, write or phone the office of the Kensington special sales
manager: Kensington Publishing Corp., 119 West 40th Street, New York,
NY 10018, attn: Special Sales Department; phone: 1-800-221-2647.

PINNACLE BOOKS and the Pinnacle logo are Reg. U.S. Pat. & TM Off.

ISBN-13: 978-0-7860-1740-9
ISBN-10: 0-7860-1740-6

First printing: December 2009

10 9 8 7 6 5 4 3

Printed in the United States of America

Prologue[*]

"No!" Lucy shouted. She jumped in front of Pearlie just as Keno fired, and the bullet struck her in the chest.

"No!" Pearlie screamed, the guttural shout a cross between an anguished cry and a roar of rage.

Pearlie's first shot hit Keno in the arm, causing him to drop his gun. Then Pearlie shot Keno in both knees. Keno went down, screaming in agony.

Pearlie shot off each of his ears, then pointed the pistol at Keno's face and fired, putting a hole right between Keno's eyes. Pearlie pulled the trigger three more times, but the hammer fell on empty cartridges.

It didn't matter.

Keno was dead.

Pearlie spun around then, and dropped to the ground beside Lucy. With each breath Lucy drew, blood frothed at her mouth. The bullet had hit her in the lungs and she was dying right before Pearlie's eyes.

* From *Violence of the Mountain Man*

"Lucy, Lucy, why did you jump out like that?" Pearlie asked.

"He would have killed you," Lucy said. "I couldn't let him kill you."

"Lucy, oh, my God, Lucy," Pearlie said. Sitting on the ground beside her, he cradled her head in his lap.

"I only wish that we could have been married," Lucy said.

"You can be," Sally said. "Smoke, you are a justice of the peace. You can marry them."

"Sally, what are you talking about? I've never performed a wedding ceremony. Why, I don't have a Bible, I don't have a book. I wouldn't know what to do," Smoke said.

"For God's sake, Smoke, this has to be done, just do it!" Sally said, cutting him off in mid-sentence. "You've been married twice now. You know what to say."

"Lucy?" Smoke said. "Do you want me to do this?"

"Yes, please," Lucy said, taking Pearlie's hand in hers and squeezing it hard. "Please marry us."

"All right," Smoke said. "Pearlie, do you take this woman, Lucy, to be your lawfully wedded wife, to love, hold, and honor, as long—" Smoke paused in mid-sentence, and when he spoke again, his voice broke. "As long as you both shall live?"

"I do," Pearlie said.

"Lucy, do you take Pearlie to be your lawfully wedded husband, to love, obey, and honor, as long as you both shall live?"

"I do," Lucy replied, her voice so weak that she could barely be heard.

"By the power vested in me by the state of Colorado, I pronounce you man and wife."

"We are married," Lucy said. She smiled through her pain. "Pearlie, you are my husband."

"Yes," Pearlie said. "And you are my wife."

"Kiss me, Pearlie. Kiss me quickly."

"Lucy?" Pearlie asked, his voice breaking.

"Kiss her, Pearlie," Sally said. "Kiss her before it is too late."

Pearlie leaned over and kissed her, holding it for a long moment before he suddenly stiffened, then raised up. He looked into Lucy's face, which, despite her death agony, wore an expression of rapture. The joy of her marriage was her last conscious thought, because Lucy was dead.

When Pearlie looked up, tears were streaming down his face. Stepping over to him, Sally knelt beside him, then held him as he wept.

One month later
Sugarloaf Ranch

As Pearlie tightened the cinches on his saddle, Sally came out to see him, carrying a cloth bag. "I baked a few things for you," she said.

"Shucks, you didn't have to do that."

"I know I didn't. But I wanted to."

"I appreciate it," Pearlie said, tying the bag to his saddle horn. He looked back toward the bunkhouse. "I thought Cal would come tell me good-bye."

"Cal's having a hard time with the fact that you are leaving," Sally said. "So am I. So is Smoke."

"Yeah," Pearlie said. He ran his hand through his hair. "Truth is, I'm having a hard time leaving."

Running his hand through his hair mussed it up a bit, and Sally licked her fingers, then reached up to smooth it out.

"It's just that, well, with what happened to Lucy and all, I need myself some time alone." Pearlie held his hand up. "This is no knock on you and Smoke and Cal," he said. "Lord, there can't no man anywhere in the world have any better friends. It's just that—" He paused in mid-sentence.

"I know what you mean, Pearlie," Sally said. "And I understand your need to get away. I just hope it isn't permanent."

"Pearlie!" Cal called, coming from the bunkhouse then.

Pearlie turned toward his young friend and smiled broadly. "Well, I'm glad you came out to see me. I was beginning to think I might have to leave without saying good-bye."

"I want you to have this," Cal said. He held out his silver hatband. "You can see that I have it all polished up for you. You have to keep it polished. Otherwise, it gets a little tarnished."

"Cal, I can't take this," Pearlie said, pushing it back.

"I ain't givin' it to you permanent," Cal said.

Sally started to correct Cal's grammar, but she realized that this was a very emotional time for the two young men, so she said nothing.

"I figure if you've got my silver hatband, you'll come back for sure," Cal said.

Pearlie looked at the hatband for a moment, nodded, then slipped it onto his hat. Without another word, he swung into the saddle and rode off.

Chapter One

When some of the hands tried to put the saddle on the horse's back, it broke loose and reared up, pawing at the air with its front hooves. Then it began running around the corral, its hooves throwing up clods of dirt. Those who were sitting on the fence had to move quickly to get out of the way as the horse seemed intent on brushing them off.

Two riders waited until the horse was at the far end of the corral, then nodded for the gate to be opened. When it was open, they rode inside, swinging lariats overhead. The two cowboys threw their loops at the same time, and both managed to get ropes around the horse's neck. They stopped the horse from running, then led him over to a pole in the center where they secured him.

One of the riders looked toward Cal with a wry grin on his face.

"There he is, Cal, all calmed down for you," he teased.

"Yeah, thanks a lot," Cal said.

Rubbing his hands together, Cal stood there looking at the horse, which, for the moment, was relatively quiet.

"Smoke, I don't think Cal should try to ride him," Sally said. Sally and Smoke were both sitting on the top rail of the fence, having just returned to their positions as they had been among those who were forced to flee when the horse began its rampage.

"The horse has to be broken," Smoke replied.

"Yes, but does it have to be Cal? Smoke, he could break his neck."

Smoke laughed. "I see. So, what you are saying is, you would rather it be me who breaks his neck?"

"No," Sally said. "You know I didn't mean that. It's just that—well, Pearlie normally did this."

"Pearlie isn't here now," Smoke said. "Cal is going to have to start taking over some of Pearlie's responsibilities."

"I know," Sally said. "But Pearlie is older and a little more experienced. It just frightens me to think of Cal trying to ride that horse."

"Sally, I don't think Cal would stop now even if I ordered him to," Smoke said. "And I wouldn't embarrass him by giving that order. Surely you know now that it is a matter of pride with him. You know how Cal is."

"I know," Sally agreed. "I just hope and pray that he doesn't get hurt."

Cal approached the horse, then stepped up to the horse's head. He grabbed the horse by the ear and pulled its head down, even with his own.

"I'm going to ride you, horse," he said. "You ain't goin' to like it all that much, but to tell you the truth, you ain't got no say-so in it 'cause I'm goin' to do it whether you like it or not. And if you think you can buck me off 'cause I ain't Pearlie, it ain't goin' to gain you nothin', 'cause I'll just climb back on and ride you again. You got that?"

"Cal, wait," one of the other hands called. He walked out into the corral carrying a blanket. "Let me put this over his head till you get on. Maybe it'll calm him down a bit—at least until you are mounted."

"All right, Jake," Cal replied.

Jake put the blanket over the horse's head, then looked at Cal. Cal climbed into the saddle and grabbed the hack rein.

The horse made no effort to prevent him from mounting, and Cal smiled.

"All right," he said. "Maybe my little talk with him did some good. Untie him and let us go."

Jake removed the blanket from the horse's head and freed him from the hitching post at the same time. Then he moved quickly to get out of the way.

For another long moment, the horse stood absolutely still, and Cal looked over toward Smoke and Sally.

"Ha!" he shouted. "Look here! I reckon this horse knows who is boss! I had a little talk with him and—ohhhh!"

The horse exploded into energy, lifting all four hooves from the ground at the same time. When he came back down, his legs were held straight, providing no spring, so that the shock was transferred up to Cal. Then the horse started running and bucking at the same time. Cal held onto the hack rein with one hand and the night latch, which was a rope tied through the gullet of the saddle, with the other.

"Hang on, Cal!" Jake shouted.

"Ride 'im into the ground, don't let up!" one of the other cowboys yelled.

The horse began spinning around. Then he reared up on his back legs, came back down, and kicked his back legs high into the air so that Cal was looking straight down at the ground. The horse ran toward the fence, again brushing everyone off, stopped suddenly, then kicked his back legs high into the air again. This time Cal came out of the saddle and slipped forward, managing to stop his fall only by wrapping his legs around the horse's neck.

Finally, the horse gave up bucking and began galloping around the corral, running at full speed.

Cal took his hat off and began waving it. "Yahoo!" he shouted at the top of his lungs.

Cal stayed with him for the entire time until the horse stopped running, started trotting, then slowed to a walk. Finally, the horse came to a complete stop and just stood there, in the middle of the corral.

Cal swung down from the horse, took off the breaking saddle and harness, then resaddled and bridled him. The animal remained as docile as a plow horse. Remounting, Cal rode around the corral, acknowledging the applause of all the ranch hands. He stopped in front of Smoke and Sally, then doffed his hat and bowed.

"Bravo, Cal, bravo," Sally said. "That was wonderful."

"I wish Pearlie had been here to see it," Cal said.

Los Brazos, New Mexico Territory

It had been over a month since Pearlie left Sugarloaf. In that time, he had maintained a southern drift with no particular destination in mind—only a need to continue to put distance and time between himself and the events that had led to Lucy being killed.

During his six-week-long sojourn, he had stayed no longer in any one town than he needed to—sometimes taking a part-time job for a couple of days or so just to earn enough money to keep going. Over the last month he had worked in a livery, had loaded and unloaded freight wagons, and had even stood in for a week as a bartender. At one ranch, he had spent a day breaking horses, getting five dollars for each horse he broke. Then, in the little town of Jasper, Colorado, he built on an extra room for a widow who earned her keep by making pies. The widow, whose name was Diane, suggested, both by word and action, that if Pearlie wanted to stay on, she would more than welcome his company. But Pearlie declined the offer as tactfully as he could.

"That's all right, cowboy," Diane, who was no more than a year or two older than Pearlie, replied. "If you ever get tired of seeing what's just over the next hill, you can always come back."

As Pearlie rode off, he wondered if he made a mistake in not taking up the widow's offer. It wasn't as if he would have been cheating on Lucy, and the diversion might have helped in the healing process. But even as he considered that, he knew that it would not have been the right thing to do—not for him, and not for Diane.

After another week of riding, he happened across the little town of Los Brazos, which lay flyblown and dying as it baked in the hot New Mexico sun. The first building he passed was a railroad depot, though there was no railroad serving the town. The age and condition of the depot indicated that it was the past expression of a misplaced optimism—rather than the sign of something to come.

Feeling the need of a beer to cut the trail dust, Pearlie dismounted in front of the Casa de la Suerte Cantina, which was the only saloon in the small town. Instead of the batwing doors with which Pearlie was more familiar, long strips of rawhide, upon which several wooden beads had been strung, hung down to cover the entrance. The beads clacked as he pushed his way through to the inside.

The inside was more pleasant than the outside had promised, with a chandelier and a long, polished bar. The bartender was Mexican, and he stood at the far end of the bar, leaning back against the wall with his arms folded across his chest and a small piece of rawhide dangling from his lips. Seeing Pearlie come in, he reached up, took the rawhide from his mouth, then walked down to stand in front of Pearlie.

"Tequila, Señor?" he asked.

"Beer."

"Beer, *sí.*" The bartender drew a mug, then set it in front of Pearlie. Pearlie blew the foam off, then took a deep drink for thirst. The next swallow was to enjoy the taste.

"Hey!" a loud angry voice yelled. "How come you serve that stranger and you don't serve me?"

"Because, Señor Dempster, already, you are drunk I think," the bartender replied. "And the more *borracho*— the drunker you get, the meaner you get. Besides, you lied to me when you said you didn't have to work today. Señor Ben had to make the run to Chama without you."

"Since when is it any of your business whether or not I go to work?" the belligerent customer replied.

"It is none of my business if you do not go to work. But it is my business if I make Señor Montgomery *enfadado.* This is his place, and he could fire me."

"Ha! He ain't goin' to fire you for sellin' me another drink. Hell, that's what saloons do, ain't it? Sell drinks to their customers?"

"Dempster, why don't you settle down?" one of the other saloon patrons said. "You been a burr under ever'body's saddle ever since you come in here."

Pearlie continued to stand there with his back to the bar, watching the exchange as he drank his beer.

"What the hell are you lookin' at, you pie-faced weasel?" Dempster said to Pearlie.

Pearlie finished his beer before he replied.

"Mister, don't try to draw me into all this. I just stopped in for a beer."

"Yeah? Well, you finished it, so get."

"Señor Dempster, to my customers like that, you no can talk," the bartender said.

"I'll talk to anyone any damn way I want," Dempster replied belligerently.

"Dempster!" a new voice called out angrily.

Turning toward the door of the saloon, Pearlie saw a gray-haired, gray-bearded man, short, stocky, and angry.

"What do you want?"

"Where were you when the stage left this morning?" the gray-haired man asked.

"There didn't nobody come to wake me up. If someone had come to wake me up in time, I wouldn't have missed the stage."

"It ain't nobody else's job to wake you up in the mornin'," the gray-haired man said. "If you hadn't been hungover, you would've been able to wake yourself up. And look at you. You're drunk now."

"Come on, Ben, I ain't that drunk. I'll be at work tomorrow mornin', just you wait and see."

"No, you won't be there tomorrow or any other day. You're fired."

"You can't fire me. You're just a stagecoach driver."

"I didn't fire you, I'm just tellin' you you're fired. Mr. Montgomery is the one who fired you," Ben said.

"Yeah? Well, who are you goin' to get to ride shotgun with you?"

"We'll find somebody before the stage leaves," Ben said.

"You're the one that talked him into firin' me, aren't you?"

"What if I am? You're supposed to be riding shotgun guard with me. You think I want a drunk sitting beside me?"

"Montgomery is going to have to find a new shotgun guard and a new driver," Dempster said. "'Cause I aim to shoot you right between the eyes."

"No, Dempster, Ben ain't armed!" one of the other customers shouted.

Glancing toward the driver, Pearlie saw that he wasn't armed. Looking back toward Dempster, he saw that the angry man was drawing his pistol.

Acting instinctively, Pearlie threw his beer mug at Dempster. The mug hit Dempster on the side of his head, and Dempster dropped like a poleaxed steer.

"Damn, mister, I reckon you just saved my life," Ben said.

"I reckon I did," Pearlie replied.

Ben sighed. "Now I'm going to have to find someone to ride shotgun with me tomorrow."

"No, you won't," Pearlie said.

"What do you mean, I won't?"

"You just found someone," Pearlie said.

"You?"

"Me."

"All right, I tell you what. I'll tell Mr. Montgomery about you. You come on down to the depot before the stage leaves tomorrow, and you talk to him. If he's willing to hire you, it's fine with me."

"What time does the stage leave?"

"It leaves at eight in the morning."

"I'll be there."

Pearlie spent the night on the ground, just outside of town. When he rode back in the next morning, he saw the stagecoach sitting out in front of the depot. The team had not yet been connected, but hostlers were over in front of the barn, putting the team into harness.

The words on the side of the coach, painted in red and outlined in gold, read, SUNSET STAGE COACH LINE. Pearlie glanced around for the driver, but didn't see him. For a moment, he considered waiting until he did see the driver; then he decided it would be best to just go on into the depot.

Inside, he saw a tall, silver-haired, dignified-looking man.

"Are you Mr. Montgomery?" Pearlie asked.

"I am."

"Mr. Montgomery, last night I met a fella by the name of Ben. He suggested I come see you, to ask about working as a shotgun guard."

"Oh, yeah, Ben talked to me about you. You're the one called Pearlie?"

"Yes, sir."

Montgomery chuckled. "Ben said you laid ole Dempster out with a beer mug. I sure wish I could have seen that."

"At the time, it seemed the thing to do," Pearlie said.

Montgomery whooped with laughter. "I don't think I've ever met you," Montgomery said. "How long have you lived in Los Brazos?"

"I'll tell you that as soon as I find a place to live," Pearlie replied.

Montgomery looked surprised for a moment; then he laughed again.

"Well, that's a straight answer. Are you married?"

"No, I—" Pearlie paused. "I was married, but my wife died."

"Oh, I'm real sorry to hear that, son. But, and don't get me wrong but I have to ask this. Have you ever been in trouble with the law?"

"I'm not a wanted man," Pearlie said.

"You're not a wanted man?"

"No, sir, I am not."

"All right," he said. "I guess that's a pretty straight answer, too. And because you gave me a straight answer, I won't go any further into it. Ben tells me you were in the saloon when he told Dempster that he was fired."

"Yes, sir, I was."

"I don't reckon it was any mystery to you why we fired him. He is a drunk. Now, let me ask you this. What were you doing in the saloon? You aren't a drunk, are you?"

"I had a long ride, and for most of that ride, I was looking forward to a beer. When I rode into town last night, that was the first thing I did."

"One beer?"

"One beer," Pearlie said. "Well, that is, part of one beer. There was still some left when I threw it at Dempster."

Montgomery laughed again. "All right, I reckon that's good enough for me. Tell me this. If I hire you, how soon can you go to work?"

"When does the coach leave?"

"In about ten minutes."

"If you hire me, I'll be on it."

Montgomery pointed to a cabinet. "There's a twelve-gauge double-barrel and a .44-.40 Winchester in there. Take one or both."

"I'll take 'em both," Pearlie said. He started toward the cabinet, then stopped and looked back toward Montgomery. "Mr. Montgomery, I think I need to tell you— I don't plan to be here for a very long time."

"Oh? Why is that?"

"After my wife was—uh, after she died, I felt like I needed to get away. Everything back there reminded me of her and the hurt was just too much. But the time is going to come when I want to get back and be around my own friends and people."

"I understand. Pearlie, is it?"

"Yes, sir, folks call me Pearlie."

"Do you have a last name, Pearlie?"

"Do I need one?"

Montgomery paused for a moment; then he chuckled. "No, I guess not. All right, Pearlie, you can work for me as long as you want, as long as you keep your nose clean, and as long as Ben is comfortable with you. When the time comes that you feel like you want to go back home, tell me. There will be no hard feelings."

"Thanks, Mr. Montgomery, I appreciate your understanding," Pearlie replied.

Montgomery stepped up to the door, then called outside. "Ben?"

"Yes, Mr. Montgomery?" Ben's voice floated in from the stable area.

"Come in here and meet your new shotgun guard."

"I already met him," Ben replied. "If he's been hired, tell him to get his ass out here and climb aboard."

Montgomery turned toward Pearlie. "Oh, uh, I didn't tell you. Ben is pretty much of what I think you would call a curmudgeon."

"A what?"

"A grouch."

Pearlie laughed. "That's all right, I like grouches. You always know where you stand with a grouch."

Pearlie grabbed the two weapons, then walked outside. The coach had been pulled into position and Pearlie put the two guns on the seat, then climbed up. Once up on the seat, he laid the guns down in the foot well, then scooted over to the left side.

"Hrmmph," Ben said. He spit out a quid of tobacco.

"At least you got enough sense to know which side of the seat to sit on."

When all of the passengers were on board, Ben clambered up onto the driver's seat, spit out another quid of tobacco, then snapped the long whip over the head of his team. The pop of the whip was as loud as a pistol shot, and the coach started forward.

They had been on the road for about fifteen minutes without either of them saying a word.

"How come you ain't asked me?" Ben asked.

"Asked you what?"

"Asked me how long it's goin' to be before we get to where we're goin'."

"You're the one drivin'," Pearlie replied. "All I have to do is just sit here. I figure we'll get there when we get there."

Ben chuckled, and it was the first time since they had met that Pearlie had seen anything other than a frown on his face.

"You figure we'll get there when we get there," Ben repeated. "Yes, sir, Pearlie, I think you may just work out all right."

Chapter Two

One hundred and seventy-five miles southeast of Sugar-loaf, at a ranch called the Tumbling Q, near the small railroad town of Santa Clara, a meeting was being held. Attending the meeting were all the ranchers whose own spreads lay within a twenty-mile radius of the Tumbling Q. The breed of choice for the ranchers was the Texas longhorn. Most had been running the longhorn ever since they started ranching. The longhorn was a hardy breed, a breed that could survive drought and find something to eat where little forage seemed available.

Today, the ranchers were complaining bitterly over the fact that the market for longhorns was dropping. The meeting had been called by Pogue Quentin, the biggest rancher in the county and owner of the Tumbling Q.

"It's these damn Herefords," Peters said. Peters owned a neighboring ranch. "That's all the slaughterhouses is wantin' now, and they ain't willin' to pay enough for our cows for us to make any money at all. In fact, at the way this is goin', by the time it's all said and done, we'll be lucky to hang on to our ranches."

Gillespie held up his hands to quiet the group; then he nodded toward Quentin, who had been watching and listening to the whole thing. So far, Quentin had said nothing.

"Quentin, you called this here meeting," Gillespie said. "So I figure that means you must have an idea or two."

"Yeah, Quentin, you said you had a way we could beat this. What have you got in mind?"

Quentin, who had been sitting quietly in a chair near the window, stood up. A very heavyset man, he was clean shaven, and had a ring of white hair that circled his head and left the top bald and shining.

"Gentlemen, the time of the longhorn has gone," he said. "We may as well face facts."

"What do you mean by face facts?" Peters asked.

"I mean, you may as well face facts that if you are running a herd of longhorns, you ain't goin' to be makin' any money from 'em. So your best bet is to get rid of 'em."

"Get rid of 'em how? If nobody wants them, what are we goin' to do, shoot 'em?"

"Oh, the market for longhorns is dwindling to be sure, but there is still some market there, so it is going to become a matter of supply and demand. If we control the supply, we can have some input into the demand."

"And just how the hell are we supposed to control supply?" Gillespie asked.

"My suggestion would be for us to form a corporation. A cattle corporation. We'll join all our ranches and our herds together. We'll be able to control supply that way, because we will approach the market as a single supplier."

"How would something like that work?" James Colby, one of the other ranchers, asked.

"It's really very simple," Quentin answered. "All we have to do is merge our ranches and our cattle into one large ranch and cattle company."

"One large ranch? I don't know about that. Who would own it?"

"We would all own it," Quentin said. "We would each own a share of the company in proportion with what we put into it."

"I still don't understand."

"All right, let's say we put all our cattle together, and we come up with one hundred head," Quentin said, starting to explain.

"Ha, I got more than a hunnert head all by my own self," Colby said.

The others laughed, and Quentin held up his hand as if telling him to wait. "I'm using a hundred head so I can explain it. Now, if we have one hundred head, and you put in two cows, Gillespie puts in six cows, and Peters puts in ten cows, you will own two percent of the company, Gillespie will own six percent of the company, and Peters will own ten percent."

"Who owns the rest?"

"We all own the rest, according to how many head of cattle we put in. I'll own most of the company, because I have the most cattle."

"And you say we're doin' that so we can control the market?"

"Yes."

"All right, I'll put my cattle in," Colby said.

"And your ranch," Quentin added.

"My ranch? What do you mean, my ranch?"

"If we are going to make this a corporation, then it has to have some substance," Quentin said. "Look, we all agree that we are going to have to switch over to Herefords, don't we?"

"Well, yes," Colby said. "That's what we need to do."

"Can you afford to do that right now?"

"No."

"Don't feel bad about it, most of us are in the same boat."

"No, we ain't," Colby said. "We're all in a rowboat, but you are in a ship. You're the biggest rancher in the county."

The others laughed at Colby's analogy.

"Yes, but compared to some of the other ranchers in the state, the Tumbling Q might be considered small. However, if we joined all our ranches into one ranch, we would be as big as anyone else."

"So, you want me to give you my ranch?"

"No, you won't be giving your ranch to me. You will be buying into the corporation with your ranch, which will make you a part owner," Quentin said. "Don't you see? With one big ranch, we'll have enough power to go to any bank in the state and take out a loan for as much money as we need to buy Herefords. I propose that we join all our ranches into one big ranch, with each of us owning a percentage of that ranch—then we sell the entire herd of longhorns, use what money we get from that sale, plus what we can borrow on the ranch, and buy Herefords."

"Sounds like a good idea to me," Gillespie agreed.

"I guess it makes sense," Peters added. "I do have a question, though."

"What is your question?"

"When this is all put together, what percentage will you own?"

"I've had Lawyer Gilmore draw up the papers for us," Quentin replied. "Mr. Gilmore, can you answer Mr. Peters' question?"

Gilmore cleared his throat, then read from a piece of paper. "Given the value of the various ranches, as appraised by the county tax commission, and the number of head of cattle each of you will be bringing to this enterprise, Mr. Quentin will own eighty-seven percent."

"Eighty-seven percent? Isn't that a lot? I mean, if we sell our herd, that means you get eighty-seven percent of the money we make?"

"It also means I'm responsible for eighty-seven percent of the cost of operation," Quentin pointed out. "Unless you want to assume a larger percentage of the expenses."

"No, no, I—I guess you are right," Peters agreed.

Quentin smiled. "But that's not the way to look at it, Peters," he said. "Remember, the whole idea is that we are partners of the whole. All of you will be part owners of the Tumbling Q ranch."

"Yeah," Gillespie said. "Yeah, I like that idea."

"Gentlemen, if you'll just sign the paper, we'll be in business," Quentin said, holding his hand out toward the desk where Gilmore stood with the paper and a pen, ready for the other ranchers to sign. Gillespie, Peters, and the other three ranchers present signed. But when it came time for Colby to sign, he hesitated.

"Are you going to sign, or not?" Gilmore asked.

"I don't know," Colby replied. "I was all right with the idea of joining our herds. But the land? I'm not so good with that. After the war, I come out here from Missouri and started cowboyin'. I liked the work, and I never worked for a boss that I didn't like. But from the time I first come here, I always had it in my mind to someday own me my own ranch. Well, after a lot of hard work, I finally managed to get my own spread. Oh, it ain't much, I guess, considerin' the size of some of the other ranches hereabout. But it's mine. Now, if I join up with this corporation you're talkin' about, it won't be mine anymore. I'll be right back where I started, just another cowhand working someone else's ranch.

"That's not true," Quentin said. "You won't be an employee of the ranch, you'll be one of the owners, a partner in a ranch that is bigger than anything you've ever dreamed of."

"Consider this, Colby," Gillespie said. "If you don't join, you'll be even smaller, compared to what we will be. You'll be squeezed out of business in no time at all."

"Listen to what Gillespie is saying, Colby," Quentin said. "He's tellin' you like it is."

"James, me an' you been friends ever since you come out here," Peters said to Colby. "I think Gillespie is makin' sense. I don't think you got no other choice, but to join up with the rest of us."

"But what about the men we'd need to work an outfit this large?" Colby asked. "Won't we have to hire a lot more men?"

"Not really," Quentin replied. "Because we'll be poolin' all our cowboys so we won't need any more men than what we already have."

"I only got two hands workin' for me and I do as much or more than either of them. Now, I don't mind doin' it for my own ranch, but looks like the way this is settin' up, I'll wind up workin' for the company."

"Ah, but don't forget. You *are* the company," Quentin said.

"A company's got to have a boss, don't it?" Colby asked.

"Yes, of course," Quentin replied. "Where would any outfit be without a boss?"

"Then that means I'll be workin' for that boss."

"By the way, how do we select the boss?" Peters asked.

"We'll vote."

"Each of us get a vote?"

"Yes."

"Well, in that case, I don't reckon it'll be all that bad," Peters said.

"One vote for each percentage point of the ranch that you own," Quentin said.

"Wait a minute. So if I own six percent, I get six votes?"

"Yes."

"And you get eighty-seven votes?" Peters asked.

"Yes."

"Then you are the only vote that counts."

"If you want to put it that way," Quentin replied.

"What the hell, Peters, Quentin is the biggest rancher here, and this was his idea," Gillespie said. "When you think about it, it only makes sense that he be the boss."

"I suppose you are right."

Although Colby was holding the pen, he had still not signed the paper. Now, he put the pen down.

"James, what are you doin'?" Peters asked.

"I'm sorry," Colby said. "I just can't do it. I worked too hard to get my own ranch. I just can't give it away like this."

"Mr. Colby," Quentin said. "I have to do what is best for all of us. That means that if you don't join us, you won't be able to survive, you will have no market for your cattle, and your ranch will be squeezed out. You'll be lucky if you have enough money to buy a ticket back to Missouri."

"Yeah? Well, at least I'll be my own boss," Colby said. "Good-bye, gents." He started toward the door.

"Colby?" Quentin called.

Colby turned back toward Quentin. "Yes?"

"Don't take this personally. It's pure business."

"I'm sure it is," Colby said.

"Gentlemen," Quentin said after Colby left, "we have made good progress here, today. I will start buying Hereford cattle to build our new herd, and to strengthen that herd, I plan to acquire at least one champion Hereford bull. I thank you for your confidence and support."

Chapter Three

Big Rock, Colorado

The stagecoach rolling out of Big Rock, bound for the nearby town of Mitchell, met four riders who were just coming into town. The stage diver nodded at the riders, who nodded back. The riders passed by the WELCOME TO BIG ROCK sign, which was just before the blacksmith shop, where sparks were flying from the heated iron wheel-band the smithy was working with his hammer. As they came deeper into town, they rode on by the butcher shop where the butcher, Stan Virden, was sweeping his front porch; by the feed store, where a wagon was being loaded; and the apothecary, where a painter was touching up the mortar-and-pestle sign that was suspended from the porch overhang.

Just up the street from the riders was a building with a huge sign that was an oversized boot.

BIG
ROCK
BOOTS
& SADDLES

An outside set of stairs ran up the north wall of the leather goods store, and at the top of the stairs the printed sign on the door read:

STEVE WARREN
Cattle Broker

Smoke Jensen, owner of Sugarloaf Ranch, had come to see Steve, to arrange a sales contract for his beeves.

At six feet one inch, Smoke Jensen was an impressive man. He was broad of shoulder and narrow of hip, and his biceps were as thick as most men's thighs. Though he was still a relatively young man, stories about him were legend, both true and false. The irony was that many of the true stories were even more dramatic than the myths that abounded.

Smoke had never really known his mother, and when he was barely in his teens, he went with his father into the mountains to follow the fur trade. The father and son teamed up with a legendary mountain man called Preacher. For some reason unknown even to Preacher, the mountain man took to the boy and began to teach him the ways of the mountains: how to live when others would die, how to be a man of your word, and how to fear no other living creature. On the first day they met, Preacher, whose real name was Art, gave Kirby Jensen a new name. For reasons known only to himself, Preacher began calling Kirby "Smoke." Later, when Smoke's father was killed by outlaws, young Kirby Jensen hunted them down and killed them. That action was the birth of the legend of Smoke Jensen.

Now, he was married and settled down as a rancher, and his Sugarloaf Ranch was known as one of the finest cattle spreads in the entire state of Colorado. And his ranch, as were many other ranches, was in the process of transition. Texas longhorns, a breed of cattle that had been the staple of Western beef production for many years now, were gradually being replaced by new breeds, such as the Angus and the Hereford.

"I hate to tell you this, Smoke, but it looks like about the best we can come up with is seven dollars a head," the cattle broker said.

Smoke was standing at the window, looking down onto the street, watching as the four men came riding into town. There was nothing particularly unusual about them—it wasn't even that unusual for four riders to arrive together. Nevertheless, there was something about them that triggered some deep-set instinct. He couldn't put his finger on it—but something about them nagged at him. He turned away from the window when he heard Steve's offer.

"Did you say seven dollars?" Smoke asked.

"That's what it looks like."

"That's not very good. Last year, I got ten dollars a head," Smoke replied. "And the year before that, I got fifteen. What's happening to the market? Are people not eating beef anymore?"

"Oh, they're still eating beef all right," Steve said. "But they've gotten a lot more particular. Now, if we were talking Herefords instead of longhorns, I could offer you twenty- five dollars a head."

"I have a few Herefords," Smoke said, turning away from the window and coming back to sit across the desk from Steve. "But not enough to sell yet. I'm just beginning to build up a herd."

"Smoke, I wish I could offer you more. As you know, I

get ten percent of the contract, which means the higher the price I can get for you, the more money I make for myself. But no matter where you go—Omaha, Kansas City, Chicago—we are running into the same thing. The most any of the meatpacking houses will pay is seven dollars per head for longhorn cattle, and if they had a hard winter, they may pay as low as four or five dollars. I've seen your herd, your beeves are in good shape, so you'll get top dollar. Unfortunately, top dollar is only seven dollars per head."

"You don't have to explain the situation. I've worked with you for a long time, Steve, and I know you are an honest man, doing the best you can. But these cattle cost me two dollars a head to raise, and at fifty dollars per cattle car, that means they are costing me a dollar a head to ship. That leaves four dollars a head," Smoke said. 'No, counting your fee, it leaves me three dollars and thirty cents a head." He sighed. "I'll ship twelve hundred head, and I'll make just over four thousand dollars. Well, I won't even make that, because that does not count the salaries I pay my men. I tell you the truth. I'll do well to break even."

"If it is any consolation to you, Smoke, this is happening everywhere and to everyone. The folks back East have gotten a taste of Hereford. Nobody wants longhorn beef anymore. But, as always, the final decision is up to you. Do you want to sell at that price?"

"No, I don't want to," Smoke replied resolutely. He sighed. "But it doesn't look like I have any choice."

"All right, I'll get you a contract. What about the train cars? Do you want me to book them for you as well?"

"Yes," Smoke said. "Oh, and tell Mr. Bidwell I'll be needing the holding pens for a couple of days."

"That'll be thirty cents a head," Steve said.

"Right. That means it will cost me another three hundred sixty dollars just to do business," Smoke said. "I don't know but what this might not work out better if I just paid somebody to take the beeves off my hands," he added with a sarcastic laugh. "At least I wouldn't have to be worryin' about feeding them and taking care of them."

"It's good you can laugh about it," Steve said.

"When you get right down to it, Steve, I have to laugh about it," Smoke said. "What else can I do?"

"I guess you have a point there. All right, once I get this all set up, how soon can you get the herd in?"

"How soon can you get everything set up?" Smoke wanted to know.

"I can send wires back to Omaha, Kansas City, Chicago. I reckon I can have everything set up by tomorrow."

"Then I'll bring my herd in tomorrow."

"I'll have everything ready for you."

The two men shook hands.

"As always, Smoke, it's good doing business with you," Steve said.

Emil Sinclair was one of the four horsemen Smoke had seen riding into Big Rock. He and the other three riders stopped just across the street from the biggest store in town. A huge, brightly painted sign that spread across the front of the store read:

Big Rock
MERCANTILE
Goods for all Mankind

The store was very large and exceptionally well stocked, and one wag had commented that when it said, "Goods for all mankind," it literally referred to all mankind.

"Why, I'll bet there's enough socks for every man, woman, and child in Colorado," he'd said.

The store was not only well stocked. It had a wide variety of merchandise from groceries, to clothes, to furniture, to tools. In one section of the store, it had baby cribs, and in another, coffins, eliciting the oft-repeated comment that the "Big Rock Mercantile can supply you with everything you need from the cradle to the grave."

"Emil, you stay here with the horses," Logan Taylor said. "Jason, Stu, you two come with me."

Emil, Jason, and Stu Sinclair were brothers. They had been recruited by Logan Taylor a week earlier to "do a job that will make us two or three hunnert dollars each, and there ain't goin' to be no risk to it at all."

"There ain't no such thing as a job with no risk," Emil had replied.

"There ain't no risk to this one. We're goin' to rob us a store."

"A store? You think we can rob a store and get a couple hundred dollars apiece?" Emil had asked. "I ain't never heard of a store with that much money."

"This one does. It's one of the biggest stores in Colorado, and does so much business that it has purt' near as much money as a bank. Only, there ain't no guards, the store clerk ain't armed, and more than likely the only customers inside will be women."

"Sounds pretty good to me, Emil," Jason had said.

"Yeah, me, too," Stu had added.

Although the whole operation sounded a little fishy to him, Emil had allowed himself to be talked into it, and now he sat on his horse, holding the reins of the other three horses as Taylor, Jason, and Stu walked across the street, then went inside.

There were seven people inside: the clerk, who wasn't armed, and six customers, all of whom, as Taylor had said, were women.

"Oh, Julia, look at this material," one woman gushed to another as they stood by a table that was filled with brightly colored bolts of cloth. The woman pulled some of it away and held it against herself. "Have you ever seen a more beautiful color? Wouldn't this make a lovely dress?"

"Oh, yes, it would be perfect with your—"

"Good afternoon, ladies!" Taylor shouted loudly. "I'm going to ask all of you to step back into the storeroom for a little while."

"What?" one of the women asked.

"Here! What is the meaning of this?" the only male, the store clerk, said.

"We're robbin' your store," Taylor said.

One of the women drew a deep breath and put her hand to her mouth. Taylor swung his pistol toward her, pulling the hammer back as he did so.

"Lady, if you scream, I'll shoot you," he said. "I'll shoot anyone who screams. Now, get back into that storeroom like I said."

This time, the women reacted and started toward the storeroom at the rear of the store.

"Jason, make sure they all get in there, then lock the door. Stu, you stand up front to take care of anyone else who comes in. Store clerk, let's me and you do some business."

* * *

Sally had asked Smoke to pick up an iron skillet for her while he was in town, so he tied his horse off out front of the Mercantile and started inside to carry out the errand.

He knew something was wrong as soon as he stepped through the door. At first, he didn't know what it was; then he realized that the store was empty. Normally, at this time of day, there would be several shoppers in the store, milling around, looking at the merchandise, or making purchases. Now there was nobody.

He stopped for a moment, every muscle in his body on the alert. Smoke was a man who had lived his life on the edge of danger—whether it be from wild animals when he was younger, renegade Indians, or desperate killers and outlaws. That lifetime of danger had given him a sixth sense, and because of his heightened awareness, he sensed, rather than heard, someone approaching him, very quietly, from behind.

Making a fist, Smoke timed his reaction perfectly, and at exactly the right moment, he whirled around, swinging as he did so. He landed a haymaker on the jaw of the armed man who was approaching him. He grabbed the man and let him down easily so that the sound of his falling wouldn't alert anyone else. It was obvious that something was going on in the store, and this man had been posted by the door to take care of anyone who might happen in, in the middle of it.

Relieving the unconscious guard of his pistol, Smoke pulled his own gun, then started moving quietly through the store. He didn't have to go too far before he saw, reflected in a dresser mirror, Eli Dawes, standing with his hands in the air. Dawes was the manager of the store. In the same mirror reflection, Smoke could also see two armed men, both of whom had their guns pointed at Dawes.

"I know damn well you got more money than this," one of the armed men said angrily. He had a flat nose and a handlebar mustache. "A store this big? I been watchin' you for a couple of days now. You do a lot of business here."

"If you really have been watching, then you know we make a deposit in the bank every day at one o'clock," Dawes said.

"You're lyin'," Flat Nose said.

"No, he isn't lying," Smoke said, stepping out to confront the robbers. "There have been times when, good-neighborly-like, I would make the deposit for him." Smoke's voice was agonizingly calm, almost as if he were having a dinner table conversation.

"Who the hell are you?" Flat Nose asked, the high-pitched, anxious tremor of his voice in stark contrast to Smoke's unruffled tone.

"I'm the man who is going to kill you if you don't drop your gun," Smoke said. Again, his voice was calm and controlled.

"Stu!" Flat Nose called. When he got no response, he called out again. "Stu, where the hell are you?"

Smoke grinned. "Stu? Would that be the man you left standing guard at the front door?" Smoke had stuck Stu's pistol down inside the waist of his pants, and now he patted it with his left hand. "I'm afraid he isn't going to be able to help you. This is the last time I'm going to say it. Drop your gun."

"Mister, are you crazy? There are two of us. There is only one of you."

"That's all right, I'll kill you first," Smoke said. He looked at the second robber. "That will leave just the ugly one there, and he and I will be all even at one and one."

"You really are crazy, aren't you?" Flat Nose asked.

"Hello, Smoke," Dawes said. "You got here at just the right time."

"Glad I could help."

"Fellas, meet Smoke Jensen," Dawes said. "I know you've heard of him."

"Smoke Jensen?" the second robber said. "Taylor, you—you never said nothin' about us havin' to go up against Smoke Jensen. I've heard of him. They say he is as fast as lightning."

"For God's sake, Jason, be a man," Taylor said.

"It's your play, boys. Taylor, Jason, what do you do now?" Smoke asked.

"Wait! I ain't no part of this!" Jason said, dropping his gun and putting his hands up.

"Jason, you cowardly son of a bitch!" Taylor shouted. At the same time Taylor was shouting, he swung his pistol toward Smoke, pulling the hammer back and firing.

The bullet whizzed by Smoke's head and plunged into a large sack of cornmeal that was part of a high stack of cornmeal sacks behind him. Smoke returned fire, hitting Taylor in the chest. Taylor's pistol twirled around his trigger finger, pointing toward the floor, then dropped. The outlaw clutched his hand over the entry wound of the bullet, staggered back a few steps, and fell.

Smoke swung his pistol toward the one called Jason, but it wasn't necessary. Since he'd dropped his pistol and put his hands in the air, Jason hadn't made a move.

For a moment, it was very quiet in the store, the only sound being the rushing sound made by the cornmeal as it oozed out of the bullet hole and poured onto the floor.

"Are you all right, Eli?" Smoke asked.

"I'm fine, but there are some lady customers locked back in the storeroom."

"You had better let them out. I expect they are all a little nervous about now."

Dawes chuckled. "I expect you are right," he said.

"Take a look at your friend," Smoke said to Jason. "Is he dead?"

Jason bent over to look down at the body of Logan Taylor, then shook his head. "Looks to me like you killed him."

"Yes, well, I didn't have time not to."

Dawes went to the storeroom, unlocked the door, and opened it. "It's all right, ladies, you can come out now," he said. "It's all over."

"Oh, thank God," one of the lady customers said. "We heard the shots and were afraid you had been killed."

"I might have been if Smoke hadn't come along when he did," Dawes said.

Stu, the robber Smoke had knocked out, was just getting to his feet then. When he saw Taylor dead and Jason with his hands up, he reached toward his empty holster.

"Are you looking for this?" Smoke asked.

Like his brother, Stu put his hands up.

"What are you going to do with us?" Jason asked.

"It's up to you, mister," Smoke replied.

"Up to us? How?"

"I'm either going to kill you, or take you down to the jail. It's your choice."

"You got no right to arrest us. Only a sheriff can do that."

"Or a deputy," another voice said as a new person came into the store. "I made Smoke my deputy a long time ago."

Sheriff Monte Carson, having heard the shooting, had come into the store to see what was going on. When he saw that Smoke had everything in hand, he relaxed.

"You want to take charge of these fellas, Monte?" Smoke asked. "Sally asked me to pick up an iron skillet for her and if I forget, I'm going to be in trouble."

Sheriff Carson chuckled. "Then by all means, you had better find that skillet. You don't want to be in trouble with Sally."

"Pick out any skillet you want, Smoke, it's free," Dawes said in gratitude.

"Well, I appreciate that, Eli," Smoke said.

Looking back toward the two would-be robbers, Sheriff Carson made a motion with his pistol. "Come along, boys," he said. "I've got a nice jail cell just waiting for you."

"Wait a minute. Where is the other one?" Smoke asked.

"The other one? What other one?" Dawes answered. "Only three of them came in."

"Yes, but I saw four of them riding into town," Smoke said. "There's another one somewhere."

Across the street from the Mercantile, Emil Sinclair had seen Smoke go in, though he had no idea who he was. Then, hearing the shots fired, he waited no more than a couple of seconds for Taylor and his two brothers to come running out. When they didn't, he tied off the three horses, then rode on up the street a little way so as not to be obvious. By the time the sheriff went into the store, Emil was all the way back to the blacksmith shop. He was watching when the sheriff came out of the store with Stu and Jason in front of him, both holding their arms in the air.

Emil noticed that Taylor wasn't with them, and he had a pretty good idea what happened to Taylor.

Stu and Jason were actually Emil's half brothers, all

three of them sharing the same mother. Because their mother was a prostitute, not one of the three knew who their fathers were. Their mother, who was called Big Nose Mary by everyone, was actually Millie Sinclair, and she had given her last name to all three of her sons.

Emil and his brothers had met Logan Taylor while all four were in the Colorado State Prison. Taylor got out three months before the Sinclair brothers did, and it was he who set up this job.

Emil waited until the sheriff and his brothers were off the street; then he returned to the horses, untied them, and led them away. The sight of a single rider leading three horses wasn't all that unusual, except that these three horses were saddled. Emil was sure that must be a very curious sight, but he rode slowly and kept his eyes straight ahead as if there was nothing at all unusual about what he was doing.

Taylor's horse had a fancy saddle with some brass trim. As soon as he could, Emil planned to transfer that saddle to his own horse. After all, Taylor wouldn't be needing it anymore. He could take the saddle and sell the horse.

He wondered how much the horse would bring. For that matter, how much would the fancy saddle bring? Then, as he thought about it, he decided he would sell not only the horse, but the saddle as well.

The closest town was Mitchell, which was about fifteen miles away. He made it there in an hour and a half.

Tumbling Q Ranch

"Wait a minute," Peters asked. "You sold all the long-horns and bought Herefords?"

"Yes. That was our arrangement, wasn't it?"

"How much did you get per head?"

"Two dollars."

"Two dollars? I could have gotten five dollars! I thought the whole purpose of us putting our herds together was to control the market and get more money?"

"Yes, well, we actually did six dollars per head, but we paid our broker two dollars per head, and our board voted to keep two dollars per head back for capital improvement."

"The board voted? When did the board vote? I don't remember any board meeting."

"As I represent eighty-seven percent of the vote, we didn't really need a board meeting," Quentin explained. "I also bought Herefords."

"How many head of Herefords did you buy?"

"I bought a thousand head at twenty-five dollars per head. In addition, I updated the feeder pens and the barn, and I put in a series of sluices and canals to give us a more dependable water supply," Quentin said.

"What do you mean, give us a more dependable water supply? Hell, the creek coming through my ranch has all dried up."

"It isn't your ranch anymore, remember? You used your ranch to buy into the corporation."

"Yeah? Well, I want my ranch back. I want out of this corporation."

"All right. As soon as you pay your share of the debt we have accrued, I'll sign your ranch back over to you."

"My share of the debt?" Peters asked, his voice strained. "What is my share of the debt?"

"Mr. Gilmore?" Quentin said. "Would you like to answer Mr. Peters' question?"

Gilmore consulted his ledger for a moment, did some figuring, then cleared his throat.

"The gross income from the sale of thirty-five hundred longhorns came to twenty thousand, nine hundred and sixteen dollars."

"All right," Peters said with a broad smile.

"The cost of shipping came to three thousand, four hundred and eighty-six dollars. The holding pen cost was one thousand, forty dollars and eighty cents. The broker fee was six thousand, nine hundred and seventy-two dollars. Likewise, capital improvement for Tumbling Q Ranch incorporated was also six thousand, nine hundred and seventy-two dollars. That leaves a net profit of one thousand, five hundred twenty-nine dollars and twenty cents. At six percent, your share of that comes to ninety-one dollars and seventy-five cents."

The smile left Peters's face and he staggered back a few feet, then sat down, hard, in a chair.

"You mean, all I made from this deal we did was ninety-one dollars?"

"Actually, you have a net loss. Your share of the money we borrowed to buy the Herefords comes to fifteen hundred dollars. Minus the ninety-one dollars and seventy-five cents, that leaves you with an obligation of one thousand, four hundred and eight dollars and twenty-five cents."

"What?"

"I'm glad you came over, Mr. Peters," Quentin said. "How soon can I expect that money?"

"I—I don't have fourteen hundred dollars," Peters said.

Quentin stared at him for a long, hard moment.

"Well, now," he said. "That does present you with a problem, doesn't it? I mean, we all agreed, when we entered into this arrangement, to share in the profit, and to be responsible for the debt, in accordance with our ownership percentage."

"But there is no profit."

"Not yet. We are in the process of building now," Quentin said.

"All right, it looks as if I have no choice but to remain in the corporation," Peters said.

"Good, good, I was hoping you would decide that. How soon can I expect the money?"

"How soon? How soon does the loan have to be paid back?"

"It was a short-term loan," Quentin said. "It's due by the end of the week."

"By the end of the week?" Peters gasped. "That's impossible."

"It was the only way we could get that much money that quickly," Quentin said.

Peters shook his head. "I would have never agreed to anything like that."

"Like I said, Mr. Peters, as eighty-seven-percent owner, I didn't need your agreement. Now, when can I expect the money?"

"I don't have that much money. Can't you, personally, carry me for a little while?"

Quentin shook his head. "You do understand, don't you, that I am obligated for eighty-seven percent of the debt? How much is that, Mr. Gilmore?"

"That is twenty-one thousand, seven hundred and fifty dollars," Gilmore said.

"I'm sure that you realize that twenty-one thousand dollars is an enormous amount of money. And I have to come up with it by tomorrow. I can't carry you beyond tomorrow."

"But what am I going to do?"

"You could sign over your interest in the ranch to me."

"You mean, just give it to you?"

"You wouldn't be giving it to me, you would be selling it to me for fifteen hundred dollars. And I will even let you keep the ninety-one dollars that was your share from the sale of the cattle."

"No, I can't do that."

"I'm afraid, Mr. Peters, that you have no choice," Gilmore said.

"What about the others?"

"Baker and Gillespie? Unfortunately, they found themselves in the same boat as you," Gilmore said. "They have already sold their interest back to Mr. Quentin. I suggest you do the same."

"This isn't right," Peters said.

"It's business, Mr. Peters. Business is a risk. Sign here."

Peters stared at the piece of paper Gilmore pushed in front of him, then, after a long moment, affixed his signature.

"I will get your ninety-one dollars," Gilmore said.

"No," Quentin said, holding up his hand. "Mr. Peters has been a good neighbor. I hate it that this has happened to him. Give him one hundred dollars."

"That's a very generous offer, Mr. Quentin," Gilmore said.

"I just wish it could be more," Quentin replied.

Peters took the one hundred dollars, then left the house without saying another word.

Quentin stepped out onto the front porch to see Peters off. When he went back inside, Gilmore was putting all his papers away. "How do you think it went?" Quentin asked.

"That was the last of them. All the land they pledged

to the corporation has now accrued to you, and that means that you own everything but Colby's land. And, with the redirection of the water that has left him only one small creek, Colby won't be able to hang on to that much longer."

Quentin laughed. "I have to hand it to you, Gilmore. Only a lawyer could make stealin' legal."

"Oh, but it isn't stealing, Mr. Quentin," Gilmore replied. "It is all quite legal. That's how I earn my fifteen percent."

Quentin stood at the front window and watched as Gilmore drove away in his surrey. Turning away from the window, Quentin walked back over to the table where Gilmore had left the papers that turned all the other ranches in the valley over to the Tumbling Q Ranch and Cattle Company.

Gilmore had made a point to tell him that it wasn't stealing. Quentin chuckled at the lawyer's insistence upon legality. Quentin didn't mind stealing if that was the only way he could get something. That's how he got enough money to buy this ranch in the first place.

Ten years earlier, down in Texas, Pogue Quentin and three other men, Emil, Jason, and Stu Sinclair, had robbed a train. They waited alongside a water tower until the train stopped, then got the drop on the engineer and fireman. After that, they decoupled the express car from the passenger cars, and forced the engineer to take the express car a mile up the track before they let him stop. When the express agent tried to resist them, Pogue shot and killed him.

Killing the express agent wasn't that hard to do. Pogue had ridden with Doc Jennison and the Kansas Jayhawkers during the Civil War. There were some who said that Jennison made Quantrill and his Bushwhackers look like Sunday school teachers. When the war ended, Quentin continued his raids, only now they were for personal gain. The train robbery in Texas was an example.

The train robbery netted five hundred dollars in cash. But because Quentin had set up the plan, he kept two hundred for himself, and gave one hundred to each of the other three.

The other three understood that the money would be divided that way and made no protest over the allocation of the proceeds. What they did not know, however, was the real reason Quentin had held up this particular train. Quentin knew that this train was carrying a bank draft worth fifteen thousand dollars, and that the draft could be negotiated by the bearer.

The Sinclair brothers also did not know Quentin's name, since he identified himself only as "Joe."

When Quentin went to Colorado, he cashed the draft, bought a ranch, then sent back to Wichita for his wife and eleven-year-old son. His wife died in the first year, leaving him with the responsibility of raising his son. It was not a responsibility he handled well. Billy Ray Quentin grew up almost like one of the feral cats on the ranch. Without the ameliorating influence of a mother or the concerned discipline of a father, Billy Ray was, as Quentin's ranch foreman, Cole Mathers, once said, "as wild as an unbroken colt."

Chapter Four

Big Rock

Emil got ten dollars for the saddle and thirty-five dollars for the horse. Both were worth more, but he had no proof that he was the actual owner, and he wasn't in any position to answer questions. Besides, forty-five dollars in his pocket was better than no money at all. And if he had kept the horse, it would just be an extra horse to keep up with.

He waited until nightfall before he returned to Big Rock; then he didn't go into town. Instead, he stopped at a little copse of trees on a small hill about a quarter of a mile from the western edge of town. Dismounting, he pulled a stem of grass from the ground, then stuck the root in his mouth and sucked on it as he stood there. From there, he could see the entire town, from the railroad depot on the east side of town to the white church with the high steeple on the west, and from the blacksmith shop at the north end of town, to the cluster of private houses at the south end. He decided to wait outside the town and not go back in until all the nighttime activity had grown quiet.

Although Emil had no watch, he knew that it had to be somewhere around ten o'clock, because by now, except for one of the saloons, there were no public buildings open at all. In addition, only a few lights showed in the residential district.

From where he was, he could hear a piano from the saloon, but he was too far away to hear any voices. Satisfied that most of the town was asleep, he got back into the saddle, picked up the reins of the other two horses, and rode into town.

He tried to ride slowly and quietly, but it seemed to him as if the hoofbeats of his horse and the other two were as loud as a drum each time they hit the hard-packed dirt of the main street. To make matters worse, the hollow, clopping sound rolled back in echoes from the buildings that fronted the street, and that managed to redouble the sound.

Leaving the street, Emil rode down the alley until he reached the back of the sheriff's office. There, he tied off all three horses. then, pulling his hat lower, he stepped up to one of the windows of the jail and peered inside.

The deputy was sitting behind his desk with his feet up on the desk, his chair tipped back against the wall, and his hat pulled low over his eyes. Emil walked around to the front, pushed open the door, stepped inside, and started toward the deputy.

The deputy awoke just as Emil reached him. Before he could speak, or react in any way, Emil brought his gun down hard on the deputy's head, and he fell from the chair onto the floor.

"I didn't figure you'd just go off and leave us," Jason said.

"Where are the keys?" Emil asked.

"In the middle drawer of the desk," Stu answered.

Emil opened the desk, got the key, then unlocked his brothers' cell.

"Let's go."

"Where we goin'?" Stu asked.

"What difference does it make, as long as it's away from here?"

Sugarloaf Ranch

Early the next morning, Smoke stood by the fire, drinking coffee as he watched his cowboys gathering the cows into a manageable herd for the ten-mile drive into town. Behind him he heard the sound of pots and pans being moved around, and he smelled the aroma of frying bacon and boiling coffee.

Although Smoke employed a full-time cook for the cowboys of Sugarloaf, on this morning Sally had volunteered to help the cook prepare breakfast for those who would be pushing the herd into town. Her biggest contribution, appreciated by all, would be her bear signs, and the sweet smell of that confectionary treat rose above even the aroma of bacon and coffee.

"Whoo-wee," Cal said when he bit into the bear sign. "Pearlie pure dee don't have no idea what he's missin'. I'll bet he ain't had nothin' like this since he has went away."

Sally shivered. "You mean Pearlie doesn't have any— oh, never mind. That sentence is so ungrammatical that I don't believe it is humanly possible to correct it."

"You ridin' into town with us, Miss Sally?" Cal asked.

"Yes, I thought I would. It's been a couple of weeks since I was in town."

"There's a lot better ways to go into town than to ride

along with a herd of longhorns, Miz Jensen," one of the other cowboys said. "Maybe you don't know what it's like."

"Ha!" Cal said. "I'll have you know that Miss Sally once helped us drive a herd of three thousand cows over a thousand miles. I reckon she knows what she's doin' all right."

"Didn't mean nothin' by it," the cowboy replied. "I was just commentin' is all."

Sally laughed. "And I didn't take any offense. But you are right, it is different riding with a herd, no matter how far you go with them."

After breakfast, all the cowboys saddled their mounts, then rode out to get the herd moving. The animals, used to the freedom of the open range, were now forced together in one large, controlled herd. That made them acutely aware of different sights, sounds, smells, and sensations, and they were growing increasingly anxious over the change in what had been their normal routine.

Embedded in the sounds of the crying and bawling of cattle, and the shouts and whistles of the wranglers as they started the herd moving, were the rattle and clacking of long horns banging together as the cattle got under way. That was a particularly poignant sound to Smoke, because he knew that the days of the longhorn were numbered.

It took them about three hours to get to Big Rock. The railroad ran north and south through Big Rock, with the track located to the east, just out of town. That meant it wasn't necessary to push the herd down Main Street. They were able to bring them up to the depot by driving them parallel with the tracks, then across the tracks, where they began pushing them into the holding pens that had been reserved specifically for Smoke's herd.

The cattle broker met Smoke as he came in with the first batch of cows.

"I have wire confirmation of a contract with the Malone Meat Packing Company in Kansas City for seven dollars a head," Steve said, showing Smoke the telegram.

Smoke nodded, and took the wire contract from him. "Thanks, Steve." He turned to look at the cows as his drovers moved them into the pens. "When will the cars be here?"

"Sometime this afternoon."

"That's good. At least I won't be eaten up by holding-pen charges."

"Speaking of which, I need to get over there and make certain all the pens are ready," Steve said.

"Smoke!" someone called to him as Steve was leaving, and looking up, Smoke saw Sheriff Carson approaching.

"Hello, Monte."

"I thought I should warn you," Carson said. "My two prisoners escaped last night."

"The boys who tried to rob the Mercantile?"

"Yes. Someone came into the jail, knocked Curley out, then let the Sinclair boys out."

"So they did have someone else with them," Smoke said. "I told you I saw four riders coming into town."

"Yeah, the other man was Emil."

"Emil?"

"It has to be. Emil, Jason, and Stu Sinclair are brothers. Emil is the one we didn't have."

"I've never heard of them," Smoke said.

"They've never really made a name for themselves, though they served time for robbing a train in which the express agent was killed."

"If the express agent was killed, why weren't they hanged? Or at least, why aren't they still in prison?"

"There was a fourth man with them and they all say he did it. The engineer and fireman corroborated their story."

"Was the man I shot the fourth man in the train robbery?"

"No. The man you shot was named Logan Taylor, and he was in prison when the robbery happened. As a matter of fact, that's where Emil and the others met him. The Sinclair brothers swear they didn't know the name of the man who was with them. They said they met him just before the job and the only name he gave them was Joe. I think that is probably true, since if they had given his name, they could have shortened their own sentences."

"You said Curley was knocked out. How is he?"

"He's all right, I guess. He has a bump on his head, and it's going to be sore for a while. His biggest problem is from the bawling out I gave him for falling asleep on the job."

"Logan Taylor, you say. I don't believe I have heard of him either."

"They didn't any of them make much of a name for themselves," Carson said. "Taylor is from Colorado Springs, and I sent a wire to Sheriff Walker this morning, telling him what happened here. Anyway, I thought I would tell you about the Sinclair boys escaping just so you could keep an eye open for 'em. But I don't think they'll be dumb enough to try and give you any trouble."

"I appreciate the information, Monte."

"Hello, Monte," Sally said, coming over to join them.

"Hi, Miss Sally," Sheriff Carson replied, touching the brim of his hat. "I need to get on back to the office. I'll see you later," he said to Smoke.

"All right, thanks for the information," Smoke replied.

"What was that all about?" Sally asked.

"Nothing much."

"One of the railroad dispatchers just told me that you were in a shoot-out yesterday."

"Yeah, I was."

"You didn't mention it."

"I didn't want to worry you."

"Like you didn't want to worry me about getting only seven dollars per head?"

Smoke sighed. "Yeah, like that," he said. "Who told you?"

"The dispatcher said that you got the best contract of anyone who has brought longhorns through in the last several weeks. I was pretty pleased with that, until he said it was only seven dollars."

"That dispatcher has a big mouth," Smoke said with a little laugh. He showed Sally the wire.

"Oh, Smoke, what are we going to do?" Sally asked. "At these prices, we can barely afford to stay in business."

"We'll do whatever it takes," Smoke replied.

The next day, Smoke Jensen stood at the edge of the porch looking out over the gently rolling pastureland of the nearly one hundred thousand acres that made up his ranch, Sugarloaf. An early morning mist hovered just over the grass, while wisps of low-lying clouds clung to the purple peaks of the Mathers Fork Range. The clouds were a luminescent orange, the light coming from a morning sun that had not yet made its appearance over the mountains to the east.

A rooster crowed.

From the barn, a milk cow lowed.

A horse whickered, then began running around inside the corral, stretching its legs as it greeted the new day. Smoke heard a low rumble of voices from inside the bunkhouse, then a burst of laughter. He caught the whiff of tobacco as some of the cowboys lit up their first roll-your-own cigarette of the day. He took a swallow of his coffee, then leaned one hand against the post that supported the porch roof.

Two of the cowboys walked out toward the corral to saddle their horses and make a morning ride around the ranch.

"Good mornin', Mr. Jensen," one of them called.

"Good mornin', Boss," the other said.

"Good morning, Jake, Dusty," Smoke called back to them.

Over in the little row of small houses where his married employees lived, he could see smoke coming from the kitchen stove stacks as the wives were preparing breakfast. Juan Mendoza, one of his oldest hands, both in age and in the length of time he had worked for Smoke, was on the back porch pumping water into a bucket.

This was Smoke's favorite time of day and, more often than not, he would make a point of watching the eastern sky change from the dark of night to the gray of predawn, then early morning pink, and finally the full light of day. He had heard a phrase once that he applied to these moments. "This is the first hour of the rest of your life."

He knew that it was probably corny, coined, no doubt, by some would-be philosopher, but he liked it.

Last year, Smoke had introduced a few Hereford cattle into his herd to see how they would do. His experience yesterday, with the small amount of money that he had received for his cattle, convinced him that it was time to start raising Herefords exclusively.

Finishing his coffee, he went back into the kitchen.

He stood just inside the door, looking at Sally for a moment, thinking how lucky he was to have found her and to have convinced the former schoolteacher to marry him. In Smoke's eyes, Sally was as beautiful today as she had been the first day he ever saw her. She sensed him looking at her, and she turned toward him.

"Have the mountains moved?" she asked teasingly.

"What do you mean, have the mountains moved?"

"I just ask because you seem to have to check them every morning."

"No, they're still there," Smoke replied.

Picking up a hot pad, Sally opened the oven door and took out a pan of biscuits. As soon as she set the pan down, Smoke reached for one of the biscuits and she slapped at his hand with the hot pad.

"Can't you even wait for breakfast?" she asked.

"Huh-uh," Smoke said. The biscuit was hot and he tossed it from hand to hand a couple of times, then took a bite. "Anyway, it's your fault," he said even as he chewed.

"My fault? What do you mean, it's my fault?"

"You are such a good a cook and the biscuits look and smell too good to pass up. I tell you the truth, Sally, as good a cook as you are, I would have married you even if you were as ugly as a fence post."

"What?" Sally shouted in feigned indignation. She threw the hot pad at him.

Smoke laughed and held up his hands to defend himself from the missile. "I'm teasing, I'm teasing!" he said. "Come on, Sally, you know that I think you are prettier than any fence post I've ever seen."

"You had better stop while you are ahead, Mr. Smoke Jensen," Sally said.

"Sally, what would you say if I told you I plan to get rid of all the longhorns?"

"You're going to get rid of all of them?" Sally asked. "I thought we were going to run both longhorns and Herefords for a while."

"Why should I? You saw what happened when we shipped this year's beeves. You pointed it out yourself, we barely broke even."

"We don't have enough Herefords."

"We'll buy more, plus a champion seed bull. I don't think we have any choice," Smoke said. "What do you think?"

"Smoke, you are the rancher here," Sally replied. "I'm just a rancher's wife."

"Ha!" Smoke said, laughing out loud. "You're *just* a rancher's wife? That's a hoot! Just a rancher's wife, my hind leg. Sally, you know full well I'm not going to do something like that unless we both agree."

"Well, I didn't say I wasn't a smart rancher's wife," Sally replied with a broad smile.

Before Smoke could respond, there was a knock on the kitchen door.

"That will be Cal," Sally said.

"Of course it will be. It's breakfast time, isn't it? Cal always manages to find some reason to drop by at breakfast time, or dinnertime, or supper time. Or if you've made a pie, or a fresh batch of bear signs."

"Cal is welcome at any meal, you know that, Smoke," Sally said.

"Yeah, I know. I was just making an observation, that's all."

"Let him in."

Smoke opened the door, and the young cowhand

stepped inside. A few years earlier, a starving and destitute Cal, who was barely in his teens at the time, made the mistake of trying to rob Sally. It was a huge mistake, because Sally was as good with a gun as any man, and she got the drop on him. Instead of turning him over to the sheriff, however, Sally brought him home and made him, not just another cowhand, but one of the family.

"Smoke, I was wonderin' if—oh, you're about to have breakfast, are you? Maybe I should come back later."

"Don't be silly, Cal. I've already set a plate for you. Have a seat at the table," Sally said.

"You've already set a plate? How did you know I would be here?"

"Like I said, Cal, don't be silly."

"Well, thank you, Miss Sally. You didn't have to do that, but, oh, sausage, eggs, potatoes, and biscuits. It does look good."

Sally brought the food to the table and they all sat down.

"Now," Smoke said as he buttered a biscuit. "What is on your mind, Cal?"

"I beg your pardon?" Cal replied.

"When you came in, you said you were wondering about something. What is it you are wondering about?"

"Oh, nothing really," Cal replied. "I was just wonderin' if you had heard anything from Pearlie is all."

"Now, Cal, you know that every time we hear from Pearlie we tell you," Sally said.

"Yes, ma'am, I know. It's just that I miss him."

"We all miss him," Sally said.

"Do you reckon he'll be comin' back?"

"I believe he will."

"The last we heard of him, he was down New Mexico way, wasn't he?" Cal asked.

"He was," Smoke said.

"Cal, did you know that Smoke is planning to get rid of all the longhorns and convert the entire herd to Herefords?" Sally asked.

"Really?" Cal asked.

"Yes."

"Oh, wow, I think that is a great idea," Cal said.

"You do?" Sally asked, surprised by Cal's reaction.

"Yes, ma'am. Me'n Pearlie—uh—that is, Pearlie and me used to talk about it."

"Pearlie and I," Sally corrected, giving in to the attitude of the schoolteacher she once was.

"Yes, ma'am, Pearlie and I," Cal said. "The thing is, there don't nobody want longhorns no more. I heard they ain't payin' near nothin' for 'em, which you didn't tell me 'cause it ain't none of my business, but I figure you didn't get much for them longhorns we drove into town last week."

Sally held up her finger and started to speak. Then she just smiled and shook her head. "You are incorrigible."

"I'm a what?"

"Never mind."

"You're right about the price we got for the longhorns," Smoke said. "We got practically nothing for them."

"Which is why I think you would be smart to switch over to raisin' Herefords. Herefords, well, they do real good on grass, and they get bigger than longhorns, and would make more beef, which means you are goin' to make a lot more money on them. The beef is better tastin', too. Why, you 'member that, Miss Sally, when we spitted and cooked that steer last fall? It was a Hereford, and ever'body just went on and on 'bout how good it was."

"Here now, Cal, you are hurting my feelings. All this

time, I thought they were just complimenting my cooking," Sally teased. "But you are telling me that I had nothing to do with it, it was just because the beef was from a Hereford."

"No, no, I didn't mean nothin' like that," Cal said quickly. "You're the best cook there is. I just—"

Sally's laugh cut him off. "I'm teasing you, Cal. But you seem to know a lot about Herefords. I must confess that I'm quite impressed."

"Yes, ma'am. Like I said, me and—that is, Pearlie and I talked about 'em some when Smoke brung the first ones in. And since that time, I've read a lot about 'em," Cal said.

"I suppose they are the way to go. But I can't help it, there is just something about longhorns that I like," Sally said. "To me they are Western icons." When she saw the blank questioning expression on Cal's face, she explained. "I think they are the symbol of the West."

"Yes, ma'am, well, there is that to be said about longhorns. Plus another thing is they are a tough breed and can near'bout raise themselves. But I do believe there will be a time when purt' near all the ranches will be raisin' nothin' but Herefords, and there won't be no—"

"Won't be any," Sally corrected automatically.

"Won't be any market for longhorns."

"Sally, why do you waste your time correcting his grammar?" asked Smoke. "You correct one sentence and he murders the next. You are like Don Quixote, dueling with windmills."

"I can't help it, it is just the schoolteacher in me. Besides, someone has to duel with windmills. Otherwise, the world would be overrun with them," Sally said, and she and Smoke laughed.

"Dueling with windmills?" Cal asked, his face mirroring his confusion. "Who would duel with a windmill? That don't make no sense a'tall."

"It's from a story about this fella named Don Quixote who went around dueling with windmills," Smoke said.

"A Mexican fella, was he?"

"No, it's—uh—"

Sally laughed. Now, this I want to hear," she said, "you explaining a novel that is farcical, but also serious and philosophical about the theme of deception."

Smoke shook his head. "I guess you are right," he said. "Cal, it's just an expression, that's all. It means wasting your time."

"Oh. Sort of like bailing out water with a sieve," Cal suggested.

Smoke laughed. "You might say that," he said.

"Well, then, why didn't you?"

"I guess I didn't think of it. Tell me, Cal, with all the reading you have done about Herefords, is it your opinion that it would be worth investing in a champion bull?"

"Do you mean a bull like Prince Henry?" Cal asked.

Smoke nodded. "That's exactly who I mean. From what I hear, Prince Henry is a true champion."

"He damn sure is!" Cal said excitedly. Then, with a flushed expression on his face, he looked over toward Sally. "I'm sorry 'bout the language, Miss Sally."

"Oh, don't be silly," Sally replied. "I've heard much worse. You know about Prince Henry, do you?"

"Yes, ma'am, I looked him up and read all about him. He's a direct descendant of one of the Seventeen."

"One of the Seventeen?"

"Henry Clay was the first to bring Herefords to America," Cal explained. "He brung seventeen of them over.

Prince Henry is a direct descendant from one of them—uh—those bulls. He would be a great bull for us. Oh, I don't mean anything by saying 'us.' I mean he would be a great bull for Sugarloaf."

"Of course you mean us, Cal. You are part of Sugarloaf and you know it," Sally said.

"Yes, ma'am, you and Smoke have sure made Pearlie and me feel like that. Are you going to buy Prince Henry?" Cal asked.

"I'll buy him if he isn't too expensive," Smoke said. "The problem is, some people get so caught up in the idea of a bull being a champion that they think he is worth more than he really is. I mean, when you get right down to it, all we really need is a bull who has an eye for the ladies, right?"

"An eye for the ladies," Cal said. He slapped his knee and laughed out loud. "Yes, sir, he sure needs to have an eye for the ladies all right."

Sally laughed as well.

"Where do you find this—handsome fellow—Prince Henry?" Sally asked.

"He is in Colorado Springs," Smoke said. "The auction is two days from now. I thought I would take the evening train—that would put me into Colorado Springs first thing in the morning and leave me a couple of days to look him over. I would also get to see who else might be bidding on him."

"Good idea," Sally said. "That way you might also get an idea as to how much you are going to have to spend."

"And, if there are several others interested in him, then it will tell me for sure that a new era in cattle breeding is coming," Smoke said. "That would be good to know, because I sure don't want to get caught a day late and a dollar short."

"You're leaving this evening?" Sally asked.

"Yes. Cal, you can ride into town with me, then bring my horse back?"

"All right."

"No need," Sally said. "I'll take you into town in the buckboard."

"I'd still like to go into town with you, that is, if you don't mind, Miss Sally," Cal said.

"I don't mind," Sally said.

"I don't have to go to Colorado Springs alone, you know," Smoke said. "Colorado Springs is a nice place to visit. You might enjoy coming along with me."

"I'll just pack a few things," Sally said, getting up from the table.

Smoke laughed.

"What is it?"

"It didn't take much to convince you to go with me, did it?"

"Ha! You were just being nice, weren't you? You didn't really expect me to go."

"To be honest, no, I didn't think you would want to go. But I wasn't just being nice. I'm glad you decided you would."

During the drive into town that afternoon, they talked about what would be required in order to convert the herd to all Herefords. One of the first things to do would be to sell off all the remaining longhorns.

"If everyone else is selling off their longhorns at the

same time, that's going to have the effect of even further depressing the market for them," Sally said.

"I know."

"I mean, we just barely broke even with what we did sell. We'll take a loss by selling all the rest of them."

"It could be worse," Smoke said. "You do remember the big freeze out, don't you? We lost thousands of cattle that year, with no compensation at all."

"Yes, I remember that," Sally said. She shivered involuntarily as she recalled the brutal winter.*

"You want to have dinner at Louie's?" Smoke suggested.

"Sure. Only, let's stop by the post office first."

*Betrayal of the Mountain Man

Chapter Five

Louis Longmont ran a saloon, but as he insisted, "Longmont's is not your run-of-the-mill warm-beer-and-bad-whiskey saloon. It is as proper a place for ladies as the finest restaurant."

The Frenchman was true to his word and, when they were in Big Rock, it was Smoke and Sally's favorite place to relax. After picking up their mail at the post office, they stepped into Longmont's.

"Smoke, *mon cher ami*!" Longmont called as he saw the three sitting at the table. "How wonderful of you to grace my establishment with your beautiful young lady."

"Louis, you make me blush," Sally said.

"Blushing becomes you, my dear. Oh, whatever you have for dinner, you must save room for my *tarte français de soie*."

"Oh, it sounds lovely," Sally said. "I shall look forward to it."

"What is, uh, whaever that is you said?" Cal asked.

"It's French silk pie," Sally explained. "Don't worry, knowing you, you will like it."

"I like any kind of pie," Cal said with a broad smile.

"*Mon jeune ami,* this isn't just any kind of pie," Longmont said resolutely.

A few minutes later, Louis served them personally.

"*Rôti de boeuf avec les pommes de terre. Bon appétit,*" he said as he set the steaming plates on the table before them.

"That just looks like roast beef to me," Cal said. "I mean, don't get me wrong, it looks like good roast beef, but it don't look like whatever that is you said it was."

Louis chuckled. "This is Hereford. I think you'll find it a bit more tender than what you are used to."

"See what I'm talking about, Sally?" Smoke said with a resigned sigh. "Even Louis is switching over to Hereford."

After their meal, Smoke began looking through the mail they had picked up at the post office. He smiled as he held one of the letters up.

"It is from Pearlie," he said.

"Read it aloud," Sally said.

Smoke opened the envelope, removed the letter, and began to read.

Dear Smoke, Sally, and Cal,

    I take pen in hand to pass on to all of you my regards and to tell you that my thoughts are often of Sugarloaf and the many fine times we have had together.

    I am still in the New Mexico Territory where I have taken a job as shotgun guard for the Sunset Stage Coach Company. Five days a week we go from Los Brazos to Chama. The trip to Chama takes about three and a half hours. We stay there for one hour, then we come back to Los Brazos.

    There is much desert land here in New Mexico, and also mountains. The cactus flowers are very pretty, but I do not think New Mexico is as pretty as Colorado.

*I have thought much about Lucy, and I have wondered
how it would be if she had not been killed. But it is not good
to think much about such things. I am glad that you are
a justice of the peace and that you were able to marry us.
I know that our getting married made Lucy very happy,
and when I think about it now, I am happy about it too.*

*Tell Cal I am taking very good care of his silver
hatband, and I promise that, one day soon, I will bring
it back to him.*

> *Your friend,*
> *Pearlie*

"Did you hear that?" Cal asked happily. "He said one
day soon, he would come back."

"He certainly did," Sally agreed.

"I wonder how soon is soon?"

Half an hour later, after having eaten Louis Longmont's
French silk pie—Cal had two pieces—the three drove in
the buckboard down to the depot that served the Denver
and Rio Grande Railroad. They reached the depot just as
the train was pulling into the station.

"Now I call that good timing," Smoke said, hauling back
on the reins as the train squealed, squeaked, rumbled, and
rattled to a halt.

"Smoke, I want you to promise me something," Sally
said as the two of them stepped down from the buckboard.

"I'll promise you anything, my love, you know that,"
Smoke replied.

"Let's not go overboard when bidding for that bull. I
think we should give ourselves a limit."

Smoke chuckled. "I've already taken care of that," he said. "I'm only taking seven hundred fifty dollars. That's as high as I will be able to go."

"Good," Sally said. "If you think having a champion bull is important, I hope we can buy him. But if we can't, then I'm sure we can find another bull who—how was it you put it? Has an eye for the ladies?"

Smoke laughed, then reached back into the buckboard to pick up their luggage. "Cal, I'm counting on you to look out for things while I'm gone," he said.

"I will, Smoke," Cal promised. "Don't you worry none about that. I will. You two have a good time in Colorado Springs, and bring back that bull."

"I'll bring him back."

"If he doesn't cost too much," Sally added.

"If he doesn't cost too much," Smoke agreed.

Smoke and Sally walked across the wooden depot platform, then stepped up into the train. Once in the car, they sat on the depot side of the train with Sally taking the window seat. As the train pulled out of the station, Sally waved at Cal, who sat in the buckboard, watching them leave. Smiling broadly, Cal waved back.

"Bless his heart, he sure misses Pearlie," Sally said as the train began gathering speed.

"I know he does. We all do," Smoke said. "But Pearlie being gone is good for Cal."

"How is it good for him?"

"One of the things about growing up is learning how to adjust to changes," Smoke said.

"Smoke, Cal was orphaned when he was barely into his teens. It was a struggle just for him to stay alive. It isn't as if he hasn't had to deal with changes."

Smoke nodded. "I guess you are right at that," he said.

He leaned back in his seat, then pulled his hat down over his eyes.

"What are you doing?" Sally asked. "Smoke Jensen, are you just going to sit there like that for the whole trip?"

"It's going to be a long overnight trip," Smoke said. "And I got up early this morning."

"You get up early every morning."

"Yeah, I do, don't I?" Smoke made no effort to remove his hat.

Sally looked at him for a moment, then reached up and took his hat off his head. Before he could say anything, she kissed him, then replaced his hat.

"What was that all about?" Smoke asked

"Don't I always kiss you good night?" she asked with a little chuckle.

As Smoke napped beside her, Sally turned in her seat to look at the countryside that was unrolling just outside the window. The scenery, now taking on the golden hue of sunset, was beautiful, and she thought again how lucky, and how unlikely, it was that she, a New England Yankee, would wind up here, married to this man who was already a legend in his own lifetime.

Growing up in New Hampshire, Sally came from a family of great wealth. She could have stayed in New Hampshire and married "well," meaning she could have married a blue blood from one of New Hampshire's old, established, and wealthy families. She would have hosted teas and garden parties, and grown old to become a New England matriarch.

But while such a future promised a life of ease and tranquility, that wasn't what Sally had in mind. She envisioned a much more active—some might suggest uncertain—

future. Thus, she announced to one and all that she intended to leave New Hampshire.

"You can't be serious, Sally!" family and friends had said in utter shock when she informed them that she intended to see the American West. "Why, that place is positively wild with beasts and savages."

"And not all the savages are Indian, if you get my meaning," Melinda Hobson said. Melinda Hobson was of "the" Hobsons, one of New Hampshire's founding families.

But Sally had a yen to see the American West, as well as a thirst for adventure, and that brought her to Bury, Idaho Territory, where she wound up teaching school.

It was in Bury that she met a young gunman named Buck West. There was something about the young man that caught her attention right away. It wasn't just the fact that he was ruggedly handsome, nor was it the fact that, despite his cool demeanor, he went out of his way to be respectful to her. That respect, Sally saw, applied to all women—including soiled doves—even though he was not a habitué of their services.

But it was the intensity of the young man that appealed to Sally—a brooding essence that ran deep into his soul.

Then, she learned that his name wasn't even Buck West, it was Smoke Jensen. And the hurt he felt was the result of a personal tragedy of enormous magnitude. Smoke's young wife, Nicole, had been raped, tortured, murdered, and scalped by men whose evil knew no bounds. They had also murdered Arthur, his infant son.

Those same men owned ranches and mines around the town of Bury. In fact, one might say they owned Bury itself, including nearly every resident of the town. If ever there was a Sodom and Gomorrah in America, Sally thought, it was Bury, Idaho Territory.

And, like the Biblical cities of sin, Bury was destroyed, not by God, but by Smoke Jensen, who, after allowing the women and children to leave, killed the murderers and the gunmen, and then put the town to the torch. When Smoke, with Sally now by his side, set out en route to the "High Lonesome," there was nothing remaining of Bury but the smoldering rubble of a destroyed town and the dead killers Smoke left behind him.

The rage that had burned in his soul was gone, and he had put Nicole and Arthur to rest in a private compartment of his heart. With the fire in his gut gone, Smoke was free to love once more, and to be loved, and Sally was there for him.

Sally knew that Smoke would always love Nicole—in fact, Sally was sure that she loved him the more because of that loyalty. And though she had never met Nicole, Sally had come to love her as well, as a sister that she'd never met.

The train rolled over a rough part of the track and the resultant jostling startled Smoke awake.

"What?" he asked.

"Nothing, darling," Sally said, taking his hand. "Go back to sleep."

Smoke squeezed her hand, and she responded. Her life may have taken some unusual twists, but had she planned every twist and turn, she could not have hoped for anything more than she had right now.

For Sally Jensen, life could not be sweeter.

Santa Clara

The New York Saloon had nothing to do with either the city or the state of New York. Rodney Gibson, the owner, was not a native New Yorker, and had never even been in New York. But the name appealed to him, so when he built his saloon in Santa Clara, shortly after the arrival of the Denver and Rio Grande Railroad ensured the survival of the struggling little town, he named his saloon after the city he had only read about.

The saloon was well appointed, with two large, hanging chandeliers as well as light sconces all around the walls. The walls were covered with a rich red paper, which filled the space from baseboard to molding.

The most talked about item of the saloon, however, was the exceptionally lifelike, as well as nearly life-size, painting behind the bar. The painting, titled *Note From Cupid*, was of a very beautiful nude woman lying on a couch of red and gilt in such a way that absolutely none of her charms were hidden from view. Hovering just over her was the artist's concept of Cupid, looking down mischievously, as the nude woman read the note he had just delivered.

It was just after seven P.M. and the saloon was at its busiest with cowboys, miners, freighters, store clerks, and the town's few professionals filling the tables and lining the bar. At the back of the room the piano player, a young man who was barely out of his teens, was bent over the keyboard, playing music that could barely be heard over the laughter and conversation of the many patrons.

"The hell I can't do the fandango!" Billy Ray Quentin shouted, his voice clearly heard above both the piano and the ambient sound. Standing up, Billy Ray reached down to the table, picked up a bottle of whiskey, and turning it to his lips, drained the rest of it in Adam's-apple-bobbing swallows. After he finished the bottle, he tossed it carelessly over his shoulder, causing the people at one of the other tables to have to dodge quickly to avoid being hit.

"Billy Ray, you can't no more do the fandango than I can," one of the other three men at the table said. Billy Ray was the son of the most prominent rancher in Huereano County, and the men at the table with him were cowboys from the Tumbling Q, which was Billy Ray's father's ranch.

"I'll just by damn show you I can do it," Billy Ray said. "And I'm willin' to put money on it, too."

"Hell, we ain't got no money to bet, Billy Ray. You know that," Jerry Kelly said. Kelly was not only the oldest of the three cowboys; he was also older than Billy Ray.

"The three of you together can come up with a dollar, can't you? I tell you what, if I can do it, you three owe me one dollar. If I can't do it, I'll give each of you a dollar apiece. How is that for a bet?"

The three men looked at each other, then nodded.

"Reeves, I'll take the bet if you will," Kelly said.

"All right," Reeves said. "Let's do it. Let's see ole Billy Ray here dance the fandango."

Billy Ray wiped the back of his hand across his mouth, then looked around the saloon until he saw one of the bar girls leaning against the piano, talking to the piano player.

"You!" he shouted, pointing toward the girl. "Come here. These here fellas have bet me that I can't dance the fandango, and I need to prove to them that I can. But I can't do it without a woman."

"Oh, Billy Ray, I don't know anything about dancing the fandango," the girl replied.

"Hell, you don't have to do anything more than just stand there, and sort of move back and forth," Billy Ray said. "I'm the one that's goin' to be doin' all the dancin'."

The girl looked over toward the saloon owner, who was now behind behind the bar, helping Lloyd Evans, the bartender.

"What should I do, Mr. Gibson?" she asked.

"Go ahead, Mary Lou," Gibson replied. "If it will keep him quiet."

"All right, if you say so," Mary Lou Culpepper replied nervously. She started toward Billy Ray.

"Hey, you, piano player!" Billy Ray shouted.

The piano player, who was in the middle of a rendition of "Buffalo Gals," didn't look around.

"Lenny, I'm talkin' to you," Billy Ray shouted. He drew his pistol and aimed toward the piano. Before anyone could stop him, he pulled the trigger. The suddenness of the gunshot quieted the room as everyone looked over to see what was going on. The bullet Billy Ray fired hit the glass bowl that sat on top of the piano, smashing it, and scattering the coins that patrons had dropped in from time to time. The piano player dived off the bench to the floor.

Billy, who was holding a smoking pistol, laughed.

"Look at that," he said. "Did you see the way Lenny jumped? Ain't that about the funniest thing you ever seen?"

"Billy Ray!" Gibson shouted, and when Billy Ray looked toward the bar, he saw that the owner was aiming a double-barreled shotgun at him. "Put that pistol down. I ain't goin' to have you shootin' up my place."

"Well, hell, Rodney, you don't have to get your dander up over it," Billy Ray said as he handed his pistol to Kelly. "I was just tryin' to get the piano player's attention, that's all."

"You shouldn't of done that," Mary Lou said. "You could have killed Lenny."

"Yeah, well, I didn't kill him, did I?" Billy Ray said. "Hey, you, Lenny. Play me a song I can do the fandango to."

"I'm—I'm not sure I even know such a song," the young man replied.

"Then make one up," Billy Ray demanded. He reached out to take the bar girl's hand. "Me'n the whore here is goin' to dance the fandango."

Lenny began playing a Spanish piece with a strong rhythmic beat, which intensified as the song progressed.

Billy Ray stepped out, whirled, stomped his feet, clapped his hands, then leaped up and tried to kick his heels together. When he did, he got his feet tangled up and he fell. He didn't get up.

Mary Lou let out a little cry of alarm.

"Oh! Is he dead?" she asked.

Kelly leaned over to look at him. "Nah," he said. "He is either knocked out or passed out drunk, but he ain't dead."

"That's a shame," the bartender said.

As the patrons of the New York Saloon stood looking down at the prostrate form of Billy Ray Quentin, an older man, with a scraggly beard, a barrel chest, and a bulging eye that didn't track with the other, stepped in to the saloon. He stopped just in front of the swinging batwing doors when he saw that everyone was quiet.

"What's goin' on?" he asked.

"Hello, Cole," Kelly said.

"Where's Billy Ray?" Cole asked.

Kelly pointed to the prostrate form on the floor.

"Is he all right?" Cole asked.

"Yeah, he's all right. If you call passed out drunk all right," Kelly said. "What you doin' here? You ain't a drinkin' man."

"I came for Billy Ray," Cole said. "His pa wants him to come home."

"I hope you come in a buckboard, 'cause ole Billy Ray sure as hell ain't goin' to be able to ride back."

"I did," Cole Mathers said. He walked over to Billy Ray, looked down at him, then sighed. "You boys get him outside, throw him in the back of the buckboard," he ordered.

Cole was able to give them orders because he was the ranch foreman. "And tie his horse to the back."

"All right, Reeves, Lewis, you heard the man," Kelly said to the other two. "Let's get him out there."

"You think he'll remember in the morning that he owes the three of us a dollar each?" Reeves asked.

"Hell, if he remembers anything, he'll probably insist that he did it and *we* owe *him*," Kelly said. "I think it best we don't say anything about it."

Cole watched as Reeves and Lewis picked up the unconscious man and carried him out.

"You might want this," Kelly said, handing a pistol to Cole.

"Why would I want that?"

"It belongs to Billy Ray."

Cole nodded, then took the pistol and stuck it down into his belt. He started toward the door, then stopped and looked back at Kelly. "You comin', or are you stayin'?"

"Mr. Quentin didn't send you after me, did he?"

"No."

"Then I'm stayin'."

Cole nodded, then walked outside, just as he saw Billy Ray being unceremoniously dropped into back of the buckboard. With a nod of thanks, he climbed into the seat, then drove off.

* * *

Two hours later, Billy Ray Quentin was back home at the Tumbling Q, sitting at the kitchen table and drinking a cup of hot coffee. He made a face. "What's in this coffee? Horse piss? It tastes awful."

"I had the cook make it very strong. I want you to sober up," Pogue Quentin said.

Pogue was sitting across the table from his son, and these were the first words he had spoken.

"All I did was have a few drinks," Billy Ray said.

"And make a damn fool of yourself," Pogue Quentin retorted.

"What did you have Cole bring me home for?"

"We're goin' to Colorado Springs tomorrow," Pogue said. "I want you sober when we get on the train."

"Colorado Springs?" Billy Ray brightened up. "Yeah," he said. "I've heard of Colorado Springs. They have a lot things you can do there. I've heard they even have a fancy gamblin' house and theater there, just like they have in the big cities."

"We aren't goin' to Colorado Springs to have a good time," Pogue said.

"Then why are we goin'?"

"We're goin' to buy a bull."

"We're goin' to buy a bull? Pa, what are you talkin' about? You can buy a bull anywhere."

"Not like this one, you can't," Pogue said. "This here is a purebred champion Hereford bull, and I aim to get him."

"Ain't we already got a herd of Herefords?"

"We've got a start," Quentin said. "But soon, there will be no longhorns left, ever' rancher in the West will be raisin' Herefords, and whoever gets started first, and with the best bloodlines, is goin' to be top hog in the lot."

Billy Ray laughed. "Hell, Pa, the way you managed to get hold of all the other ranches in the county, you are already top hog in the lot."

"Yeah, I am," Pogue said. "And I aim to stay here. So you get yourself packed, then get a good night's sleep. We'll be leavin' on the mornin' train."

"To buy a bull?" Billy Ray asked.

"To buy a bull," Pogue said.

Chapter Six

Los Brazos

An article in a Western newspaper gave hints for those who traveled by stagecoach, and the proprietors of the Sunset Stage Line had it printed up on flyers to be handed out to the passengers as they bought their tickets. Pearlie, who had been a shotgun guard for the stage line for nearly six weeks now, leaned back against the wall with his arms folded across his chest as he watched the passengers take the little handbill, then find a seat in the waiting room to read the material.

Helpful Instruction *for* Stagecoach Passengers

1) When a driver asks a passenger to get out and walk, you are advised to do so, and not grumble about it.
2) If the team of horses runs away, remain seated and let the skilled and experienced driver handle it. Passengers who attempt to jump from the rapidly moving coach may be seriously injured.
3) Smoking and spitting on the leeward side of the coach is discouraged.

4) Drinking spirits is allowed, but passengers should be generous and share.
5) Swearing is not allowed.
6) Sleeping on your neighbor's shoulder is not allowed.
7) Travelers shouldn't point out spots where murders have occurred, especially when "delicate" passengers are aboard.
8) Greasing one's hair is discouraged because dust will stick to it.

As he had written in his last letter to Smoke, Sally, and Cal, the Sunset Stage Coach Line was a small company that ran only from Los Brazos to the railroad depot at Chama. The coach departed Los Brazos at eight A.M., and at an average speed of eight miles per hour, would arrive at Chama just before noon. It would leave Chama at one P.M., and arrive in Los Brazos just before supper.

Although you could crowd nine passengers into the coach, it would be making the journey today with only five, the passenger manifest consisting of a man, his wife and child, a banker, and a territorial mining official. The official was an overbearing man, impressed with his position and authority. He had already let the ticket agent and the driver know who and what he was, and how important it was that he reach Chama in time to take the two o'clock train.

"It is vital business for the territorial government of New Mexico," he insisted. "I'm not sure you quite understand the significance of that, but as an official representative of the territory of New Mexico, it is imperative that I not be impeded."

"You are due to arrive by noon," the ticket agent said. "I'm sure we will be able to get you there by two o'clock."

Just outside, the hostlers were hitching up the team and

readying the coach for the trip. The driver, a man with white hair and beard, stuck his head in through the door.

"How many today?" he asked.

"Hello, Ben. Looks like five, unless someone else comes before we leave," Pearlie said.

Ben pulled a pocket watch from his shirt pocket, opened the face, and examined it.

"Well, if anybody else is plannin' on makin' the run, they'd better get themselves here in a hurry," he said. "Otherwise, they'll be waitin' here till tomorrow."

"Your team is all hitched up, Mr. Dooley," one of the hostlers called to him.

"Thanks, Mike," Ben said. "Pearlie, you go ahead and climb up to your seat. I'll get the passengers loaded."

"Yes, sir."

Pearlie used one of the horizontal spokes of the front wheel to climb up into the high seat. Scooting over to the left, he looked down into the boot and saw both a double-barreled shotgun and a Winchester, 44.40 rifle. Breaking down the shotgun, he saw that both barrels were loaded. He closed it, then let the hammers down. The rifle was loaded as well.

A moment later, Ben came out of the depot with the passengers and stood by the door as they boarded. That done, he climbed up beside Pearlie, released the brake, picked up the reins, and snapped them against the back of the team.

The coach left the depot with the team moving at a rapid trot. Ben always did this, holding the trot until they were well out of town. Not until then would he slow the team to a more sustainable gait.

Shortly after he came to work with the stage line, Pearlie asked Ben why he did that.

"It's to make a show for the people in town," he said.

"Most folks, when they see the stage leave town like that, have the idea that we keep the speed up all the way to where we are goin'. That way, if they're thinkin' on goin' somewhere, the idea of usin' a stage ain't all that hard for 'em to take. But if they was to see us leave at a slow walk, they would, more than likely, want just about anything other than a long, slow stagecoach ride."

Pearlie chuckled. "I reckon there's some truth to that when you think about it."

"Of course there is," Ben said. He leaned over to spit out the quid of chewing tobacco he had been working on.

Ben was married and had a daughter who was just a little younger than Pearlie. When Pearlie first came to work for the stage line, Ben hinted that his young shotgun guard might take an interest in Mindy. Mindy was a pretty girl, and any other time, Pearlie might have been interested. But the loss of Lucy was still too fresh. Pearlie told Ben about Lucy, and how she had died. Ben understood, and never brought up the subject of his daughter again.

Up on the box, Pearlie rode silently while the driver worked the horses. Ben had named the horses and he was constantly talking to them, cursing one of them for slacking off, praising another for doing well, often playing them against each other.

"Well now, Rhoda, what do you think? Do you see how Harry is showin' off for you? You aren't going to hurt his feelings now, are you? Come on, pick it up, show him what you can do."

Because Ben was busy with his horses, Pearlie was left alone with his thoughts. He wondered what was going on back at Sugarloaf. Did they miss him? Would they welcome him back when he returned? He had already given notice that this would be his last week, that he was going back home.

Home? Was Sugarloaf home?

Yeah, the more he thought about it, the more he was sure that Sugarloaf was home. It was certainly more of a home to him than anyplace else he had ever lived in his life.

A few years earlier, Pearlie had been a gunman, hired by a man who wanted to run Smoke off so he could ride roughshod over those who were left. But Pearlie didn't take to killing and looting from innocent people, so he quit his job. He had stopped by to warn Smoke of the plan against him, and to tell him that, because he wanted no part of it, he would be leaving the valley. To Pearlie's surprise, Smoke offered to hire him.

Since that time, Pearlie had worked for Smoke and Sally. He stood just a shade less than six feet tall, was lean as a willow branch, had a face tanned the color of an old saddle, and a head of wild, unruly black hair. His eyes were mischievous and he was quick to smile and joke, but underneath his slapstick demeanor was a man that was as hard as iron, as loyal to his friends as they come, and very nearly as good with a gun as Smoke was.

There were three other stagecoaches in Chama when Ben hauled back on the reins and set the brakes at the conclusion of their journey. Like Pearlie's coach, the other three coaches represented towns that had no railroad of their own, and so their main routes were back and forth from their towns to the depot in Chama.

A couple of hostlers who worked for Sunset met the coach as it arrived, then unharnessed the team and led them off for a twenty-four-hour rest. Before the coach started back, a new, fresh team would be connected.

Pearlie laughed the first day when they started back because, when Ben started talking to the teams, calling the horses by name, he saw that he was using the same names.

"They don't mind, they're just horses," Ben explained.

"And if I use the same names for all of·them, it makes it easier for me to remember."

Pearlie couldn't argue with that.

The drivers and shotgun guards of the stagecoaches always took their lunch at the Railroad Diner. They were free to go somewhere else if they wanted to, but if they ate at the Railroad Diner, their meals were paid for by their respective stage lines.

The drivers generally ate at one table and the shotgun guards at another. Pearlie was neither the oldest nor the youngest of the guards, so he fit in well with them, and generally enjoyed his visits with them.

Today, two of the other guards were in the middle of an argument when Pearlie joined them.

"He ain't nowhere near as good," one of them said.

"The hell he ain't," the second guard said. "I've read books about my man. I ain't never read nothin' about your man."

The guard shook his head. "First of all, he ain't my man."

"Well, he's the one you're sayin' is so good."

"Hello, Mack, Zeb. What are you two talking about?" Pearlie asked.

"Zeb says that Snake Cates is a better man than Smoke Jensen," Mack said.

"No, now, I ain't said no such a thing," Zeb said, holding his hand out in denial. "I ain't talkin' about who is the better man. There ain't no doubt in my mind but what Smoke Jensen is the better man. Fact is, I ain't never heard nothin' bad about him. All I'm a sayin' is that iffen it was to come down to a gunfight betwixt the two of 'em, I think Snake Cates would win."

"What makes you think that?" Pearlie asked.

"Well, think about it. Near'bout ever one knows that Snake Cates kills folks for a livin'. What I mean is, if somebody has someone he wants kilt, why, all he has to do is pay Cates enough money and Cates will do it. Hell, there ain't no tellin' how many men he's kilt by now. But this fella Smoke Jensen, now, I'm sure he's good 'cause I've heard a lot about him. But he don't go around killin' people as a job, does he? So, when you get right down to it, that means Snake Cates would more than likely kill Smoke Jensen if they was to get into an out-right gunfight," Zeb said, finishing his explanation.

"What do you think, Pearlie?" Mack asked. "Iffen the two of them was to get into a gunfight, which one do you think would win?"

"I don't know," Pearlie replied. "But I tell you this, don't sell Smoke short."

"What do you mean by don't sell 'Smoke' short?" Mack asked.

"What do you mean, what do I mean?"

"I mean the way you said 'Smoke' as if you know him. You ain't goin' to try an' tell us you know him, are you?"

"No," Pearlie said. "I'm not going to tell you I know him. All I'm saying is, if it came right down to it, I wouldn't bet against Smoke Jensen."

"There you are, Zeb," Mack said. "Pearlie agrees with me."

"Ha! And that's supposed to change my mind, be-cause Pearlie agrees with you?"

For the rest of the meal, Pearlie made no more contri-butions to the conversation. He had never told anyone of his relationship with Smoke Jensen, and he really didn't plan to tell anyone. He had no specific reason for keeping quiet about it, though he knew, intuitively, that if he did tell someone, he would face two types of people. The first group would be those who would attempt to get a rise out of him by heaping scorn on Smoke Jensen. The second group would be those who didn't believe him, and they would be just as uncomfortable to be around as the first.

Because Pearlie did not participate in the conversation, the subject soon changed so that, by the time they were all ready to leave the diner to make their return run, there were no arguments and they were laughing and joking together.

"So, this here feller," Zeb was saying, "went into a bank pullin' his wife along with him. 'Look here,' he says to the bank teller. 'Iffen I was to give you forty dollars, would you give me two twenties?'

"'Why, yes, I would,' this here bank teller answers.

"So this feller, what he done is, he pushed his wife up in front of the teller and he says, 'This here woman is forty years old. I'd like me two twenty-year-olds, please.'"

Zeb laughed hard at his own joke.

"I don't get it," Danny said. Danny was the youngest of the shotgun guards.

Now all of them laughed even harder.

"Mack," one of the drivers called from the other table. "Time for us to be gettin' started back."

"Yeah, us, too," another driver said, and the four drivers and four shotgun guards left the restaurant to the good-byes of the regulars who ate there every day.

"Pearlie? Can I speak to you for a moment?" Ben asked as they walked from the diner back to the coach. The new team had been attached and the six horses stood waiting in their harness.

"Sure thing, Ben," Pearlie replied.

"Can you use a gun?" Ben asked.

"Well, sure I can, if I have to," Pearlie replied. He chuckled. "I wouldn't be much good in this job if I couldn't now, would I?"

"The reason I asked is, you might want to be particularly ready for this trip."

"Why is that?"

"I've just been told that there is over ten thousand dollars in cash in the strongbox," Ben said. "It's for the New Mexico Mining Company, cash comin' back to 'em for the last shipment of gold they sent out."

"We're goin' to be carrying ten thousand dollars?"

"That's what the dispatcher told me."

"That's a lot of money."

"It sure is. Of course they're tryin' to keep it quiet, but when there's that much money, it has a way of getting out. So I think you better be on your toes."

"Thanks for the warning. I will be," Pearlie said.

Pearlie thought about the money they were carrying. Ten thousand dollars was a lot of money, and the truth was, there was a time in his life, before he met up with Smoke, when ten thousand dollars would be a big temptation to him.

He looked over at Ben as the older man concentrated on driving the team.

Pearlie wouldn't have to hurt Ben. All he would have to do is point his gun at the driver, reach down into the boot, pick up the strongbox, then jump off the coach.

"No!" he said aloud.

"What?" Ben asked, startled by Pearlie's unexpected outburst.

"Oh, nothing," Pearlie replied. "I was just thinking aloud, that's all." Thinking thoughts he had no business thinking, Pearlie told himself. There was no way he would ever do anything like that. In fact, there was no way he would have ever done anything like that, even when he was at his wildest.

Still, if he wanted to foil a holdup attempt, it probably

didn't hurt to think like the outlaws. Take this route, for example. He knew that if anyone had a notion to jump the stage, the best place to do it would just ahead of where they were right now, where the canyon walls squeezed in so tight alongside the road that the coach would have to move at a snail's pace.

Pearlie looked through a gap in the canyon ahead, and as he did so, he saw two men who seemed to have an intense interest in the progress of the coach. It also appeared that they did not want to be seen, as they would peek around the edge of a large boulder, then jerked back quickly, then peek again, repeating the process. The amount of time they were exposed to view was so brief that, to any but the most experienced eye, they would have gone unnoticed.

"Ben, I just saw them," Pearlie said.

"You sure about that?"

"Yeah, I'm sure."

"What makes you so sure?"

"Because they are watching us and they don't want to be seen watching us. They are waiting up at the bend."

"Damn, you are probably right. I've been thinkin' all along that if they was going to hit us, more than likely they would do it here. We're goin' to be easy targets when we go through the pass."

"Or *they* will be," Pearlie said.

"What do you mean?"

Pearlie reached down into the boot for the rifle. "I'm goin' to hop down here," he said. "You go on through as if you don't suspect a thing. I plan to cut across the top here while you keep goin'. Slow down just a little bit to give me time to get into position. If I'm lucky, they'll be so busy keepin' an eye out for the stage that they won't see me comin'."

"Yeah, that sounds like a good idea," Ben said.

"I'll climb up on that rock just ahead," Pearlie offered.

"You keep your head down, young feller," Ben said with genuine concern.

"Don't worry, I will. And if everything goes all right, I'll see you on the other side."

"Right," Ben answered.

Pearlie climbed up onto the top of the stage. Then as they passed particularly close to the canyon wall, he stepped off the stage onto a rock. From the rock, he climbed on up to the top, then crouched low as he ran across the top of the canyon wall. A moment later, he saw the two men exactly where he thought they would be. Both had their guns drawn, and both were looking toward the opening in the canyon where the stagecoach would appear.

"You two boys mind tellin' me what you're doin' here?" Pearlie called out to them.

"What the hell? Who are you?" one of them yelled. When the two men turned around, Pearlie recognized one of them as the shotgun guard whose firing had led to Pearlie taking this job.

"Drop your guns, both of you," Pearlie ordered.

It looked for a moment as if the two men considered shooting it out with Pearlie, but he had a bead on them and they knew that, at the very best, at least one of them would be killed. After a quick glance at each other, they dropped their pistols, then put their hands up.

"Get on down there on the road," Pearlie ordered, motioning with the rifle.

As the two men climbed down onto the road, Pearlie went down behind them, all the while keeping them covered. In the distance, Pearlie could hear the whistles and shouts as Ben worked his team through the narrow pass and around the curve.

When Ben saw Pearlie standing in the road in front of him, with his rifle covering two men who held their hands in the air, he pulled the coach to a stop.

"I'll be damn," Ben said, as he saw the two men. "Dempster, is that you?"

"Hi, Ben," the former shotgun guard said quietly.

"Pearlie, I reckon you remember Bob Dempster, don't you?"

"I remember him," Pearlie answered.

"Dempster, I can't believe you would have robbed me."

"I know you was responsible for me a-losin' my job," Dempster said. "I was just takin' what I figure is owed me, that's all."

"You're the one that caused you to lose your job," Ben said. "You was drunk more times than you wasn't. I kept warnin' you. If I'm goin' to have someone lookin' after me, they damn well better be sober."

Ben reached under the seat and threw down two pair of hand shackles. "Get these on 'em, Pearlie, then get 'em up on top of the coach. I've had these things for nigh on to five years, and I ain't never had to use them before."

"Here!" one of the passengers in the coach called out. "You don't intend to take those men on this stage with decent folk, do you?"

"We got no choice, mister. We can't leave 'em out here," Ben called back. "They'll be ridin' up on top of the coach. You'll never see them."

"I want you to know that I intend to make my protest known about this," the passenger said.

Ben leaned over and spit out a quid in the general direction of the irate passenger. The passenger had to jerk his head in quickly to keep from being hit.

"You do that," Ben said.

Working quickly, Pearlie put the shackles on the two

would be road agents, then ordered them up onto the top of the coach. Once they were on top, he loosened their shackles just long enough to pass the chain through one of the luggage guards. Then he reconnected them before joining Ben on the driver's seat.

"You ready?" Ben asked.

"I'm ready," Pearlie replied.

Ben nodded, then whistled at the team, and the coach continued on its way.

It was late afternoon when the coach pulled into town. Because the coach was the town's major physical connection with the outside world, it always garnered attention. That was partly because Ben made his arrivals, just as he made his departures, with the horses pulling the coach along at a rapid trot.

Today, though, the coach attracted even more attention as it was very obvious that there were two men shackled to the roof of the coach. And one of them the townspeople recognized right away.

"Hey! That's Dempster!" someone shouted.

"Dempster, what are you doin' up there?"

"You remember Dempster, don't you? He used to be a guard for the stage. Now they got him shackled up there on top."

Chapter Seven

Colorado Springs

Although the train ran through the night, it had neither Pullman cars nor pull-down berths; therefore, Smoke and Sally had to sleep as well as they could on the seats. Smoke, who could sleep almost anywhere, had a much easier time of it than Sally, who sat by the window, staring out into the darkness for most of the trip. After leaving Big Rock, they had to change trains in Como, then again in Denver, both changes made in the middle of the night. It was harder in Como, because they had to wait for one hour in the small depot with only hard, wooden, and backless benches to accommodate them.

The depot in Denver was much larger, and would have been considerably more accommodating if they had had to wait, but the train for Colorado Springs was on an adjacent track, already taking on passengers, even as they were arriving.

Sally finally fell asleep on this, the last leg of their trip, but it was more because of exhaustion than anything else. She woke up just as they were coming into Colorado Springs, and was surprised to see that it was now light outside.

"Ahh, good, you are awake, I see," Smoke said.

"Barely," Sally mumbled.

"If you want, I can just leave you on the train. Whenever you finally wake up, you can take the next train back," Smoke teased.

"Ohh," Sally groaned. "I don't want to see another train, ever."

"That's interesting. You plan for us to walk back, do you?"

The couplings began rattling and the brakes squealing as the train slowed on its approach to the station.

"What do we do first?" Sally said. "And I truly hope it is find a hotel."

"That's what I plan to do, then I'll look up Tom Murchison," Smoke said.

"Who is Tom Murchison?"

"He is a lawyer here. Jim Robison recommended him to me. In fact, I would be surprised if Jim hadn't contacted him already."

Jim Robison was a lawyer back in Big Rock who was not only a friend, but who'd done some work for Smoke.

"Well, if Jim recommends him, that is good enough for me," Sally said.

Finally, the train jerked to a halt and the other passengers in the car started securing their things, preparatory to exiting.

"Oh, what a handsome-looking train station," Sally said as she and Smoke stepped down from the train.

The building that had caught Sally's attention was the Denver and Rio Grande Depot. Built of brick, it was one of the more impressive-looking buildings in town. The depot had a red-tiled roof with dormers and a cupola on top from which the yardmaster could observe train traffic on the eight sets of tracks that made up the marshaling area.

Sally saw him first, a young man standing on the platform, holding up a sign.

SMOKE JENSEN

"Smoke, look over there," Sally said, pointing the young man out to her husband. "Oh, I hope that isn't Mr. Murchison. He is so young."

"Lawyers aren't born old, you know," Smoke replied. "They are all young at some point."

"I suppose so. But I do prefer a little seasoning."

"Let's go meet him," Smoke said, leading Sally in the direction of the young man. "I'm Smoke Jensen," Smoke said when they reached him.

"Mr. Jensen, my name is Roy Clinton."

"Good," Sally said.

"I beg your pardon?"

"I mean, I thought you were Mr. Murchison."

"No, ma'am. Mr. Murchison asked me to pick you up and take you to the hotel. He has already secured a room for you, and he said he would join you for breakfast."

"Oh, I'm too tired for breakfast," Sally said.

"You may as well eat," Smoke said. "Besides, a good breakfast will refresh you."

"How far is the hotel?" Sally asked.

"Your room is at the Homestead Hotel. It's a nice place, and it's close by," Roy said. "Do you have luggage?"

"Yes, it's on the luggage car."

"That's the surrey over there. Why don't you go climb

aboard? I'll make arrangements to have your luggage sent directly to your hotel room."

"All right, thanks," Smoke said.

Smoke was carrying a small grip with him, and he and Sally walked over to the surrey and climbed in. As they waited in the surrey, Smoke watched Roy speak to one of the railroad officials and give him some money.

"He seems like a nice young man," Sally said.

"Aren't you ashamed of yourself now?"

"Why should I be ashamed?"

"For saying you are glad it wasn't Murchison."

"No. I'm still glad he isn't Mr. Murchison."

Roy came back to the surrey.

"All taken care of," he said as he climbed into the surrey, then picked up the reins.

"Are you a lawyer in Tom Murchison's office?" Smoke said.

"Yes and no," Roy replied. "I'm reading for the law, but I am not yet a practicing attorney. I'm apprenticed to Mr. Murchison."

"Well, you seem quite efficient, so I'm sure you will make a very good lawyer," Sally said.

"Thank you, ma'am," Roy replied, beaming at the compliment.

Smoke and Sally checked into the hotel, then went up to their room.

"Oh, look, a bed," Sally said. "Couldn't we just send our regrets and meet Mr. Murchison for lunch?"

"I tell you what. You go ahead and take a nap," Smoke said. "I'll meet Mr. Murchison for breakfast."

"You are a dear," Sally said, kissing Smoke.

* * *

When Smoke went downstairs to the dining room, he was met by the maître d'.

"I'm to meet Mr. Murchison for breakfast," Smoke said. "I've never met him, so I don't know what he looks like. When he comes in, I would appreciate it if you would send him over to my table."

"He is already here, sir," the maître d' replied. "Follow me, please. I'll take you to him."

Tom Murchison was rather short, with thinning hair that had once been red, blue eyes enlarged by his glasses, and a spray of freckles. He stood as Smoke approached.

"Mr. Jensen," Murchison said. "I have heard so much about you. It is a pleasure to finally meet you. Please, have a seat."

"Thank you," Smoke said, taking a seat that put his back to the wall and allowed him to have a view of the room and the door.

"I was led to believe that Mrs. Jensen was with you. Will she be joining us?"

"No, not right away. Later perhaps."

"Very good. Oh, I've researched the bull that is being auctioned. Prince Henry's sire is Gold Nugget, and his dam is Gladys of Farleigh, both of whom have won awards in cattle shows. Prince Henry has already proven himself to be a good breeder, and his progeny are all well framed, heavy muscled, moderate at birth, but with a tremendous growth curve, correct off their feet and legs, and with great eye appeal."

"So he is what they claim him to be?"

"Yes, every bit of it. He will be a prize for whoever gets him."

"Do you have any idea how many people will be coming to the auction?" Smoke asked.

"About a hundred, I think."

"Whoa! A hundred?" Smoke asked in surprise.

"Yes, there is to be a dinner tonight for all who will be at the auction tomorrow."

"Will they all be bidding on Prince Henry?" Smoke asked.

"Very few will actually bid on Prince Henry. I mean when you think about it, he's the crème de la crème of the auction and he is probably out of the price range of all but a few. But there will be several other bulls and cows in the auction, and that is what is attracting most of the others who will attend."

A waiter brought their breakfast then, and it wasn't until he left the table that Smoke resumed his questioning.

"About how many do you think will be bidding on Prince Henry?" he asked.

Murchison chuckled. "I thought you might ask that," he said, "so I made some inquiries." He pulled a piece of paper from his inside jacket pocket and began to read.

"It looks like there will only be about four serious bidders. Miller Smith owns Sky Meadow Ranch. He will be bidding. Smith is pretty stout and will be able to take the bidding up for quite a way. Tucker Phillips, of Backtrail Ranch, will also be bidding. But Phillips only manages Backtrail, he doesn't actually own it. The owner lives in England, and I'm sure that means Phillips probably has a limit as to how much he can spend."

Smoke laughed. "We all have a limit as to how much we can spend," he said.

"Yes, but Mr. Phillips' limit will be absolute. There will be one other serious bidder there, and he may be the one who will be your biggest competition. His name is Pogue Quentin."

"Pogue Quentin? I don't think I know him."

"He owns the Tumbling Q down at Santa Clara," Dan said. "From what I can determine, he moved there from Texas about ten years ago. Now he is the biggest rancher in Huereano County."

"That's a pretty short time to become such a big rancher. He must have come well heeled."

"From what I understand, he did arrive with a considerable amount of money and was able to buy some land when it was at a depressed value," Murchison said. "He's recently enlarged his holdings by incorporating neighboring ranches, though I don't know how he did it."

"Let's discuss the bull," Smoke said. "Where is Prince Henry now? Will it be possible for me to see him?"

"Yes. He's down at the auction barn. They are keeping him in a private stall, separated from the others. By all means, go down and take a look."

Smoke waited until Sally had finished her nap so she could accompany him when he went down to the sale barn to see Prince Henry.

There were several cows in pens waiting to be sold, but Prince Henry was all alone in a clean and roomy stall. He was eating when Smoke and Sally stepped up to the pen to have a look at him. Prince Henry looked over toward them with only mild interest, then returned to the task at hand—eating.

"Oh," Sally said. "Isn't he beautiful?"

"Careful, don't be too loud with your compliments," Smoke said. "He's got a big enough head already."

Sally laughed. "What do you mean, he has a big enough head?"

"Look at him," Smoke said. "He knows he is the center of attention. Why, he is positively arrogant."

"That's all right, Prince Henry," Sally said. "You are smart, and you are beautiful. Be arrogant all you want."

"You are impressed with him, are you?"

"Oh, Smoke, we have to buy him," Sally said. "We simply must."

"Ha! And you are the one who was telling me I had to stay within a spending limit."

"Well, don't go overboard. But I do want him."

"I tell you, it's him," Stu Sinclair said to his two brothers.

"How do you know it's him?" Emil replied.

"The son of a bitch hit me right in the face. Do you think I can't remember someone who hit me right in the face?"

Emil, Stu, and Jason Sinclair were sitting at a table at the Bucket of Blood Saloon. Out of curiosity, Stu had gone down to the auction barn, but returned to tell the others that he had seen Smoke Jensen.

"What would Smoke Jensen be doing here?" Jason asked.

"How the hell do I know?" Stu replied. "All I know is I saw him."

"I don't believe it."

"Believe him," a new voice said. "Smoke Jensen is here."

The three brothers looked up at the new voice, irritated that a stranger was interrupting their conversation. Then, Emil recognized him.

"You!" he said. "You are the one who—"

Pogue Quentin held up his hand to stop Emil in midsentence. "Do you want to stand up and shout to the whole world that you once robbed a train?" he asked quietly.

"Won't bother us none," Jason said. "We done served our time for it."

"And was damn near hung 'cause you kilt the expressman," Stu added.

"I appreciate you boys staying quiet about that."

"Hell, we didn't have no choice," Jason said. "If we had know'd who you really was, we would have told 'em and maybe got some time off. But we never actually know'd your name, other than Joe."

"And that ain't your real name, is it?" Emil asked.

"No. My real name is Pogue Quentin."

"Pogue Quentin? Damn, I've heard of that name. You're a rich man now, ain't you?"

Quentin nodded. "I am a rich man, yes," he said.

"Damn, that ain't right. I mean, here, the four of us robbed a train, but we went to jail and you got rich."

"We all took the same risk," Quentin said. "The only difference is, you got caught and I didn't."

"Yeah? Well, I'll bet there's a reward out for you," Stu said. "What would keep us from just turning you in to the sheriff for that reward?"

Quentin laughed.

"You think it's funny, do you?" Stu challenged.

"Emil, you seem to have more sense than the other two," Quentin said. "Tell him why that is a dumb idea. You do know, don't you?"

Emil nodded. "Yeah, I know. For one thing, you have become a very rich and very powerful man in this state. It would be our word, three former convicts, against yours. And nobody would take our word against yours."

"You have a price on your head, don't you?" Quentin said. "Trying to rob a store, were you?" He shook his head and made a clucking sound. "You boys have come a long way down from the last time I saw you."

"Yeah, well, we ain't rich like you," Stu said. "We needed the money, which is why I think we should turn you in. There's bound to be a reward on you, and the sheriff might believe us."

Quentin laughed.

"You think that's funny, do you?"

"I think it is stupid. I can give you three reasons why trying to tell the sheriff about me would not be a good idea."

"And what are those reasons?" Emil asked.

"Number one, you have a price on your head, which makes going to the sheriff and calling attention to yourselves pretty stupid.

"However, and this is number two, you wouldn't have to worry about winding up in jail, because if you do go to the sheriff, even though he wouldn't believe you, I would have you killed."

"What do you mean you would have us killed?" Stu asked. "There is only one of you, there are three of us."

"Oh, don't get me wrong. I wouldn't do it myself," Quentin replied. "I said I would have you killed. As we have discussed, I am a very wealthy man. I will simply hire someone to do it."

"You said there were three reasons," Emil said. "What is the third reason?"

"The third reason is you will miss out on the opportunity to make some money."

"How much money?"

"That depends."

"Depends on what?"

"On how much money Smoke Jensen brought with

him. And since he plans to participate in the big cattle auction tomorrow, I suspect he has brought quite a bit with him."

"What's that got to do with us?" Jason asked.

"If you play your cards right, that could be your money," Quentin replied.

"How much money are we talking about?" Stu asked.

"I heard that bull they're sellin' might bring in five hundred dollars or more," Emil said.

"Five hundred dollars for one bull? I don't believe it," Stu said.

"Believe it," Quentin said.

"So what if he does have five hundred dollars? You still ain't said what that has to do with us," Jason said.

"I don't want Smoke to take part in the auction tomorrow. I'm willing to give you boys a hundred dollars apiece to see to it that he doesn't. And consider this. In addition to the three hundred dollars I'll give you, you can also have whatever money you find on him."

"Find on him?" Stu asked. "What do you mean, find on him?"

"I'll let you figure that out," Quentin said.

"Find on him," Emil repeated. He nodded. "Yeah. Yeah, I know what you are saying." He chuckled. "Yeah, find on him. I like that."

Quentin removed a twenty-dollar bill from his billfold and put it on the table in front of the three brothers. "Here," he said. "Drink, eat, buy yourself a woman, but don't go anywhere and don't do anything until you hear from me again."

"How long will that be?" Emil asked.

"As long as it takes."

Chapter Eight

The Colorado Cattlemen's Association sponsored the dinner that night, holding the event in the Association Hall. Smoke wore a suit, only because Sally had had the presence of mind to pack one for him. A banner, spread across the front of the ballroom, read:

Colorado Springs
welcomes
Colorado Cattlemen

The room was a kaleidoscope of the muted gray, brown, and blue suits of the men, among which flitted, like butterflies, the brightly colored gowns of the women. Smoke was glad that Sally had come with him because, in his mind at least, she was clearly the most beautiful woman present.

The guest list included Colorado's leading citizens. In addition to the state's most successful cattlemen, there were others present, like Owen Goldrick, founder of Colorado's first public school; William Byers, editor of the *Rocky*

Mountain News; and William Palmer, best known as the builder of the Denver and Rio Grande Railroad.

"Mrs. Jensen," Goldrick said, greeting her. "How wonderful to see you here tonight. You are not only Colorado's best schoolteacher, but clearly you are our state's most beautiful."

"Mr. Goldrick, you have not lost the ability to charm," Sally replied with a chuckle. "And you must know that I am no longer teaching."

"Sadly, I do know," Goldrick said. He turned to Smoke. "And, Mr. Jensen, I want you to know that I shall forever hold you responsible for denying the state the gift of her teaching."

"I plead guilty," Smoke said, smiling as he accepted the good-natured gibe.

"Smoke, could I see you for a moment?" Tom Murchison asked.

"Sure. What is it?"

"I have someone I think you should meet."

Murchison led Smoke through the crowded ballroom toward a man who was standing apart from everyone else. The man was about fifteen years older than Smoke, about the same height, but considerably heavier, as evidenced by the fact that his vest strained against the buttons. He was clean shaven and bald, except for a narrow ring of white hair that encircled his head, and was smoking a cigar.

"Smoke Jensen, this is Pogue Quentin," Murchison said.

"Mr. Quentin," Smoke said with a nod of his head. Quentin had given no hint that he was about to offer his hand, so Smoke kept his by his side as well.

"I've heard of you, Jensen," Quentin said, not removing the cigar from his mouth as he spoke. "I hear you've got a pretty nice little ranch up there around Big Rock."

"I'm pleased with it," Smoke replied.

"You would have been better off staying up there and tending to your business," Quentin said. "You've wasted your time coming here."

"Oh? And how is that?"

"You came here to buy Prince Henry, right? Only, you ain't goin' to get him. I plan to buy him myself."

"You don't say? Well, that should make for a spirited bidding tomorrow then, shouldn't it?"

"One way or another, Jensen, I generally get what I go after," Quentin said.

Someone rang a small bell then, calling all the attendees to the table for the meal. As they were being served, the auctioneer stepped up to a podium to say a few words.

"Ladies," he said, acknowledging the women who were in attendance, "and gentlemen. I want to welcome you to Colorado Springs, and to the Hereford auction we will be conducting tomorrow. As a special treat, and to give you an idea as to what the future of the beef industry is, tonight you will be dining on steaks prepared from Herefords. Enjoy."

Smoke had eaten Hereford beef before, so he wasn't surprised at how much better the meat was than that from a longhorn. There were several who were surprised, though, and the conversation during dinner was about the superiority of Hereford beef.

Pogue Quentin was sitting at a table that was on the other side of the room from Smoke. As the waiters started serving the dinner, the chair beside Pogue was empty, but his son came in to sit before the waiters reached their table.

"Did you take care of it?" Pogue asked his son.

"Yeah, I took care of it," Billy Ray said.

"You're sure?"

"I'm sure."

"Where were they?"

"Just where you said they would be. They were in the Bucket of Blood Saloon."

"Good."

"Pa, they said they had done business with you before."

"They have."

"I can't imagine you ever doin' business with anyone like those three men."

"Billy Ray, you'll learn someday that a man in my position has to do business with all sorts of people."

"They just don't seem to me like they are our kind of people," Billy Ray said.

"Oh? Tell me, Billy Ray, what are our kind of people?"

"People like what's in here," Billy Ray replied, taking in the room with a wave of his hand. "People with money."

When Emil, Jason, and Stu stepped into the lobby of the Homestead Hotel at three o'clock the next morning, it was dark, except for a single lantern that burned on the front desk. They walked lightly across the lobby, the carpet cushioning their steps so that they made little or no noise.

The desk clerk was sitting in a chair with his head back against the wall. His mouth was open and he was snoring loudly.

Emil turned the registration book around and ran his fingers down the list of names.

"Here it is," he said quietly. "Smoke Jensen, Room 210." He looked up at a peg board that hung on the wall just on the other side of the desk. There were several hooks on the board and from some of the hooks, two keys hung. There was only one key hanging from the hook numbered 210. Emil reached over to get it. Once he had the key in his hand, he turned to the others.

"Let's go," he said to the others.

A moment later, the three men stood at the top of the stairs.

"Emil, are you sure this fella has money?" Jason asked.

"You heard what Quentin said, didn't you? Jensen is plannin' on biddin' for that high-priced bull. He couldn't do that if he didn't have any money on him."

"Where do you reckon his room is at?" Stu asked.

"He's in Room 210, so if I figure it right, that will be the last room on the left, down at the far end of the hall."

Jason stubbed his toe on the top step. "Damn!" he said, barking the word out in pain.

"Hush," Emil whispered.

"I stubbed my toe," Jason said.

"If you don't hush up, I'm goin' to stub your head," Emil warned. "You want to tell the whole world we're a-comin'?"

"You worry too much, brother. Who's goin' to hear us at this hour of the night?" Stu asked.

"Just keep quiet."

The hallway was well lit by a series of kerosene lanterns that were mounted on the walls on both sides.

"Jason, Stu, you boys get them lights snuffed out," Emil said, pointing to the lanterns.

Following his instructions, Jason and Stu began moving quietly down the hallway, snuffing out the flickering yellow lanterns as they advanced. The hallway grew progressively darker as each light was extinguished, until finally it was illuminated only by the pale gleam of moonlight that splashed in through the window at the far end.

When they reached the room, Emil motioned for the other two to draw their pistols. He pulled a long-bladed knife from his belt scabbard, then used the key to unlock the door. He pushed it open very slowly, thus avoiding any sound.

Smoke wasn't sure what awakened him, but when he opened his eyes he perceived something was amiss. Looking toward the door, he saw immediately that the small crack of light that had been shining under the door was gone. Although there was no longer any light coming under the door, the room was surprisingly well illuminated by the fall of soft silver light from a full moon that splashed through the window.

"Sally," he whispered. "Get under bed, now."

Although his instruction had awakened her from a very sound sleep, Sally didn't question Smoke's unusual request. Instead, she acted instantly to roll out of the bed, then slip under it.

Smoke's holster was hanging from the head of the bed, and reaching up for it, he pulled his pistol. Then, he too rolled out of bed, only instead of getting under it, he moved quietly across the room, stepping into the shadows of the corner, then looking toward the door. He felt a slight movement of air in the room, and realized that the door had just been opened.

Three men came in, shadows within the shadow of the dimly lit room, and moving quietly, they crossed the floor toward the bed. Something flashed, a soft reflection from the moonlight, and Smoke could see that what glistened was the blade of a knife being carried by the one who was in the lead. He could see that the other two had their guns drawn. The one with the knife plunged it into the bed.

"Damn!" he said. "He ain't here."

"Oh, I'm here, all right," Smoke said. "I'm just not in bed. You boys drop your weapons."

Smoke stepped to one side as soon as he spoke. The two men with guns turned toward the sound of Smoke's voice and fired. Smoke returned fire, using the flame patterns of their pistols as his target. Even as the sound of gunfire faded, he heard a crash of glass and realized that the third man, the one with the knife, had jumped through the window. Moving quickly to the window, he got there just in time to see the third man get to his feet on the ground below, then run into the alley, disappearing into the darkness.

"Sally, are you all right?"

"Yes," Sally's muffled voice came from under the bed.

"You can come out now."

"What is it? What's going on?" someone shouted from down the hall.

"Was that gunshots?" another asked.

"What happened to the lanterns in the hall?"

"Someone go for the sheriff!"

Smoke lit the lantern in his room, then walked over to look down at the two men he had shot.

"Are they dead?" Sally asked. She was tying the waist of the silken robe she had just put on over her nightgown.

"Yes."

"Hello? Is anyone alive in there?" someone called from the hotel hallway.

"It's all over, folks," Smoke called back.

One brave soul appeared in the doorway, carrying a pistol. Seeing him, Smoke aimed his pistol at him; then, from having met him at the dinner last evening, he recognized Tucker Phillips. Phillips was one of the men who would be bidding against him tomorrow. Smoke eased the hammer back down on his pistol and lowered it.

"Mr. Phillips, I'd be much obliged if you'd lower your pistol," Smoke said.

"Right, right," Phillips said. "I just thought—well, uh, right, I'll put the gun down. Are you and Mrs. Jensen all right?"

"Yes, we're fine, thank you," Smoke answered.

As Smoke had done a moment earlier, Tucker Phillips looked down at the two men on the floor. Both were dead, but the fact that they were clutching guns in their hands and were fully clothed, whereas Smoke was wearing the long underwear he had been sleeping in, clearly told the story that Smoke was the innocent participant in the shooting.

By now, several others had gotten brave enough to venture down to the room and look inside.

"There's two dead men in there," someone said from just outside the door to Smoke's room.

"Two dead men," another said, and Smoke could hear the refrain repeated up and down the hallway as the crowd of hotel guests gathered.

It took about fifteen minutes for the deputy sheriff to arrive. He looked down at the men, prodding each of them with the toe of his boot to convince himself that both were dead.

"You're Smoke Jensen, aren't you?" the deputy asked. "Come to bid on the bull at the big auction?"

"Yes," Smoke said.

"Well, then, there's not much of a mystery here, is there? These two galoots probably found out who you are, and they come in here to rob you."

"And maybe more," Smoke said.

"What do you mean?"

"This one is Stu Sinclair, this one is Jason Sinclair," Smoke said, pointing out the two men.

"You know them?"

"In a manner of speaking, I do." Smoke told about his encounter with the two men who had tried to rob the Mercantile in Big Rock. "They broke out of jail on the first night," he concluded.

"Ahh, then it was probably a little of both. Revenge, and to rob you."

"And maybe more," Smoke repeated.

"More? What more could there be?"

"Look in Jason's shirt pocket," Smoke said.

The deputy knelt beside the one Smoke had identified as Jason Sinclair, then reached into his shirt pocket. From the pocket, he extracted three one-hundred-dollar bills.

"I'll be," he said. "This is three hunnert dollars. Who would have thought that a galoot like this would have three hunnert dollars on him?"

"It's not just three hundred dollars, it is three one-hundred-dollar bills," Smoke said. "I believe that money was given to them tonight."

"Well now, that's kind of strange," the deputy said. "Why do you suppose someone would give them three hundred dollars?"

"I think someone paid them to kill me."

* * *

"I'm sorry about what happened to you last night," Sheriff Walker said to Smoke the next day. "If I had known the Sinclair boys were in town, I would have had them in jail. There is paper out on them now."

"There were three of them," Smoke said.

"Yes, Emil, Jason, and Stu."

"Emil is the smart one."

"You mean because he got away last night?"

"He got away the last time, too."

Sheriff Walker stroked his chin. "Yeah, well, no doubt he's a long way from here by now."

"I'm not so sure about that. I think he is still here."

"If he is, I'll have my deputies keep an eye out for him. Can you tell me what he looks like?"

"I've never actually seen him up close," Smoke said. "I only saw him once, and then from a distance, when he and the others rode into Big Rock the day they tried to hold up the Mercantile. I saw him last night, of course, but it was so dark that I couldn't make out any features."

"So what you are saying is, you could pass him on the street and not recognize him?"

"Yes, that's what I'm saying."

"Well, if that's the case, there really ain't no need for him to be gone, is there? Not if you can't even recognize him."

"That's true," Smoke replied. "Tell me, Sheriff, will I be needed for an inquiry or anything?"

"No, I don't think so," the sheriff answered. "From everything I can determine, and from the statements I took from the other hotel guests, it seems pretty obvious they were coming into your room to rob you. Besides, Mr. Jensen, I know you and I know your reputation. If anything does come up, I certainly know how to get hold of you."

"Yes, I'll be here until after the auction today. After that, you can reach me at Sugarloaf, my ranch."

"You came to make a bid for Prince Henry, didn't you?"

"If he is all he is cracked up to be. And if I can afford him," Smoke replied.

"Well, from what folks say about him, he's quite a bull. I reckon he would make a good addition to anybody's herd. And after this, you can probably afford to bid a little higher than you'd planned."

"What do you mean?"

"Like I said, there was paper out on those two men who tried to rob you last night. There is a five-hundred-dollar reward on each one of them. That means you are a thousand dollars richer today than you was yesterday. If you stop back by my office just before the auction, I'll have your money ready for you."

"You don't say. Well, now, that's good to know," Smoke said. "Thanks, Sheriff Walker."

Chapter Nine

Tucker Phillips, Miller Smith, and their wives joined Smoke and Sally for lunch at the Manitou Restaurant, advertised in the *Colorado Springs Gazette* as "Colorado's Finest Restaurant." Sally, Mrs. Phillips, and Mrs. Smith had gone shopping that morning, and Mrs. Smith had bought a new hat at Wilbur and Woulf, an emporium on Tejon Street. She was wearing it now and Sally, after giving Smoke a small kick under the table, nodded toward Mrs. Smith.

"Mrs. Smith, what a pretty hat," Smoke said, getting the signal.

"Why, thank you, Mr. Jensen," Mrs. Smith replied, beaming at the compliment.

"I wonder why Pogue Quentin didn't join us," Tucker Phillips said. "From what I understand, he is the only other person who will actually be bidding on Prince Henry."

"Do you know anything about Quentin?" Smith asked.

Phillips shook his head. "Not really, just that he is a pretty big rancher."

"I don't know him, but a fella who used to cowboy for me, James Colby, went down to Huereano County and bought himself a small ranch. He sent me a letter not too long ago, said that this man, Quentin, had cheated every other ranch owner in the county out of his ranch," Smith said.

"How did he do that?" Phillips asked.

"Somehow or the other, he got them all to agree to join their ranches together as a single ranch, with each of them owning shares. Only, after a short while, he turned out to be the sole owner."

"What about your friend, Colby?"

"Colby didn't join him," Smith said. "He hasn't lost his ranch, but he is really struggling to hang on. I hate to see that, too. He was one of the best men I ever had workin' for me."

"Do you know Quentin, Mr. Jensen?" Phillips asked.

"I never met him before last night," Smoke said, "And there was something about him that I didn't like. Hearing how he cheated his neighbors out of their land, I'm glad to see that my instincts are still working."

"Speak of the devil," Smith said. "There he is now."

Smith nodded toward the door of the restaurant where Pogue Quentin and his son, Billy Ray, were just coming in. They were shown to a table on the opposite side of the room, but shortly after they were seated, Quentin came over to speak to Smoke and the others.

"Mr. Jensen, I heard about your little ruckus last night," Quentin said. "I'm happy to see that you weren't hurt."

"Thanks," Smoke replied.

"They had obviously come to rob you. Of course, I guess that could have been any of the four of us, seeing as we are all carrying large sums of money."

"Except that doesn't explain the three one-hundred-dollar bills that were found in the shirt pocket of one of them," Phillips said. "To me, that's proof that they weren't there just to rob Mr. Jensen. I believe they had come to kill him, and someone had paid them to do it."

"That's not very likely, is it?" Quentin asked.

"Maybe not," Smith replied. "But then, how likely is it that a man could build up one of the largest ranches in Colorado by stealing land from all his neighbors?"

The smile on Quentin's face had been forced from the moment he walked over to the table. Now, even the forced smile left his face, to be replaced by an irritated scowl.

"Are you suggesting I did that?" Quentin asked.

"No, I'm just repeating what I've heard others suggest," Smith said.

Quentin stood there for a moment longer, then nodded. "I'll see you men at the auction," he said.

When Smoke stepped into the sale barn a little later that afternoon, his entry didn't go unnoticed. Most of the town had heard of the incident in his hotel room the night before, and several came over to speak to him about it, offering their sincerest appreciation that he had come through the robbery attempt unscathed.

The gathering of all the ranchers was congenial, because most had no intention of bidding on Prince Henry, and as there were cattle and bulls enough to go around, there was no competition between them. And Smoke, Smith, and Phillips had established a friendly relationship so that the competition between them wasn't in the least acrimonious. The only person to show a bit of hostility toward the others was Pogue Quentin, but even that didn't cause a problem as he and his son kept to themselves until the auction began.

"Gentlemen, if you will all take your seats, we'll get the auction under way," Lindsey Beck, the auctioneer, said.

The buzz of conversation quieted as the ranchers all found a place to sit.

"Before we begin the bidding, I need to go over the rules with you once more. Only those of you holding a valid ticket will be authorized to bid. The ticket will cost you one hundred dollars. If you bid successfully, that one hundred dollars will be applied to your bid. If you do not buy anything, the one hundred dollars will be refunded at the conclusion of the bid.

"Also, you understand that all transactions are to be in cash and payable immediately, so I caution you not to make any bid higher than the amount of cash you have on your person right now. If you cannot come up with the cash for your purchase, the next highest bidder will be declared the winner.

"And I should not have to tell you that all bids are final. Are there any questions?"

There were none.

"Gentlemen, if there are any among you who have not yet purchased your bidding ticket, I invite you to do so now."

For the next few minutes, several of the ranchers, most of whom were late arrivals at the auction, hurried over to the clerk's table to make the purchase.

"Now, gentlemen," the auctioneer began. "Our first sale will be one bull and ten heifer calves. Though they are not of champion stock, they are all purebred Herefords and will be a good addition to your existing herds, as well as a good means of starting your Hereford herd. We will sell all eleven animals in a single lot, so your bidding will be for all eleven. Do I have an opening bid?"

"Fifty dollars," one of the ranchers shouted.

"I have fifty, do I hear fifty-five, five, five, five, do I have fifty-five?"

"Five."

"Fifty-five, now sixty, sixty, sixty, fifty-five now sixty," the auctioneer droned on in an almost lyrical, singsong voice.

There were several ranchers at the auction, and through all the early rounds the bidding was brisk. Then the excitement reached its crescendo when Prince Henry was introduced.

Although there as many as one hundred people at the auction, there were, as Murchison had pointed out, only four who could realistically bid for the bull, and the auctioneer and everyone else present knew who they were. The four were sitting in different parts of the bleachers, having, for this particular sale, purposely separated themselves from each other.

Prince Henry was a fine-looking specimen, and as he was led into the circle, he held his head high.

"Here he is, gentlemen, Prince Henry, the bull you all came to see, but only one of you came to buy."

The audience laughed at the auctioneer's joke.

"Prince Henry weighed ninety-five pounds at birth, is guaranteed to be completely free of defects or any history of illness or injury, and now weighs thirteen hundred and fifty pounds.

"The seller has stated that the opening bid must be five hundred dollars or higher. Do I have an opening bid?"

"Five hundred and five dollars," Tucker Phillips called out.

"And ten," Miller Smith said.

"Five hundred fifty dollars," Smoke bid.

"Gentlemen, let's quit pussyfooting around here," Pogue Quentin said. "I bid six hundred fifty dollars."

"Six-fifty, fifty, fifty, fifty," the auctioneer barked. "Do I hear seven hundred, seven hundred, seven, seven, seven—"

"Six hundred seventy-five," Smith said.

"I have six hundred seventy-five, seventy-five, six hundred seventy-five, do I hear seven hundred? Seven hundred, seven hundred, now six seventy-five, seven hundred?"

"Seven hundred," Tucker Phillips called.

"And fifty," Quentin shouted.

"Seven hundred fifty," the auctioneer said. "I have seven hundred fifty. Mr. Phillips, do you wish to increase the bid?"

Phillips made a dismissive motion with his hand. "Too rich for me," he said.

"Mr. Smith?"

"Eight hundred," Smith said.

"Nine hundred," Quentin shouted.

"I'm out," Smith said.

Quentin smiled broadly. "Looks like I've bought a bull."

"Nine hundred fifty," Smoke said.

"One thousand," Quentin shouted back angrily.

"Fifteen hundred dollars," Smoke said resolutely.

The audience gasped at the size of the jump in the bid, and for a moment, even the auctioneer was surprised.

"One thousand five hundred?" he asked, not in the singsong voice, but a conversational tone, as if to be certain he wasn't making a mistake. "Mr. Jensen, do I understand the bid?"

"One thousand five hundred dollars," Smoke repeated. When he left Sugarloaf, he'd had no intention of ever paying this much, but the unexpected bonus of the reward money enabled him to do so.

"Mr. Quentin, do you wish to respond?" the auctioneer asked.

"I—I will need some time to raise a little more cash," Quentin said.

"I'm sorry, Mr. Quentin," the auctioneer said. "The rules are quite specific. The terms are cash, due at the time of the purchase."

Quentin sat in his seat for a moment; then, without a word, but casting an angry glare toward Smoke, he got up and left the room.

"One thousand five hundred once, one thousand five hundred twice, one thousand five hundred three times," the auctioneer said. He slammed his gavel on the podium. "Prince Henry is sold to Smoke Jensen for one thousand five hundred dollars."

The others in the sale barn applauded as Smoke walked down front to take possession of the animal.

"You've bought yourself a good bull, Mr. Jensen," R.J. Billings, the seller of the bull, said as he received the money, then turned over the bull and his bill of sale.

"Thanks," Smoke said. "I've recently introduced Herefords, and I'm hoping Prince Henry will strengthen my herd."

"Oh, he will, I promise you that," Billings said.

"I noticed that Mr. Quentin seemed quite upset," Billings said. "He left the building without so much as a fare-thee-well."

"Yes, he did. Well, if he was all that upset, I'd just as soon not have to deal with him. I've had enough conflict in my life. I don't need any more," Smoke said.

"Yes," Billings said with a chuckle. "I heard about your conflict last night."

"It would seem that everyone in town has heard."

"I'm glad it turned out as it did. From all I have heard about you, you are a good man. I would not want to have seen you hurt."

"Ha!" Smoke teased. "What you mean is, you would not want to have lost the sale."

Billings laughed out loud. "Well, there you go, Mr. Jensen, you have found me out," he said. "But I'm also glad that Prince Henry has found a home with a gentleman like you. How will you be getting Prince Henry back to your ranch?"

"By train."

"If you wish, I will make the transportation arrangements for you. A bull like this needs special accommodations. Also, having raised him from a calf, I'd like a moment to tell him good-bye if you don't mind."

"I don't mind at all," Smoke said. "If you need me for anything, I'll be down at the saloon."

Chapter Ten

As Pogue Quentin stood in the hotel hallway unlocking the door to his hotel room, Emil Sinclair stepped out of the broom closet.

"Sinclair, are you a damn fool? The whole town is looking for you. What are you doing here?" Quentin asked.

"I got to get out of town," he said.

"Well, you aren't going to get out of town standing here."

"I ain't got no money."

"What do you mean, you don't have any money? I gave you three hundred dollars."

"Jason wanted to hold on to the money until we was done," Emil said.

"That's not my problem," Quentin said. "If I hadn't given you that money, I would have been able to raise the bid. And if you and your brothers hadn't been so incompetent, you would have a lot of money now and I would have Prince Henry."

"You wound up gettin' both my brothers killed," Sinclair said.

Quentin shook his head. "That was your bungling."

"They was killed doin' somethin' you wanted done. You owe me."

Quentin shook his head. "I don't owe you a damn thing."

"There's things I could tell people about you, Quentin, about things we done together down in Texas."

"So you told me," Quentin said. "But like I told you, I am a successful rancher, and you are a wanted man. Who is going to believe you?"

"That ain't right, Quentin. That ain't no way right. My two brothers got kilt and I damn near did. All I need is a little travelin' money."

Quentin opened the door to his room. "Come inside for a moment," he said. "I don't want to talk out here."

Sinclair followed Quentin into his room, then stood to one side as Quentin locked the door behind him.

"I'll give you one hundred dollars," Quentin said.

A huge smile spread across Sinclair's face. "A hunnert dollars? Yes, that's enough. That's more than enough."

"You have to earn it."

"Earn it? Earn it how?"

"Smoke Jensen bought a bull today."

"Yeah, I know."

"I want you to find that bull and kill it."

"Ain't that supposed to be some champion bull worth a lot of money?"

"Yes."

"Wouldn't it be better to try and steal it?"

"Now you tell me just how in the hell you are going to steal it," Quentin replied. "What are you going to do? Drive him down the middle of the street for everyone to see?"

"Oh, yeah, I guess I see what you are talking about," Sinclair said. "But I don't understand. Why do you want me to kill the bull?"

"If I can't have him, then I don't want anyone to have him," Quentin replied.

"Where is the bull now?" Sinclair asked.

"I imagine it's down at the railroad station, waiting to be put on the train. Wherever he is, it's your job to find him. Find him and kill him."

"What about Jensen?"

"What about him?"

"You want me to kill him, too?"

"I'm not giving you any more than one hundred dollars," Quentin said. "At this point, I don't care what happens to Jensen."

Sinclair held out his hand. "You just give me the money, Mr. Quentin. I'll kill the bull for you, and throw in killin' Jensen for free. I owe the son of a bitch for killin' my two brothers."

Quentin gave the one hundred dollars to Sinclair, then opened the door. "Make this the last time we see each other," Quentin said.

"Don't worry, it will be. After I take care of business, I'm heading for California."

As Sinclair started toward the stairs, Billy Ray Quentin was just arriving. He passed Sinclair by without saying a word, but when he got to the room where his father was standing in the open doorway, he gave in to curiosity.

"What was Sinclair doing here?"

"We were taking care of some last-minute business," Quentin said. "Did you get the train tickets?"

"I got 'em, Pa," Billy Ray said, holding them up for his father to see.

* * *

"Mr. Jensen, won't you and Mrs. Jensen join us for dinner?" Tucker Phillips called. The ranch manager and his wife were sitting with Miller Smith and his wife.

"We would be happy to," Smoke said.

Phillips and Smith stood as Smoke pulled out a chair for Sally; then all took their seats.

"Well, this was quite a spirited auction today, wasn't it?" Phillips asked.

"Perhaps a bit too spirited," Smoke replied with a smile. "I paid a lot more for Prince Henry than I intended."

"I think it will work out for you," Phillips said. "Prince Henry is a fine bull, and if my owner had given me permission to bid whatever I wanted, I would have continued the bid."

"I believe you made an enemy today," Smith said.

"You would be talking about Pogue Quentin, I take it," Smoke said. He looked around the saloon. "Mr. Quentin, isn't here, I see."

"I haven't seen him since he left the auction," Phillips said. "Which is fine by me. From what I have heard of the man, the more distance I can keep between us, the better it is."

A waiter brought their dinner then, and the three men and their wives carried on a pleasant conversation until it was time for the train. As Smoke and Sally stood, the other two ranchers stood as well.

"Mindy, Carol, you two must visit us at Sugarloaf," Sally said. "I feel that I have made two new and good friends during this trip, and I would love to entertain you sometime."

"I can think of nothing that would bring me more pleasure," Mindy Phillips said.

"Nor I," Carol Smith added.

* * *

Although there was a cab available in front of the restaurant, the depot was only a couple of blocks away, so Smoke waved the driver off, saying he would rather walk.

"The Phillipses and the Smiths were nice people, weren't they?" Sally said.

"Yes, I enjoyed their company."

"I'm so glad you invited me along. And I'm so happy we got Prince Henry. I'm going to treat him like a house pet."

"Ha! Does that mean we're going to keep an animal that weighs three quarters of a ton in the house?" Smoke asked.

Sally laughed. "Well, maybe not a house pet," she amended. "I am glad we bought him, though."

"Even though we paid a lot more than we intended?"

"Yes. I think he will pay off in the long run," Sally said.

"I think you are right. At least, I hope you are right."

"Jensen!" a loud, angry voice shouted.

Smoke had not seen Emil Sinclair standing in the shadows of the alley between the apothecary and a feed store. He whirled toward the sound of the shout, drawing his pistol as he did so. He didn't have to use it, though, because even as Sinclair raised his own gun to fire, Sheriff Walker stepped up behind Sinclair and brought his gun down hard on Sinclair's head.

Smoke put his pistol back in its holster.

"Lucky for me you came along when you did," Smoke said.

"More 'n likely, it was luckier for Sinclair," Sheriff Walker said. "I saw him sneaking in here and figured he was up to no good, so I followed him."

"You're a good man, Sheriff Walker."

Walker smiled broadly. "Comin' from you, Mr. Jensen, that's quite a compliment," he said.

When Smoke and Sally reached the depot, they saw several people gathered around one of the stock pens.

"Who would do such a thing?" someone asked.

"Never mind who, why would they do it?" another asked.

Curious, Smoke walked over to the pen, but before he even got there, he saw a Hereford lying on the ground. He quickened his pace.

"What happened?" he asked.

"Somebody shot this bull," one of the bystanders said.

Smoke pushed his way to the fence, then looked at the animal. He saw someone squatting beside it.

"I just paid two hundred and fifty dollars for this bull," the man said, shaking his head in anger. "I'd like to get my hands on the son of a bitch who did this."

Smoke's first reaction was one of relief that it wasn't Prince Henry. But that was followed quickly by a sense of guilt for feeling such relief, since he knew that the man who had bought the bull was out the money.

"Mr. Jensen?" someone called.

Turning from the pen, Smoke saw the railroad dispatcher.

"Yes?"

"Your bull has been loaded onto a private stock car," he said. "I have the bill of lading here. It's all taken care of."

"Thanks," Smoke said, walking over to retrieve the papers.

"A terrible thing, that," the dispatcher said, nodding toward the cow pen and the dead bull.

"Did you see what happened?" Smoke asked.

"No, sir, nobody did," the dispatcher said. "Ken and I were in the depot when we heard the shot. When we looked out, we saw the bull lying on the ground." He shook his head. "It takes a special kind of meanness to kill an animal for no reason," he said.

Santa Clara

When Pogue and Billy Ray Quentin stepped down from the train, they were met by the foreman, Cole Mathers, and two other cowboys from the Tumbling Q.

"Where at's the bull, Mr. Quentin?" Mathers asked.

"I didn't get him," Quentin replied with a growl.

"You didn't? Why not? Was there somethin' wrong with him?"

"No, he was a good bull. But some fool by the name of Jensen outbid me."

"Ha. I didn't think there was anyone who could outbid you," Mathers said. "You got more money that Croesus."

"Yeah, well, I won't keep it if I throw it away in a foolish bidding war," Quentin said. "I wouldn't be surprised if Jensen and the seller weren't in cahoots, bidding against me just to run the price up." He chuckled. "If they were together, I snookered them, 'cause once it reached a certain point, I quit bidding."

"Yes, sir. Well, there ain't never been nobody say you wasn't smart," Mathers said.

"Did you bring our horses?"

"Yes, sir, they're tied up out front."

"All right, good. Come on, Billy Ray, let's go home," Pogue said.

"Pa, I'll come along later," Billy Ray said. "I ordered me a pair of boots to be made, and I'm goin' to go see if Donovan has 'em done yet."

* * *

A little bell attached to the top of the door tinkled as Billy Ray stepped into Donovan's Leather Goods shop.

"I'll be right there," a voice called from the back of the shop.

Donovan was a small man with thinning hair that he kept combed over the top. He was wearing a leather apron with a full pocket, in which he kept some of his tools.

"Ah, Mr. Quentin," he said. "Come for your boots, have you?"

"Yes," Billy Ray said.

"I have them right here," Donovan said, taking a pair of boots down from the shelf. "Beautiful, aren't they?"

"Yeah," Billy Ray said. "They are. Let me try them on."

"Please do," Donovan invited.

Billy Ray sat down, pulled one of his old boots off, then stuck his foot down in the new boot. It didn't go on easily, and he worked with it until he finally got it on. Then, when he stood up, he winced in pain as he took a step.

"They are too small!" he said. "You dumb son of a bitch! You made them too small!"

"They are still new, they will loosen up," Donovan said. "I made them to the exact measurements."

"I paid good money for these boots! And they don't fit."

"They will fit as soon as they are broken in, I assure you."

Billy Ray sat down and pulled the boot off, then threw it through the front window. The glass shattered with a loud crash.

"Mr. Quentin!" Donovan gasped. "You broke my window!"

"Yeah, and that ain't all I'm goin' to break," Billy Ray

said as he picked up a bench, then slammed it into a leather cutter.

After leaving Donovan's, Billy Ray walked down to the New York Saloon.

"Whiskey," Billy Ray said to Lloyd Evans, the bartender. "Leave the bottle."

Evans took a bottle from beneath the bar and put it in front of Billy Ray. Billy Ray pulled the cork with his teeth, then spit it into one of the nearby spittoons.

"Billy Ray, that means you just bought that whole bottle," Evans said. "There ain't no way we can re-cork it now."

"I asked for the whole bottle, didn't I?" Billy Ray replied with a snarl. He poured himself a glass.

Doc Patterson was standing at the bar just a few feet down from Billy Ray.

"Hello, Billy Ray," Doc Patterson said. "How was your trip?"

"What trip?" Billy Ray replied. He tossed down the glass of whiskey.

"Didn't you and your pa go up to Colorado Springs to buy a bull?"

"What? Oh, yeah," Billy Ray said. He poured himself another glass. "Yeah, I guess we did." He drank that glass as well.

"I'll be anxious to see him," Doc Patterson said. Doc was a veterinarian, and as he was the only veterinarian in the county, he did a lot of business with the Tumbling Q. "Tell your pa I'll come out and look him over whenever he wants. I've read about him, sure will be nice to examine a champion. What's he like?"

"What's who like?" Billy Ray poured himself a third glass of whiskey.

"Why, Prince Henry, of course. I'm talking about the champion bull you bought," Doc said.

"We didn't buy no bull," Billy Ray said. He tossed down the third glass, then poured a fourth, spilling a little of it onto the bar.

"You didn't? I thought that was why you went."

"That's why my pa went," Billy Ray said, tossing down still another glass of whiskey.

"Say, you'd better go easy on that. It's not good to drink that much whiskey that fast," Doc said. "Why don't you slow down a little?"

"And why don't you mind your own damn business?" Billy Ray replied. This time, when he poured the whiskey, he got more on the bar than he did in the glass. "You ain't a people doctor anyway, you're a horse and cow doctor. What the hell do you know about what's good for me and what ain't?"

"Nothing at all," Doc said, holding up his hands and backing away. "I was just making conversation."

"Yeah? Well make it somewhere else." Billy Ray looked around the bar and seeing Mary Lou toward the back, he called out to her. "Hey, you! Whore! Let's me an' you go upstairs."

"You're drunk," Mary Lou said.

Billy Ray walked toward her, stumbling into a chair and knocking it over, almost falling, but catching himself at the last minute by putting his hand down on a table.

"All right, if you won't go upstairs with me, come have a drink with me."

"I'd rather not."

"What do you mean, you'd rather not? Ain't that what you're supposed to do? Drink with your customers, then go upstairs with them when they want?"

"Mr. Gibson lets us choose who we go upstairs with," Mary Lou said. "And I don't choose to go upstairs with you."

"Gibson, our ranch does a lot of business in this saloon," Billy Ray said. "How would you like it if I said nobody who works for us can come in here any more?"

"I'm not going to make her go upstairs with you if she doesn't want to," Gibson replied.

"All I want is to have a drink or two with her. Just till I get calmed down. Donovan—" With an unsteady hand, he pointed toward the street. "Donovan, that cheatin' son of a bitch, just cheated me out of a pair of boots."

"Have a drink with him, Mary Lou," Gibson ordered. "You don't have to do any more than that."

"All right," Mary Lou replied in a nervous voice. With a little look of apprehension, Mary Lou walked over to him. Thinking it would be better to have him calmed down, she forced a smile. "All right, cowboy," she said. "Let's have that drink."

Billy Ray smiled at her, but there was something about the smile that alerted Mary Lou, as if the smile was a reflection in a flawed mirror. Suddenly, the smile left Billy Ray's face, to be replaced by a snarl.

"I'll teach you not to say no to me when I tell you I want you to go upstairs with me!" Billy Ray said. He swung at her, hitting her in the face with his doubled-up fist.

Mary Lou went down.

"Now, I'll carry you upstairs," Billy Ray said as he bent over to pick her up.

Billy Ray didn't see Gibson coming up behind him.

Gibson brought a small wooden club down on Billy Ray's head, and Billy Ray went down and out.

Everyone else in the saloon was shocked into silence.

"What do we do now, Boss?" Evans asked.

Gibson sighed. "I don't reckon we have much choice," he said. "Go get the marshal."

"The marshal? Are you kidding? You know Quentin controls the marshal."

"Go get him," Gibson said again.

Tumbling Q

When Pogue Quentin awakened the next morning, he got dressed, then walked down the hallway to his son's room.

"Billy Ray? Billy Ray, you in there?"

Getting no answer, he opened the door and looked inside. The bed had not been used.

Leaving the big house, Quentin walked out to the bunkhouse. Several of the cowboys were already up and about, including Cole Mathers.

"Cole, have you seen Billy Ray? I looked into his room. It doesn't look like he even came home last night."

Cole cleared his throat, then looked over at a cowboy who was standing nearby.

"Well, sir, uh, accordin' to what Reeves just now told me, Billy Ray got hisself into trouble yesterday. I was about to come tell you that Billy Ray is in jail."

"Reeves, are you saying Billy Ray got into trouble yesterday but you are just now telling us?" Quentin asked angrily.

"Yes, sir, well, the thing is, I got drunk yesterday, and spent the night in jail my ownself," Reeves said. "And that's where Billy Ray is. I couldn't tell you before this mornin' 'cause the marshal didn't let me out till this mornin'."

"If it was just drunkenness, why didn't he let Billy Ray out at the same time?"

"With Billy Ray, it was a little more than just bein' drunk," Reeves said.

"What has Billy Ray done now?" Quentin asked with a long-suffering sigh.

"Well, sir, you may remember that he ordered himself a new pair of boots and had the shoemaker make 'em for him. But when he went down to try 'em on, they didn't fit, so he got mad and busted up the boot store pretty good. He threw a bench through the window, broke up some of Mr. Donovan's tables, even broke one of his machines."

"Surely Dawson didn't have to put him jail for that, did he?" Quentin asked. "He knows I would have paid Donovan for the damage Billy Ray did."

"Yes, sir, and I think if that had been all there was to it, the marshal would have let him go. But Billy Ray still had a mad on when he come into the New York Saloon, and he beat up Mary Lou."

"He beat up who?"

"Mary Lou Culpepper. She's one of Gibson's whores."

"Dawson put my son in jail, just for beating up a whore?"

"Yes, sir. From what the marshal was sayin' this mornin', there was lots of folks pretty upset about it."

"Cole, get my horse saddled," Quentin ordered.

"Yes, sir, I'll get him ready."

It took about fifteen minutes to ride the three miles into town. Quentin rode down the street toward the marshal's office, which was located at the far end of town, and as he did so, several citizens of the town paused to nod at him, or to raise their hands to their eyebrow in a respectful salute. Reaching the marshal's office, he dismounted, tied the horse off at the hitching rail, then stepped inside.

Marshal Dawson was sitting at his desk, playing a hand of solitaire.

"I figured you'd be comin' in here as soon as you got into town," Dawson said without looking up. He put a red queen on a black king.

"What the hell is Billy Ray doing in jail?" Quentin asked.

"Maybe you ain't heard the whole story."

"I heard he broke up some furniture and windows over at Donovan's Leather Goods. Hell, Dawson, you know I'm good for whatever damages he might have caused. You didn't have to put him in jail."

"Did you also hear about the girl he beat up?"

"I heard he slapped a whore around a bit. You can't tell me that's the first time that's ever happened to her. Whores get slapped around all the time. It's the nature of their business."

"He did more than just slap her around. He broke her nose. There was some folks got pretty upset over it. I figured the best thing to do was to put Billy Ray back in jail until you come into town today. Else there might have been even more trouble. You know how he is."

"No, how is he?" Quentin asked, a sharp edge to his question.

"Come on, Pogue, you know how he is. Billy Ray's got about the quickest temper of anyone I've ever known. You need to talk to him about that. One of these days he's goin' to get mad at the wrong person."

"You let me worry about my boy," Quentin said. "He's my problem, not yours."

"That ain't entirely right. He's my problem, too, as long as I'm marshal of this town."

"Yeah, well, that's another thing, Dawson. You are marshal of this town only as long as I say you are marshal of this town."

"I know that, Pogue," Dawson said obsequiously. "I didn't mean nothin' by what I was sayin'."

"Find out how much damage was done to Donovan's store and I'll make it good."

"What about the whore?"

"What about her?"

"It cost her two dollars to have the doctor look at her. Plus, she ain't goin' to be makin' a lot of money as long as she's got a broke nose and two black eyes."

Quentin took out a twenty-dollar bill. "Give this to her," he said. "This should be enough, don't you think?"

"Yes, sir, this ought to more than satisfy her," Marshal Dawson said.

"Now, turn Billy Ray loose."

"I hope I didn't get you upset none by me puttin' him in jail."

"When I get upset with you, Dawson, you'll know it," Quentin said.

"Wilson," Dawson said to his deputy.

"Yes, sir?"

"Go back and let Billy Ray out of his cell."

Quentin walked over to the wall and stared at the wanted posters for a moment as he waited for his son to be brought out to him.

"What you should be doin' is lookin' out for people like this, instead of wastin' your time puttin' my son in jail," Quentin said. He leaned over to examine two of the

SAVAGERY OF THE MOUNTAIN MAN   133

posters more closely. "I'll be damn," he said. "No wonder he had enough money to bid against me."

"What? What are you talking about?"

"These two men here, Jason and Stu Sinclair. It says here there was a five-hundred-dollar reward on each of them."

"Yes, sir, there still is."

Quentin shook his head. "Not anymore there isn't," he said. "That's how come Jensen was able to go as high in the bid as he did. He had that reward money."

"Are you saying someone has collected the reward on those two?"

"Yeah. Them two got themselves killed by Smoke Jensen."

"How do you know?"

"Because it happened back in Colorado Springs while I was there," Quentin said.

At that moment, Deputy Wilson brought Quentin's son out.

"What the hell, Billy Ray. Can't you stay out of trouble?" Quentin asked.

"Them boots didn't fit, Pa," Billy Ray said. "I paid good money to have him make 'em special, and when I tried 'em on, they was too little."

"That didn't give you cause to tear up his place. It's going to cost me a couple hundred dollars just to make things right."

"He should'a made the boots the right size."

"Where's your horse?" Quentin asked.

"I don't know. Last I seen of him, he was tied up in front of the New York Saloon."

"He's in the stable out behind the jail," Marshal Dawson suggested.

"Come on, let's get your horse and get back to the ranch."

Chapter Eleven

Big Rock

It was dark when the train pulled into Big Rock, but Cal was at the depot to meet them.

"Look at him, Cal," Sally said as Prince Henry was led down from the private cattle car. "Have you ever seen a more magnificent-looking animal?"

"No, ma'am, I don't reckon I have," Cal answered.

"And here I thought you came down to the depot to meet us," Smoke said. "Little did I know you were just here just to meet Prince Henry."

"Well, I came to meet you two also," Cal said.

"Also?"

"Uh, well, I don't mean nothin' by that. You know what I think of you an' Miss Sally."

"For heaven's sake, Smoke, quit teasing him," Sally said.

"That's all right, Miss Sally, I know'd, uh, I knew he was just teasin'. Say, don't you wish Pearlie was here? He's been after you to buy a champion bull for nearly a year now."

"I think he would approve," Smoke said.

"Do you think Pearlie will come back?" Cal asked.

"I'm sure he will," Sally said.

"He's the best friend I ever had," Cal added.

"You loaned him your silver hatband, didn't you?" Sally asked.

"I sure did."

"Well, when a friend borrows something from another friend, don't you think he will bring it back? Especially if you are best friends?"

Cal smiled. "Yes, ma'am, I expect you are right about that. But I don't mind tellin' you, I sure do miss him."

"We all miss him, Cal," Sally said. "He's like a part of the family." She smiled, then ran her hand through the young man's hair. "Like you. You are part of the family."

"Let's get this bull home," Smoke said.

"Did you have to pay a lot for him?" Cal asked.

"Look at the confirmation of that animal," Smoke said. "Yes, sir, he is a champion all right."

"How much did you have to pay for him?"

"Can you imagine the calves we will get from him? Why, we'll have a fine herd of Herefords in no time at all."

Sally laughed. "Do you get the hint, Cal? He doesn't want to tell you."

"Yes, ma'am, well, truth to tell, it ain't none of my business nohow."

"Fifteenhundreddollars," Smoke said, speaking so quietly and running the words together so Cal couldn't understand.

"How much?"

"Fifteen hundred dollars," Sally repeated, saying the words clearly. "Which is exactly twice as much as he intended to spend."

"Yes, but . . . I came into a little extra money while I was down there."

"How?"

By now, all were mounted and they were leading Prince Henry toward the ranch. As they rode through the night, Smoke told the story of the break-in at his hotel room.

"If them boys had known what room they was breakin' into, they would of never done it," Cal said. "They ain't nobody can beat you."

"Cal, haven't you ever heard the old cowboy adage?" Smoke asked.

"No. Uh, what's an adage?"

"A saying."

"I don't know, I've heard lots of cowboy sayings."

"Try this one," Smoke said. "There's never been a horse that can't be rode, and there's never been a cowboy that can't be throwed."

Cal laughed, then said, "I don't get it."

"It means you should never think that you can't be beaten."

"Oh," Cal said. "Oh. You mean there might be someone somewhere who is better with a gun than you?"

"Maybe."

"Let's don't talk about this anymore," Sally said.

Los Brazos

It had been two weeks since the attempted holdup of the stagecoach. The last ten runs had been tiring, but without incident. It was dark when the stage returned from its round-trip run to Chama, and it rolled down the main street with its corner lanterns gleaming.

"I tell you the truth," Ben said as he handled the reins. "I'm so tired I don't even plan to eat supper tonight. I'm going to go right to bed, soon as I get home."

The coach passed in front of the cantina and as it did, a burst of laughter spilled out into the street. Pearlie turned in his seat to look toward it, and Ben chuckled.

"What is it?" Pearlie asked. "What are you laughing at?"

"Here I am so tired I'm going to go bed without even eating supper, and you can't wait to get to the cantina."

"I thought I might drop in for a little while," he said. "I'm not ready for bed yet."

"That's because you are still a young man," Ben said. "Wait until you are as old as I am."

"Ben, I don't mean anything by this, but what's a fella your age doing driving a stagecoach anyway? Couldn't you find something a little easier to do?"

"You think I'm too old to handle the ribbons, do you, boy?"

"No, no, not at all," Pearlie said. "I didn't mean anything like that. It's just that—"

Ben laughed. "Don't get all in a twitter over it. I'm just teasin' you. I know you didn't mean anything by it. I know I complain about getting tired, but driving a stage is what I do. I've been drivin' one for thirty years. Wouldn't know how to do anything else. Wouldn't want to do anything else."

"I'll give you this," Pearlie said. "You're good at it. I've seen a lot of drivers in my life, and you are the best."

"Well, thank you, boy, I appreciate that," Ben said as he pulled the coach into the depot, then halted the horses and set the brake.

"Here we are, folks!" he shouted down to the passengers.

Pearlie climbed down, then opened the door to help the passengers out. After all had exited the coach, he climbed back up to gather up the rifle and shotgun, then went inside the depot and put the weapons into the rack.

"No trouble?" the dispatcher asked.

"Not a bit."

After putting his two weapons in the gun rack, Pearlie started toward the door.

"You going down to the cantina, are you?" the dispatcher asked.

"Yeah, I thought I might."

Under the soft, golden light of three gleaming chandeliers, the atmosphere in the Casa de la Suerte Cantina was quite congenial. Half a dozen men—Mexican and American—stood at one end of the bar, engaged in friendly conversation, while at the other end, the barkeep stayed busy cleaning glasses. Most of the tables were filled with vaqueros or cowboys, laborers, and storekeepers laughing over stories they exchanged, or flirting with the *niñas del bar* whose presence added to the agreeable atmosphere.

"Señor Pearlie, do you want a tequila?" the bartender asked.

"Yeah, you may as well give me one, Manuel."

The bartender laughed. "I remember when only beer you would drink."

"Yeah, well, you've ruined me," Pearlie said.

Pearlie was standing at the end of the bar, nursing a tequila, when one of the girls sidled up to him. She had long black hair and was wearing a low-cut red dress that showed a generous amount of cleavage.

"*Tú vas a beber a solas, Señor Pearlie?*" she asked.

"Come on, Rosita. You know I don't comprehend your lingo that well," Pearlie replied.

"I asked if you were going to drink alone."

Pearlie smiled. "Not if I can get a pretty girl like you to dr ink with me," he said. He looked toward the bartender. "Manuel, tequila for the beautiful Rosita, *por favor.*"

As she waited for the drink, Rosita reached up to remove Pearlie's hat. She touched the band, which gleamed brightly in the soft light of the cantina.

"*Plata,*" she said.

"What?"

"The hatband. It is silver."

"Yes."

"It is beautiful. Where did you get it?"

"It isn't mine," Pearlie said. "It belongs to a friend. I borrowed it."

"He must be a very good friend to let you borrow such a beautiful thing."

"Yeah," Pearlie said as he looked at the hatband for a moment. "He is a very good friend."

"It is a good thing to have *buenos amigos.*"

"*Sí,* it is very good to have friends."

Rosita smiled. "I am your friend, am I not?"

The tequila was delivered, and Pearlie picked it up and handed to her. "*Sí,*" he said. "You are my friend."

"What is your friend's name?"

"The one who gave me the hatband is Cal. But I have two more very good friends. Smoke and Sally."

"*Humo?*" Rosita asked, her face registering confusion at the name. "You have a friend who is named *Humo?*" She made the motion as if smoking. "Smoke?"

"His real name is Kirby, but everyone calls him Smoke."

"That is a funny name. Does he smoke *mucho?*"

"No. I don't know why everyone calls him Smoke."

"And Sally? She is your woman?"

"No, she is Smoke's wife."

"I am glad she is Smoke's wife. You do not have a wife, no?"

The smile left Pearlie's face, to be replaced by an expression of great sadness. He tossed down the rest of his drink.

"No," he said. "I do not have a wife."

Whether it was a byproduct of her profession, or inherent in Rosita's personality, she was a very perceptive young woman, and she saw immediately that her question had caused Pearlie some pain. She put her hand on his arm.

"You had a wife but something bad happened, yes?"

"Yes," Pearlie said. "She—she died." He did not go into the details of how Lucy died, but whether it was to spare Rosita or himself, he wasn't sure.

"I am very sorry, Señor Pearlie," Rosita said. "I did not wish to cause you sorrow."

"That's all right," Pearlie replied. "It's been a while now."

"Is that why you are here, and not with your friends? Because being with your friends brings too much sadness?"

Pearlie nodded, but didn't speak.

"Señor Pearlie, I think maybe you should go to your friends now," Rosita said. "I think if you were with your friends, things will be better for you."

Pearlie was surprised by Rosita's comment, but he knew as soon as she spoke that she was right. It was time to get back to his friends, to start living his life again, and to put the hurt and the sorrow behind him. He didn't want to put Lucy behind him, not now, not ever. For the rest of his life she would occupy a part of his heart. But life must go on.

He finished his drink and put his hat back on his

head. "Rosita, you are right," he said. "I think soon I will go home."

"*Vayas con Dios, Señor Pearlie,*" Rosita said.

Pearlie could feel the young woman's eyes staring at the back of his neck as he pushed through beaded curtains that hung over the door of the cantina.

It would be good to get back home. He would leave as soon as Montgomery could find a replacement for him.

Because the next day was Saturday, there was no stage run. Pearlie was having his lunch at the City Pig Café when two men came in. One of the men was C.D. Montgomery, the owner of the stage line. Pearlie had no idea who the man with Montgomery was, but the man was wearing a three-piece suit, so Pearlie assumed he was a man of some importance.

"There he is," Montgomery said, pointing out Pearlie. As the two approached his table, Pearlie stood.

"Young man, my name is Kyle Abernathy. I'm with the New Mexico Mining Company. A couple of weeks ago, you saved our money shipment, and I want to thank you personally."

Abernathy stuck out his hand and Pearlie took it. "Well, I appreciate you coming here to thank me, but I was just doing my job."

"Yes, sir, and doing it very well, too, if I may say so," Abernathy said. He reached into his inside jacket pocket and pulled out an envelope. "This is for you, Pearlie. A little expression of our thanks."

Pearlie looked inside the envelope and saw several bills. "You—you didn't have to do that," he said.

Abernathy laughed. "It's two hundred and fifty dollars,"

he said. He reached for it. "But if you don't want it, I'll take it back."

"No, no, I wouldn't want to seem ungrateful. I'll keep it," Pearlie said, pulling the money back, and both Abernathy and Montgomery laughed.

"I'm sorry we interrupted your lunch, but I just wanted to see you to thank you," Abernathy said.

"Anyone can interrupt my lunch anytime for something like this," Pearlie said with a chuckle.

The following Friday, after returning from his run, Pearlie saw Montgomery sitting at his desk, working on a ledger book.

"Have you changed your mind?" Montgomery asked.

"No, sir," Pearlie replied. "I think it's about time I went home. And I'll be honest with you. When Mr. Abernathy gave me that money, it made it a lot easier."

Montgomery laughed. "I was afraid of that," he said. "That's why I almost told Abernathy not to give it to you. I wanted to keep you on. You've been a good man."

"I appreciate that. But I think Tony will make you a good employee. And with a wife and baby, he needs the job."

"You're right. I've already told him to be ready to start on Monday." Montgomery got up and extended his hand. "We're goin' to miss you around here, Pearlie. If you ever get back down this way again, drop in and see us."

"I will," Pearlie said. He took one last look around the depot, then walked outside, mounted his horse, and started the long trip back to Sugarloaf.

Chapter Twelve

Santa Clara

Even though it was only mid-afternoon, the New York Saloon was fairly crowded. Mary Lou Culpepper, whose face, two weeks after the fact, still showed the effects of her encounter with Billy Ray Quentin, was standing at the end of the bar, having a beer with Lenny York, the young piano player.

At twenty-one years of age, Lenny was actually two years older than Mary Lou, but life's circumstances had forced Mary Lou onto "the line" when she was only sixteen years old. As a result of her worldliness, Mary Lou seemed older than the young musician.

"How's your ma doing?" Mary Lou asked.

"Oh, she's doing fine," Lenny answered.

"That's good. Your ma is a very nice woman. Everyone in town thinks so."

"Mary Lou, I wish you would quit your job here and go work with Ma. She would love to have you."

Mary Lou smiled. "What? And leave you here in the

saloon all by yourself? Why, who would look out for you? Besides, your ma runs a restaurant. What do I know about working in a restaurant? Bein' a whore is the only thing I know."

"I wish you wouldn't call yourself that," Lenny said.

Mary Lou chuckled, then put her hand on Lenny's cheek. "That's just it, Lenny, I am a whore," she said. "That's all I've ever been, and that's all I'll ever be, until I'm too old to whore anymore. You need to know that, and you need to quit spending so much time with me and go find yourself a nice, churchgoing young woman."

"You don't need to be a whore," Lenny said. He reached up to touch her swollen nose, and though his touch was very gentle, she winced under it. He pulled his hand away quickly. "Sorry."

"You didn't hurt me. I was just overreacting, is all."

"If you worked for my ma, you wouldn't have to worry about something like this happening ever again," he said, lifting his hand to nearly, but not quite, touch her broken nose.

Mary Lou chuckled. "Lenny, you are very sweet. But don't you know that if I worked in your ma's restaurant, it would drive away customers? Nobody wants to eat in a place where a whore works."

From one of the tables there was a loud burst of laughter, and looking toward the sound, Lenny and Mary Lou saw Billy Ray Quentin.

"I see Billy Ray is being his usual obnoxious self tonight," Lenny said.

"I try and stay away from him now," Mary Lou said. Unconsciously, she raised her hand to her face. "Since he did this to me, he doesn't find me pretty anymore, so he hasn't been bothering me."

"You are beautiful, Mary Lou, with or without a busted nose," Lenny said.

"And you are sweet," Mary Lou replied. She laughed. "You are blind for saying I'm beautiful. But sweet nevertheless."

At that very moment, no more than a mile outside of town, Pearlie was on his way back to the Sugarloaf. He had been following a railroad track for the last several miles. Now, as he rounded a curve in the tracks, the town appeared in front of him. He had not come by this route on his way south, so he had no idea what town this might be, but it was not unlike the many other towns he had visited during his prolonged odyssey. It was a scattered array of buildings that were barely distinguishable from the hills and clumps that rose from the prairie floor.

As he rode into the town, he took a look at the row of false-front buildings that lined the street. Only two of them showed any sign of ever having been painted. The rest were made of raw, ripsawed lumber that was left to dry and gray as it was weathered by the elements.

Pearlie had learned long ago that his first impressions could tell him a lot about a town, so he made a thorough perusal of the town as he rode in. He saw a freight wagon backed up to the loading dock at Quentin's Warehouse. Two men were busy unloading the wagon, though they weren't talking.

Someone was sweeping the front porch of Quentin's Hardware Store, and though Pearlie looked over toward him, and even touched the brim of his silver-banded hat by way of greeting, the sweeper made no acknowledgment of him whatsoever.

Pearlie hadn't bothered to check the sign that hung on the railroad depot as he came into town, so as he rode down the street he had no idea where he actually was, though he was fairly certain he was back in Colorado now.

Pearlie rode by Quentin's General Store, Quentin's Apothecary, Kathleen's Kitchen—which was a restaurant and boardinghouse, then Quentin's Hotel, until he reached the New York Saloon.

"Hmm, I wonder how this fella Quentin has missed buying the saloon?" Pearlie said to the horse. Over long, solitary rides, Pearlie often talked to his horse—doing so in order to hear a human voice, even if it was his own. And in his mind, talking to his horse was more acceptable than talking to himself.

Stopping in front of the saloon, Pearlie tied his horse off at the hitching rack. Hanging under the porch roof of the saloon was a carved and painted mug of beer. It squeaked slightly as it moved back and forth in the hot, dry wind. Green bottle flies buzzed around a horse apple that lay next to the steps.

Once inside, Pearlie saw a large nude painting behind the bar. Surprised to see such a thing, he stopped to admire it for a moment.

"She's quite a looker, isn't she?" the bartender asked.

"Indeed she is," Pearlie agreed.

"They say she is the illegitimate daughter of the Czar of Russia. He won't claim her, so she has to model for nude paintings in order to make a living."

"Is that true?" Pearlie asked.

The bartender laughed. "Hell, I don't know if it is true or not, but Mr. Gibson—he owns the place—has told us to tell that story to all our new customers. What will it be?"

"A beer," Pearlie said.

"Mr. Evans, could we have another beer please?" a young woman called from the far end of the bar.

"Hold your horses, Mary Lou, till I take care of this fella," the bartender answered.

"I'm in no hurry," Pearlie said. "You can serve the young lady first." He nodded toward her, noticing that her nose was swollen and her eyes black.

"What happened to her?"

"She got beat up by an angry customer," Evans replied.

"I hope you have stopped him from coming in here anymore."

"I wish I could say that I did stop him, but he still comes in here on a regular basis," Evans said as he held two mugs under the spigot of the huge barrel of beer.

Evans served both the scarred young woman and the young man who was with her, then returned to Pearlie.

"Now, stranger, you ordered a beer, I believe?"

"Yes, please," Pearlie replied.

"Coming right up." The bartender held another mug under the spigot of the barrel, then filled it with a foam-crowned, golden liquid.

Pearlie put a nickel on the bar, picked up the mug, then turned his back to the bar to look over the room. He saw a card game in progress.

"Well, boys, I've lost five dollars here today. If I lose any more than that, my wife won't let me back in the house tonight," one of the players said, getting up from the table then.

"Damn, Deckert, you didn't play very long. You're breakin' up the game," the youngest of the players said.

"Better I break up the game than my wife break my nose," Deckert said, and the others laughed.

Pearlie walked over to the table and asked if he could join the game.

"What's your name?" one of the cardplayers asked.

"I'm called Pearlie."

"Pearlie?" the player replied. He chuckled. "Well, that's not a name you hear every day, but then, I don't have room to talk. My given name is Carroll Patterson, and when folks hear it, they think it's a woman's name. But I'm a veterinarian now, so most folks call me Doc."

Doc pointed to the other two players in the game. "That fella is the newspaper editor—his name is Elmer Brandon, and the young one there is Billy Ray Quentin."

"Glad to meet you," Pearlie said. He shook hands with Doc and Brandon, but when he reached across the table to Billy Ray, Billy Ray pointedly began shuffling cards.

"You got 'ny money, Pearlie?" Billy Ray asked. "I don't intend to waste my time with some saddle bum who can't afford to play."

"Billy Ray, that's no way to greet a stranger," Brandon said.

"This isn't some welcoming cotillion," Billy Ray said. "I asked you if you have any money."

"I've got enough for a few hands, I suppose," Pearlie replied, sizing up the unpleasant young man.

Extending his leg under the table, Billy Ray kicked the chair out. "All right, you can play till you run out of money. Have a seat."

"Thanks."

"Don't pay Billy Ray any mind," Doc said. "He just got out of the wrong side of the bed this morning."

"Hell, Doc, what makes you think Billy Ray's bed has a right side?" Brandon asked, and those close enough to overhear the conversation laughed.

"If you fellas don't mind, I think I'll just pull another chair up close and watch," Deckert said. "That way I can enjoy the game without losin' any more money."

"Fine with me if nobody else cares," Doc said.

No one else at the table complained, so Deckert pulled up a chair to watch.

Pearlie, Cal, and some of the other hands at Sugarloaf often played poker for matches. It was a game he enjoyed, and it was one at which he had some skill. He spent the first few hands observing the playing habits of the others, folding twice, once sacrificing only his ante, and once losing a little more. He lost the third hand as well, refusing to match a raise.

Without asking for permission, Billy Ray reached across the table and turned over Pearlie's cards. The others seemed deferential to him.

"Ha!" Billy Ray said. "You had three fours, and you folded to two pair. I'm glad you decided to join us, mister. It's goin' to be fun takin' what little money you have."

"I don't have all that much left," Pearlie said. "And I didn't want to take too much of a chance."

"A fella as scared as you probably ought not to play," Billy Ray said as he raked in the pot.

Pearlie knew exactly what he was doing. By now he had not only picked up some of the strategy of the other players, he had also established in the minds of the others that he was a very cautious player. He had also noticed that Billy Ray was not only arrogant, but reckless. It was a character trait that Pearlie would be able to use.

The cards were dealt again, and this time Pearlie drew a pair of kings. He discarded one card, then smiled as he drew his new card, though in fact it was a five of diamonds, which did nothing to improve his hand.

Pearlie matched the bets, then when Billy Ray raised by five dollars, he watched as the others matched the raise.

"You goin' to fold again, are you?" Billy Ray asked.

"No," Pearlie said. "In fact, I think I'll see your five-dollar raise and raise it by five more."

"Too steep for me," Doc said.

Brandon matched the raise, but Billy Ray, as Pearlie knew he would, raised again.

"Ten dollars," Billy Ray said.

"Damn, Billy Ray, now you've run me out of the game as well," Brandon said.

"I'll see your ten, and raise you twenty more," Pearlie replied.

"I ain't got that much money on me," Billy Ray said.

"What a shame," Pearlie said as he reached for the pot.

"Wait a minute, do you know who I am?"

"They told me your name is Billy Ray. Is that not right?"

"It's Billy Ray, all right. Billy Ray Quentin." An arrogant smile spread across the young man's face. "I reckon that names means somethin' to you."

Pearlie shook his head. "No," he said. "To tell you the truth, Billy Ray, the name doesn't mean a thing to me. Should it?"

"You damn right it should!" Billy Ray said angrily. "What's the matter with you? Are you blind? Didn't you see the name when you come into town? I near'bout own this town."

"Actually, Billy Ray, that would be your pa that owns the town, not you," Brandon said.

"It's the same damn thing and you know it," Billy Ray insisted. He looked across the table toward Pearlie. "Now here is the way it is, mister. I'm goin' to see your twenty, and raise you by one hundred dollars," he said. "You can either match that raise, or throw in your cards. What do you think of that?"

"I think if you are going to be raising me, you need to put the money in the pot," Pearlie replied.

"I told you, I ain't got it on me, but I'm good for it."

"Mister, I've played poker in saloons and gambling halls all over the West," Pearlie said. "And everywhere I've ever played, when a fella is raised, you either call, or raise with what money you brought to the table. Now if you have the money, put it out there. Otherwise, you're goin' to have to fold."

"The hell you say!"

"Billy Ray, Pearlie is right," Deckert said. "We've always played that way, and you know it."

"What the hell business is it of yours, Deckert? You done dropped out of the game," Billy Ray said angrily. "You lend me the money, Doc. You know I'm good for it."

"I don't have that much money on me," Doc replied. "Brandon?"

"Billy Ray, I've got a pretty good hand here myself," the newspaper editor replied. "If I had enough money, I would have matched his raise. I don't have the money."

"All right!" Billy Ray said angrily. He took his hat off and ran his hand through his hair. "All right, take your damn money."

"Thank you," Pearlie replied, raking in the pot.

"What did you have?" Billy Ray asked.

"You know better than that, mister," Pearlie said in a friendly voice. "If you didn't pay to see my cards, then I don't have to show them."

"I aim to see them damn cards," Billy Ray said. He reached across the table and flipped over the cards Pearlie had laid before him facedown.

"What?" he shouted when he saw them. "All you had was a pair of kings?"

Deckert laughed out loud. "Whoowee, Billy Ray. Looks to me like this young feller run a bluff on you. Yes, sir, he dangled that line down and hooked you just like a fish."

Several other patrons in the saloon laughed as well.

"Why, you cheatin' son of a bitch!" Billy Ray shouted, leaping up quickly from his chair. "You ain't about to make a fool out of me!"

Billy Ray started for his pistol.

The first thing Pearlie noticed was how incredibly slow the man was. When he started his draw, Pearlie thought he was going to have to kill him, but Billy Ray's draw was so slow and deliberate that Pearlie realized he had another, better option.

Pearlie drew his own pistol, easily beating Billy Ray, then wrapping his hand around it, he brought it down hard on Billy Ray's head. The arrogant man went down like a poleaxed steer.

Reaching down, Pearlie picked up Billy Ray's pistol, then walked over to the bar and dropped the gun into a large, brass spittoon, specifically choosing one that was full.

A couple of the other people in the saloon chuckled.

"Ole Billy Ray isn't goin' to like findin' his gun in the spittoon," Lenny said.

"I don't like this. Billy Ray isn't the type to take this. I'm afraid the stranger has let himself in for trouble," Mary Lou said.

Doc got down on the floor beside Billy Ray and, gingerly, ran his hand over the bump on Billy Ray's head.

"How is he, Doc?" Evans called from behind the bar.

"He's all right. He'd going to have a headache, but he's all right."

Brandon grabbed his hat. "If nobody objects, I think I'll leave before Billy Ray comes to."

"I'll join you," Doc said, following the newspaper editor to the door, then outside.

Pearlie stepped up to the bar. The bartender was standing at the far end, and he stood there for a moment longer before he moved down.

"You might want to leave, too, while you've still got the chance," the bartender said.

"Why is that?"

"Billy Ray ain't goin' to be too pleasant when he comes to."

"Well, maybe I can make friends with him," Pearlie said easily. "But for now, I'd like another beer please, Mr. Evans," Pearlie said, remembering the bartender's name. "I'm afraid my other one got spilled in the ruckus."

"I'll get the beer, but mister, my advice to you is to drink it quick, then ride on out of town."

"Thanks. Maybe I'll just do that."

"What's your name, mister?" one of the others in the bar asked.

Pearlie waited until the beer was put in front of him. Then he picked it up, took a swallow, and wiped some of the foam off his lips before he turned to face his questioner.

"Folks call me Pearlie," Pearlie said pleasantly. "And you are?"

"Kelly, Jerry Kelly. I work at the Tumbling Q. And the reason I asked your name is, I was just wonderin' what name to tell the undertaker to put on your tombstone, is all."

"Well, I appreciate your concern, Mr. Kelly, but I don't

figure on that bein' any part of your problem," Pearlie replied. "After I finish my beer, I plan to be on my way."

"You better drink fast then. You got 'ny idea who that fella is that you just riled?"

"Isn't his name Billy Ray?"

"That's right. Billy Ray. Quentin," he added pointedly.

"Yeah, he said that, too."

"Don't that name mean anything to you?"

"He tried to tell me he was someone important," Pearlie said easily. "I know I did see the name a few times as I was ridin' into town."

"A few times? Pogue Quentin damn near owns the whole town, plus one of the biggest ranches in the state," Kelly said.

"Pogue Quentin?"

"Yeah, that's Billy Ray's pa. And he ain't one to get riled."

"Well, Mr. Kelly, I didn't rile Pogue Quentin," Pearlie said easily. "I riled his son."

At that moment, Billy Ray regained consciousness. Getting up groggily, he looked around the room and, seeing Pearlie standing at the bar, let out a loud, angry roar. He reached again for his pistol, but this time found only an empty holster.

"Where at's my gun?" he yelled.

"In there," Pearlie said, pointing to the spittoon.

Billy Ray looked at the spittoon, then glared at Pearlie. After a moment, he walked out without saying another word.

Chapter Thirteen

"I'll be damned," Deckert said after Billy Ray left so quietly. "I never thought I would see anything like that. Billy Ray's got the worst case of temper of anyone I've ever seen."

"Yes, who would think he would just walk out of here like that without doing anything?" Lenny said.

"Maybe he just—" Mary Lou stopped in mid-sentence, and glancing into the mirror behind the bar, Pearlie understood why. In the reflection of the mirror, he saw Billy Ray rushing back in through the batwing doors like a mad bull. This time he had a shotgun in his hands.

"You son of a bitch! Nobody does me that way!" he bellowed. He let loose a blast as soon as he cleared the doors.

Because Pearlie had seen Billy Ray in the mirror, he was able to launch himself onto the floor just as the big man pulled the trigger. Despite Pearlie's quick reaction, he felt the sting of four or five of the pellets. Fortunately, the biggest load hit the bar, taking out a significant chunk of it.

Enraged that he missed, Billy Ray swung the shotgun toward Pearlie.

"You son of a bitch!" he shouted. He pulled the hammer back on the second barrel. "I'm going to leave your guts on the floor!"

Pearlie had drawn his pistol even as he dived to the floor and now, lying on his back, with his face bleeding slightly from the puncture wounds of the pellets that did strike him, he raised up, pointed his pistol at Billy Ray, and pulled the trigger. His bullet caught Billy Ray in the forehead, and the shotgun-wielding big man fell backward onto the boardwalk in front of the New York Saloon.

Pearlie was just getting to his feet when two men, wearing badges, came into the saloon. Both were carrying shotguns and, seeing Pearlie struggling to his feet, bleeding from the shot that had hit him, they pointed their guns at him.

"Drop your gun, mister!" one of the men said.

"No need for all that, Marshal," Pearlie said. He nodded toward Billy Ray, whose body was now lying half in and half out of the saloon. "It's all over now."

"You the one that killed him?"

"I am."

"Then it ain't all over, boy. Not by a long shot, it ain't over. It's just startin'."

"Marshal Dawson, Billy Ray is the one who started this. He came in here, shooting first," Lenny said. "You can see there at the bar, he fired the shotgun and took out part of the bar. Hit this man, too. This man had no choice but to shoot back, considering Billy Ray was ready to shoot again."

"If I need any comment from you, Lenny York, I'll ask for it," the marshal said. "You do the piano playing. I'll do the marshaling around here." He made a gesture with his shotgun, thrusting it toward Pearlie. "Shuck out of that gun belt, boy, and let it fall, real easy like, to the floor."

"Marshal, Lenny is right," Deckert said. "Billy Ray come after this fella. Seems to me this fella didn't have no choice."

"Lenny and Mr. Deckert are telling the truth, Marshal," Mary Lou said.

"So now the whore puts her two bits," Dawson said dismissively. "Anybody else got anything to say?"

Pearlie looked around, and when no one else said anything, the marshal spoke again.

"I know Billy Ray had a temper," he said. "But he wasn't in the habit of goin' after someone, especially with a shotgun, unless he had a good reason. Why did he come after you?"

"We were playing cards. I won the hand and he took issue with it."

"Who else was playin'?"

"I had been playin' but I dropped out," Deckert said.

"Were you the only one?"

"No, Doc and Brandon were playin', too," Deckert said.

Dawson looked around the saloon. "Where are they?"

"They left before the shootin'," Evans said.

Dawson turned his attention back to Pearlie. "So you're saying that Billy Ray get mad just because he lost a hand of poker?"

"That's what I'm saying."

"Well, now, I'll admit that Billy Ray had a temper. But I don't think even he would fly off the handle like that just because he lost a hand of poker."

"It might have been the way he lost, Marshal," Deckert said.

"Oh? And how was that?"

"This here young fella, Pearlie, he said his name was, run a bluff, only it weren't no ordinary bluff."

"You mean he cheated?"

"No, wasn't nothin' like that. But he sorta set Billy Ray up, you might say, playin' like he didn't quite know what he was doin', then when Billy Ray stepped into it, why, Pearlie here, closed the trap slick as a whistle."

"You a cardsharp, are you boy? I don't like cardsharps."

"I enjoy playing. I'm not a cardsharp."

"Uh-huh. Tell me, boy, how do you make your livin'?"

"I'm a cowboy."

"Is that a fact? Who do you work for?"

"Well, I, uh, haven't cowboyed the last six months," Pearlie said.

"How have you been supporting yourself?"

"Doing odd jobs here and there," Pearlie said. "I just came off a job of bein' a shotgun guard on a stagecoach. I worked there for nearly three months."

"Doing odd jobs here and there, you say. Where was you a shotgun guard?"

"Down in New Mexico."

"Why you wanderin' around so?"

"No particular reason," Pearlie answered. He wasn't about to tell the marshal about Lucy. That was none of his business.

"Boy, I get real suspicious of folks that can't stay in one place. I'll just bet that if I go back down to my office, I'll find some wanted dodgers on you."

"I'm not a wanted man," Pearlie replied.

"Uh-huh. You ever been in trouble with the law?"

"I'm not a wanted man," Pearlie repeated.

"That ain't what I asked. I asked if you have ever been in trouble with the law."

"Nothing to speak of," Pearlie answered.

"How much did you win tonight?"

"About forty dollars."

"So you killed a man over forty dollars?"

"No. I killed him because he was trying to kill me. Mr. Deckert, Lenny, and the young lady are tellin' the truth," Pearlie said. "Billy Ray came after me. I didn't have any choice."

"It's easy enough for you to get a couple of friends to lie for you," the Marshal said.

"What?" Pearlie looked over toward Lenny. "Lenny is not my friend. I've never even met him before. And the only reason I know Mr. Deckert is because he was sittin' at the table with us, watching the game."

"Then how did you know York's name?"

"York? I thought it was Lenny," Pearlie said.

"It's Lenny York," the marshal replied. "Anyone else in here want to back up what York and Deckert just said? How about you, Evans?" he asked the bartender. "You got 'nything to say?"

"Tell you the truth, Marshal Dawson, when the shootin' started, I ducked down behind the bar," Evans said.

"Who shot first?" Pearlie asked.

"I don't know, mister," the bartender answered. "It happened so fast that it seemed to me like it all started at the same time."

"Anybody else got 'nything to add?" Marshal Dawson asked.

"Yeah, I do," Kelly said. "This here fella started it." He pointed at Pearlie.

"Was you playin' cards with 'em?" Dawson asked.

"No, but you might take a look in that spittoon there," Kelly suggested.

"Now, why the hell would I want to do that?" Dawson replied.

"Because this fella dropped Billy Ray's pistol into it."

"Is that right?" Dawson asked Pearlie. "Did you actually drop Billy Ray's pistol into the spittoon?"

"Yes, that's right."

"Why did you do that?"

"We were playing cards, and Billy Ray got a little upset. I thought if I took the gun away from him, it might keep him from using it to shoot me."

"Didn't you stop to think that might make Billy Ray mad?"

"Like I said, he was already mad at me. I just figured the best thing I could do is put his pistol where he couldn't get to it so easy."

"How'd you get his pistol in the first place?"

"I took it from him when he tried to draw on me," Pearlie said.

"You took it from him?"

"Yes."

"Billy Ray don't seem like the kind of person you could just take a pistol away from."

"I hit him over the head with my gun and knocked him out before I took it. You can ask Mr. Deckert here. He saw it all."

"That's right, Marshal," Deckert said. "Like I told you, Billy Ray mad at the way Pearlie won the pot."

"But you say he wasn't cheatin'?"

"No, he wasn't cheatin'. He bluffed Billy Ray out of the hand. Also, I guess you could say he bought the pot."

"He bought the pot? From Billy Ray Quentin? How the hell could anyone buy a pot from Billy Ray Quentin?" The marshal looked back at Pearlie. "Are you rich, mister?"

"No."

"Well, the Quentins is rich. So you want to tell me how you could buy the pot from Billy Ray Quentin?"

"I raised the pot to more money than Billy Ray had brought to the table with him," Pearlie explained.

"And you wouldn't let him go get anymore?" the marshal asked.

"No."

"Why not?"

"Because I figured he probably had a better hand than I did. I was playing cards to win, Marshal, not to be a good sport."

"Mister, the more you talk, the deeper you are getting yourself into trouble."

"I'm just tellin' you the truth," Pearlie said.

"Put the shackles on him, Wilson."

"Yes, sir, Marshal," the deputy replied enthusiastically, as if this was the first time he had ever been involved in anything that offered such excitement.

Deputy Wilson took a pair of iron wrist cuffs from his belt, told Pearlie to put his arms behind his back, then cuffed them.

"There," the marshal said. "I reckon that'll hold you till we get you down to the jail."

"Jail. What are you taking me to jail for?"

"Murder, boy," Marshal Dawson said. "You shot down Pogue Quentin's boy in cold blood. You're goin' to stand trial for that, and if Pogue Quentin gets his way, well, sir, I reckon you're goin' to hang."

"Wait a minute, Marshal, this was self-defense!" Pearlie said. "Ask anyone in here, they'll all tell you, it was self-defense!"

"Now, son, you seen me ask, didn't you? Kelly says you started it, the bartender says he didn't see it. That leaves you, Decker, Lenny, and the whore. Deckert, are you really willing to go to court? Hell, you ain't got nerve enough to even stand up to your wife. Do you think you can stand up to Pogue Quentin, and tell him that his boy was at fault here?"

Deckert looked at Pearlie, who was now in shackles, and at Dawson and the deputy.

Deckert was quiet for a long moment. "No, I—I reckon not," Deckert said. "Now that I think back on it, it all seemed to happen so fast that I ain't exactly sure what happened."

"Deckert, that ain't true and you know it! You seen ever'thing!" Pearlie said.

Deckert didn't answer. Instead, he looked toward the floor so he could avoid looking into Pearlie's eyes.

"That leaves you with nobody but the piano player and the whore. And ever'body knows they didn't neither one of them like Billy Ray. Let's go, mister," Dawson said, waving his pistol toward the front door. "I've got a nice cell waitin' for you down at the jail."

The jailhouse was at the far end of the street from the saloon, and as Marshal Dawson marched Pearlie down the street, many followed along so that, by the time they reached the jail, there were at least forty or more townspeople who had fallen in behind them, creating a regular parade.

"When you goin' to hang him, Marshal?" Kelly asked.

"Yeah, let's string 'im up now!" another said.

"Just hold off, the both of you," Dawson said. "He's goin' to hang, all right, but it's all goin' to be done fit an' proper, soon as we get the judge down here."

"Who you goin' to get to try him? Won't do now to get someone who is all too highfalutin," Kelly said.

"I'll be sendin' for McCabe," Marshal Dawson said.

"Yeah, that's it, send for the Hangin' Judge," one of the others in the crowd said. "Yeah, that'll do just real good."

Marshal Dawson pushed Pearlie into the cell, then closed the door. "Turn around and back up to the bars and I'll get those shackles off," he said.

"Thanks," Pearlie said, turning around while the marshal unlocked the chains.

"Boy, I don't know what made you come into our town, but you would have been a lot better givin' Santa Clara a wide berth."

"Santa Clara?" Pearlie said. "Is that the name of this town?"

"You mean to tell me you don't even know where you're at?" Dawson asked.

"I didn't notice the sign when I rode in."

"So what you done is, you just come into a town you didn't even know, just so's you could kill one of our leading citizens."

"If the fella I killed is one of your leading citizens, then your town is in sorry shape," Pearlie said.

"Yeah? Well, we see what kind of shape we're in when you're danglin' from the gallows."

"You got a doc in this town?" Pearlie asked. "I mean other than Doc Patterson, who said he was a veterinarian."

"Yeah, we got a doc. What of it?"

"I've got a few shotgun pellets in me. You might of noticed that."

"Don't worry about 'em. They ain't a-goin' to kill you afore we hang you," the marshal said.

Chapter Fourteen

When Lenny York stepped into the jail that night, he was carrying a tray covered with a cloth.

"What have you got there?" Deputy Wilson asked.

"I brought the prisoner his supper," Lenny said.

"Who told you to do that? The marshal didn't leave me no money to pay for the prisoner's supper."

"I paid for it myself," Lenny said.

"Why?"

"Because I saw what happened and I know this man didn't have any choice. If he hadn't killed Billy Ray, Billy Ray would have killed him, and maybe even someone else in the saloon, the way he was using that scattergun."

"Damn, if you feel like that, maybe I better check just to make sure you ain't carryin' him in no gun or nothin'," Wilson said.

Wilson took the cover off, revealing a bowl of beans and a small plate that had two corn bread muffins. He picked up one of the muffins and took a bite.

"Hey, put that back! That isn't yours," York complained.

Wilson laughed. "I'm the deputy," he said. "There's

been some hard feelin' about this man, seein' as he kilt Billy Ray Quentin. I need to make sure you wasn't poisonin him or nothin'."

Wilson ate the corn bread muffin with obvious enjoyment, then made a dismissive motion with his hand.

"Go ahead, you can take it to him," he said.

Lenny nodded, then walked back to the cell.

"I brought you something to eat," he said.

"Thanks," Pearlie replied. "I haven't eaten since this morning and I was getting pretty hungry."

Lenny passed the bowl and plate through the bars, then turning the tray on edge, passed it through as well so Pearlie would have something to eat on. Pearlie sat on his bunk, put the tray on his knees to use as a table, and began to eat.

"This is very good," he said. "Or else I'm just very hungry."

"No, it is really good," Lenny said. "I know, because my ma fixed it. She runs Kathleen's Kitchen and Boarding House."

"Really? Yes, I saw that as I rode by it while coming into town," Pearlie said. "I almost stopped there before I went to the saloon. I should have. If I had done that I wouldn't be sitting here right now."

"You shouldn't be here now anyway," Lenny said. "What you did was in self-defense."

"Yes, well, when we have the trial, with you, the young lady, and Deckert testifying, I shouldn't have any problem convincing the jury."

Lenny shook his head. "Deckert isn't going to testify in court."

"Why not? He spoke up back at the saloon."

"Yes, but remember when the marshal questioned him

again, he backed down. He isn't going to testify because he's too afraid."

"Afraid of who? The marshal?"

"He's afraid of Pogue Quentin," Lenny said. "Everybody in town is afraid of him."

"Are you scared of him?"

Lenny nodded. "He is not a man I would want to cross."

"Does that mean you aren't going to testify for me?"

"No, I'll testify for you. I'm scared of Pogue Quentin all right, but that doesn't mean I won't testify."

"Well, Lenny, I appreciate that," Pearlie said. "From the way the marshal talks, your testimony may not do much good, but I appreciate that you are willing to do it."

"Your cheek looks like it's beginning to swell up some from the shotgun pellets," Lenny said. "How come the doc didn't take 'em out?"

"I haven't seen a doctor."

"That's not right. The marshal should have gotten him to look at you. I'll get him to come by."

"If the marshal doesn't ask him to come, I doubt he'll do it," Pearlie said.

Lenny shook his head. "No, he'll come if I ask him," he said. Lenny smiled. "Dr. Urban is a single man, and my ma is a widow. Dr. Urban has been callin' on her."

"I appreciate that, Lenny." Pearlie put his finger on one of the pellet wounds on his cheek and winced. "You think you could get the doctor to come look at me pretty soon?"

"I'll get him," Lenny said.

"Lenny, are you sure you want to get involved in this?" Lenny's mother asked a few minutes later when Lenny told her what had happened.

"Doesn't seem like I have any choice, Ma," Lenny replied. "You have always said I should do what is right, regardless of what anyone else thinks. Well, this is the right thing to do."

"I always said you should play the piano in concerts in grand theaters, too," Kathleen York said. "And where do you play? In a saloon."

Lenny chuckled. "How many grand theaters are there in Santa Clara?"

"You don't have to stay here."

"I know I don't have to stay here, but I want to I mean, you are here, aren't you? Besides, I'm not really good enough to play anywhere except a saloon." Lenny chuckled. "But I'm not complainin'. Playing the piano certainly beats mucking manure out of a stable over at the livery—and that's about the only thing else I would be qualified to do."

"I'm not the only one keeping you here, am I?"

"What do you mean, Ma?"

"Are you still seeing that—uh—woman over at the saloon?"

"Only in a matter of speaking. Mary Lou Culpepper is a good woman, but she doesn't want to have anything to do with me."

"Surely she doesn't think she is better than you?" Kathleen asked.

"No, Ma, it's just the opposite. She doesn't think she is good enough for me."

"Well, who am I to judge?" Kathleen said. "After your father died, it was quite a struggle keeping food in our mouths and a roof over our heads. If I hadn't managed to make a go of the restaurant and boardinghouse, who knows what I would have done?"

"You've done well, Ma," Lenny said. "We never went hungry, and you even found enough money to pay for my piano lessons."

Kathleen smiled, and put her hand on her son's cheek. "You think it is important that you help this man the marshal has in jail, do you?"

"Yes, ma'am, I do," Lenny replied.

"All right. I'll go over to David's office now, and ask him to step down to the jailhouse to take a look at your friend."

"Thanks, Ma."

The lettering printed on the side of the doctor's medical bag read: DAVID URBAN, M.D. He set it on the edge of Deputy Wilson's desk.

"What are you doin' here?" Wilson asked.

"I've come to have a look at your prisoner," Dr. Urban replied.

Wilson shook his head. "Huh-uh, no, you don't. I ain't been authorized to pay you nothin'."

"I'm not asking for any money, Deputy. All I'm asking is that you let me see your prisoner."

"I can't let him out of the cell—you'll have to stay in there with him. And he's a dangerous man, seein' as he's already killed one man."

"That's all right. I'll take my chances with him. And I can work as well inside the cell as outside," Dr. Urban said.

"I'll take you back there and let you in, but I'm going to have to lock the door behind you."

"I understand."

Pearlie was lying on the bunk when the three men approached his cell.

"Pearlie, I brought the doctor," Lenny said.

Pearlie sat up. "Good for you. I appreciate that."

Wilson put the key in the cell door, but before he turned it, he looked over at Pearlie. "Don't you get up off that cot till these folks is inside and I've locked the door behind 'em."

Pearlie didn't answer, but neither did he make an attempt to get up. Wilson opened the cell door, held it for a moment, then slammed it shut behind Lenny and Dr. Urban.

"When you are ready to come out, just let me know," he said.

"I'm ready to come out," Pearlie said, and Lenny and Dr. Urban laughed.

"You're a real funny man, ain't you?" Wilson said with a sneer as he turned and walked back toward the front of the building.

"Let me take a look at your face," Dr. Urban said, examining the wounds.

"How do they look?" Pearlie asked.

"Right now, it's not a face the ladies will fall in love with," Dr. Urban answered. "But it shouldn't be all that hard to get the pellets out. And they are going to have to come out before they fester up on you."

Dr. Urban searched through his bag until he found something that looked like an extended pair of tweezers. "Lenny, grab that plate that his dinner was on, and hold it while I dig these out, will you?"

"Yes, sir," Lenny replied.

Lenny stood by, holding the plate as Dr. Urban dug each of the little balls of shot out of Pearlie's face. As he pulled them out, he dropped the pellets into the plate. Pearlie winced with each extraction.

"I'm sorry," Dr. Urban said.

"It's all right," Pearlie replied.

Dr. Urban cleaned the wounds, then poured alcohol on them.

"Ouch!" Pearlie shouted.

"Sorry, but we've learned a lot in the last few years," Dr. Urban said. "And one of the things we've learned is that alcohol helps to prevent the wounds from festering."

"I know, and I appreciate it," Pearlie said.

"All right, that does it," the doc said, standing up and cleaning his own hands. "Try and keep your hands away from the wounds if you can."

"I'll try," Pearlie said. Pearlie looked up at Lenny. "Lenny, I'm goin' to ask you do to a favor for me. A big favor."

"All right. Whatever you say."

"I want you to go up to the town of Big Rock. When you get there, ask directions for Sugarloaf Ranch. At Sugarloaf, you'll find a fella by the name of Smoke Jensen. Tell him where I am, and what kind of a fix I'm in. Also, tell him how much money it cost you to go there. He'll pay you back."

"I will if I can get off," Lenny said.

"If you can get off? Get off what?"

"You don't know, because I wasn't working when you were there, but I play piano for Mr. Gibson."

"Gibson?"

"He's the man that owns the saloon. He wasn't there when you were there. In fact, he's not even in town now. I'll have to wait until he comes back so I can ask him."

"There may not be enough time to wait," Pearlie said. "From the way the marshal was talking, they're going to try to get this done very fast."

"You're right," Lenny said. He sighed. "All right, I'll go. It may cost me my job, but I'll go."

"It's not going to cost you your job, Lenny," Dr. Urban said. "I'm sure you know that Rodney Gibson is a very good friend of mine. I'll make things right with him."

"I appreciate that," Lenny said.

Pearlie reached over to pick up his hat. The silver band flashed once in the sun. "When you get to Sugarloaf, give this hat to a young fella there named Calvin Woods. Tell him I said, 'Thanks for the loan.'"

"Thanks for the loan?"

"Yeah, he'll know what that means. And it will prove that you didn't steal it, that you're actually carrying a message from me."

"All right," Lenny said, taking the hat. "I'll do that."

"Don't let me down, Lenny," Pearlie said. "And hurry, or my friends might get here just in time to visit my grave."

"I don't know, Lenny," Lloyd Evans said as he stood behind the bar, polishing glasses. "I ain't your boss. Rodney is. And he's up in Denver for a few days, you know that."

"Yeah, I know," Lenny replied. "But Dr. Urban is a real good friend of Mr. Gibson's. He said he would take it up with him and make it right."

"If Dr. Urban offered to do that, you'll probably be all right then," Evans said. "They are good friends. Why, you've seen yourself how many times they've sat at that table back in the corner, playing chess."

"How soon are you leaving?" Mary Lou asked.

"Pearlie is right. If I don't go as soon as I can, it may be too late. That's why I'm takin' the next train north."

"Lenny, are you sure you are doing the right thing?" she asked.

"What do you mean?"

"Pogue Quentin is a very powerful man," she replied. "He may not like it if he thinks you are helping the man who killed his son."

"Come on, Mary Lou, you saw it just like I did. You know Pearlie didn't have any choice but to shoot Billy Ray."

"I know. It was self-defense."

"I might not get up there and back in time—and even if I do, I don't know that his friends will be able to do anything. But I have to try."

"Who are his friends?" Evans asked. "Did Pearlie tell you their names?"

"Well, one of them owns a ranch and Pearlie used to work for him. His name is Smoke Jensen."

Evans stopped polishing the glasses and looked up in sharp surprise. "Did you say Smoke Jensen?"

"Yes. Why? Do you know him?"

"I can't exactly say that I know him," Evans said. "But I've seen him in action."

"Seen him in action? What kind of action?"

"He's the fella that single-handed cleaned out the town of Bury, Idaho. I'll tell you this—if there is a man alive who can help this boy, it would be someone like Smoke Jensen."

"In that case, I have to get back in time," Lenny said.

"Lenny, if you'd like, I'll come down to the depot with you and see you off," Mary Lou offered.

A broad smile spread across Lenny's face. "Mary Lou, I can't think of anything I would like more," he said.

* * *

Kathleen York also went down to the depot to see her son off. Lenny was the only passenger leaving at this hour, so the waiting room was empty except for the single ticket clerk, who sat behind the ticket counter reading the newspaper, and the telegrapher, who was at his incessantly clacking key, nosily listening to the messages, even though none of them were being sent to Santa Clara.

"Ma, promise me that you'll take food down to him while I'm gone," Lenny said.

"Are you saying you don't think the marshal will feed him?"

"I don't know. You know that Marshal Dawson is Pogue Quentin's man, and if Quentin doesn't want Pearlie fed, Dawson would more than likely just starve him."

"I'll do what I can," Kathleen said. "But you know yourself that sometimes I get pretty busy in the restaurant. I might not always be able to get away."

"You've got to feed him, Ma."

"Like I said, I'll do what I can. I'm not going to let him starve," Kathleen promised.

"You'll like Pearlie, Ma. He's really a very nice person. And he has been just real friendly to me."

"How nice can he be? He killed Billy Ray Quentin."

"I told you, he didn't have any choice," Lenny said, glancing toward the door. He had been glancing toward the door every minute or so since they had arrived, half an hour ago.

"What are you looking for?" Kathleen asked.

Before he could answer his ma's question, a young woman stepped through the door. She smiled when she saw Lenny and she started toward him, then stopped when she saw Lenny's mother with him. The smile left her face, to be replaced by a look of concern.

"Mary Lou, I'm glad you could come," Lenny called to her. "Come on, I want you to meet my ma."

"Lenny, I don't think . . ." Kathleen began, but Lenny cut her comment off with a stare.

"Ma, watch what you say," he said quietly. "I don't think you want to insult the girl I'm going to marry, now, do you?"

"Lenny, you can't be serious."

"I am, Ma. She just doesn't know it yet."

Lenny walked over to take Mary Lou by the arm and lead her back to his mother.

It was obvious that Mary Lou was nervous, but to Lenny's relief, his mother smiled graciously, then extended her hand.

"Mary Lou," she said. "I've heard so much about you. I'm glad you are here to help see Lenny off."

The tense expression left Mary Lou's face, and she relaxed visibly. "It is nice to meet you, Mrs. York," she said, taking Kathleen's proffered hand.

"Oh, hey, Ma, I've got an idea," Lenny said. "On those times when you can't get off long enough to take a meal over to Pearlie, you can let Mary Lou do it for you."

"Oh, Lenny, I couldn't ask her to do that," Kathleen said.

"I don't mind," Mary Lou said. "I'd be glad to do that for you."

Kathleen paused for a moment, as if considering all the consequences. Then, smiling, she nodded. "Thank you, that will be wonderful," she said.

* * *

By mid-morning of the next day, a polished black coffin, liberally trimmed with silver, was on display behind the big window in front of Quentin's Hardware Store. Throughout the morning, nearly the entire town had stopped by at one time or another to have a look. The top half of the coffin was open so the body could be seen lying on a bed of white silk. Billy Ray was wearing a black suit, a ruffled white shirt, and a black bow tie.

A sign posted alongside the coffin read:

A Noble Young Life
Brought to an *untimely end*
by a murdering Stranger

The article in the *Santa Clara Chronicle* was more neutral:

Shooting in The New York Saloon.

A quiet evening of pleasant conversation, moderate imbibing, and recreational cardplaying erupted into gunplay Thursday last. Billy Ray Quentin, the son of Huereano County's most affluent citizen, was hurled into eternity by the accurate placement of a .44-caliber ball, said ball the result of a pistol discharged by a visitor to Santa Clara, a man who has identified himself only as Pearlie.

Shortly after the dramatic confrontation, Marshal Clem Dawson and Deputy Deke Wilson arrived on the scene, whereupon Pearlie was immediately placed under arrest. Pearlie is now awaiting trial for murder, though the prosecutor may have a difficult time in establishing his case. There are some who were eyewitnesses to the shooting who have made the statement that the stranger had no choice but to return fire. These witnesses report that Billy Ray started the fight by firing a twelve-gauge shotgun at Pearlie, with the obvious intent of killing him. It will be up to a jury to make the final decision as to whether Pearlie's arrival in our fair town, surely with no aforethought to killing another human being, shall now result in his being hanged.

Billy Ray Quentin will be buried tomorrow in the Santa Clara Cemetery.

The funeral parade to the cemetery was led by members of the volunteer fire department, proudly showing off their pumper, its highly polished brass boiler shining brightly in the afternoon sun. Following the fire pumper was the town's marching band, its members elegantly attired in their red and gold uniforms, the bright color offset somewhat by the black armbands they were wearing. The band was playing Chopin's stately *Funeral March*, and they proceeded along the route in slow, measured steps, keeping pace with the somber music.

Next came the highly polished white, glass-sided hearse, bearing Billy Ray's black and silver coffin. The head of the coffin was somewhat elevated so that the spectators who lined the street on both sides could see the body. The hearse was driven by Josiah Welch, the undertaker, who, like Billy, was dressed in a black suit, with a ruffled white shirt and black bow tie. The only difference was that Welch was wearing a high-crown silk hat.

Pogue Quentin, who was also wearing a black suit, rode in an elegant open carriage behind the hearse. The carriage, as were the horses pulling it, was draped in black bunting. As the cortege passed by, the people began following it to the cemetery.

Because there had been no rites in the church, the body was taken directly from its place of display in the show window of the hardware store to the cemetery. Once the cortege reached its destination, the coffin was removed from the hearse and placed on the ground alongside the open grave. Not until then was the top part of the coffin closed, after which the Reverend Charles Landers stepped up to the head of the grave.

"Dear friends," he began. "We are gathered here in the sure and certain hope of the resurrection and eternal life of our brother, Billy Ray Quentin, and I ask you to now—"

"Hold on there, Preacher," Pogue Quentin called, interrupting the funeral rite. "I want to say a few words."

"I—uh—very well," Landers said, surprised by Quentin's unexpected outburst. He stepped aside, assuming that Quentin would take his place, but Quentin didn't move from where he had been standing.

"Folks," Quentin began. "The man who murdered my boy, in cold blood, is down there in the jailhouse." He pointed in the general direction of the jail. "We'll be havin' his trial soon as Judge McCabe gets here, and that means there will be a jury selected. That jury will come from this town, most of which is here now. If you are selected to be on that jury, I want you to understand that I expect the murderer to be found guilty and to hang."

He held up a copy of the *Santa Clara Chronicle* and pointed to the front-page story.

"Brandon, there will be no more stories like this one. Why, if someone didn't know any better, they could read this story and think maybe that the man who killed my son was justified."

"Mr. Quentin, you must know that there are some who

witnessed the event who say that it was justifiable homicide," Brandon replied.

"I want you to know, Brandon, that I will be keeping my eye on you and on any more stories you write like this one. And I'm givin' you fair warning now not to do it."

"Are you threatening the right of a free press, sir?" Brandon asked.

"I'm just tellin' you, that's all," Quentin said. "And for rest of you, any of you who might be on the jury," he continued, looking out over those who had gathered in the cemetery for the purpose of interment, "hear me good. I won't take too kindly to anyone who doesn't do their duty and find that son of a bitch guilty. I aim to see to it that my son's killer is hung by the neck until he is dead."

"Mr. Quentin, we are having a funeral," Landers said. "Such language is unseemly."

"Yeah? Well, you got your language and I got mine, Preacher," Quentin said. "But I've got my piece said now, so you can get on back to the buryin'."

Chapter Fifteen

Sugarloaf Ranch

Although Prince Henry had his own stall, he had been brought outside and was now tied to a post in the middle of the corral. This was, in fact, the same post to which horses were tied before being broken.

Cal approached the animal carrying a brush in one hand and a bucket of soapy water in the other. Setting the bucket down beside Prince Henry, he patted him on the head.

"I don't know, Prince Henry," he said. "You bein' a champion and all, it could be that you been scrubbed down before. But I have to tell you the truth. I ain't never washed no bull before, and I never thought I would do it. But Miss Sally's taken a shine to you, and she wants you all spruced up, so that's what I'm goin' to do."

Dipping the brush into the water, Cal began scrubbing down the bull. Prince Henry offered no resistance at all to the procedure.

"Well, I'll be damn," Cal said, smiling broadly. "You

have had this done to you before, haven't you? I swear, I believe you are likin' it."

"Hey, Cal, it ain't even Saturday night!" Jake called. "What are you doin' givin' him a bath?"

Some of the other cowboys laughed at Jake's tease.

"I got to get him cleaned up," Cal called back. "He ain't goin' to do us no good if the ladies don't take to him. And what heifer is goin' to turn down a bull that is clean and smells good?"

The cowboys laughed again.

Cal scrubbed on the animal for about half an hour. Then he led Prince Henry up to the back of the ranch house and called out.

"Smoke! Miss Sally, come out and take a look!"

A moment later, Smoke and Sally appeared on the back porch.

"Oh, my," Sally said. "I've never seen him looking so good. You did a wonderful job, Cal."

"Thank you, Miss Sally, I'm right proud of it myself." Cal patted Prince Henry on the head again. "Tell me, do you think the ladies will like him now?"

"Oh, I'm sure of it," Sally said. "If I were a lady cow, I would certainly be attracted to him."

"Whoa, hold it," Smoke said. "Now you are making me jealous."

Cal and Sally laughed.

"Shucks, Smoke, I don't think you need to be . . ." Cal stopped in mid-sentence and looked over toward a rider who was coming through the gate. What caught his attention was a flash of sunlight on the silver hatband. "Pearlie?" he said.

"What?" Sally asked, turning toward where Cal was looking.

"That's not Pearlie," Smoke said.

"No, sir, it is not," Cal said. "But whoever it is, he's a-wearin' Pearlie's hat."

Smoke and Sally came down off the back porch and stood alongside Cal as the rider approached. As soon as Lenny reached them, he dismounted, but before he could say a word, Cal stepped toward him.

"Where at did you get that hat?" he shouted angrily.

Lenny leaned back away from Cal.

"I got it from Pearlie," he said.

"What do you mean you got it from Pearlie?"

"Are you Calvin Woods?"

"Yeah, I'm Cal." Cal was a little taken aback at being called by his name. "How do you know who I am?"

Lenny took the hat off and handed it to Cal. "Well, sir, I got the hat from your friend Pearlie. He said I was supposed to give this here hat to you and tell you thanks for the loan."

"That's what he said? Thanks for the loan?"

"Yes, he said if I said that, you would know that he gave me the hat to give to you. And I'm also supposed to see a man by the name of Smoke Jensen."

"What about?"

"Well, sir, I reckon that's for me to tell Mr. Jensen," Lenny said.

"I'm Smoke Jensen," Smoke said. "And you are?"

"My name is Leonard York, Mr. Jensen, but most folks just call me Lenny. Mind if I water the horse? I came up here by train, and rented the horse in town. I didn't know it was going to be this long of a ride out here, and I wouldn't want the horse to go down on me before I can get him back to the livery stable."

"No, by all means water your horse," Smoke said.

"Excuse me for not making the offer. It's just that, well, Pearlie has been gone for a while and when we saw you with his hat and hatband, we were concerned."

"Yes, sir," Lenny said as he led the horse to a large, round, watering tank. "The thing is, Mr. Jensen, you got a right to be concerned."

"Why?" Sally asked. "Is Pearlie in trouble?"

"Yes, ma'am, he is. In fact, he is in a great deal of trouble," Lenny said as he stood there, watching the horse drink. "That is, if you figure getting hung trouble."

"Oh, my God!" Sally gasped. "Pearlie's been hung?"

"Oh, no, ma'am, not yet," Lenny said quickly. "I'm sorry, ma'am, I should have thought before I spoke. I certainly didn't intend to give you that idea. But the truth is, the marshal has Pearlie in jail for murder and they are bringing in a judge that's pretty much known as a hanging judge, so I reckon they'll be getting around to it right soon."

"Pearlie may have killed someone," Cal said. "But I don't believe for one minute that he would commit murder."

Lenny shook his head. "You're right, I don't think any reasonable person could say that what Pearlie did was murder. I know, because I saw what happened. Pearlie had no choice in the matter. If he had not killed Billy Ray, it is for certain that Billy Ray would have killed him. Billy Ray came after Pearlie with a double-barrel shotgun with the intention of shooting Pearlie in the back."

"You say you saw it?" Smoke said.

"Yes, sir, I saw it all very clearly," Lenny replied.

"Why didn't you tell the marshal what you saw?"

"Oh, I did tell him, Mr. Jensen. So did a couple of others who were in the saloon at the time. But the truth is that the marshal works for Pogue Quentin more than he works for the town. And Billy Ray, the man that Pearlie killed, was Pogue Quentin's son."

"Pogue Quentin?"

"Yes, sir. Do you know him?"

"Smoke, isn't Pogue Quentin the unpleasant man we met in Colorado Springs?" Sally asked.

"Unpleasant, yes, ma'am, that would be him. I reckon you do know him," Lenny said. "Because if you were going to describe Pogue Quentin, well, unpleasant would sure be the way to do it."

"You are talking about Pogue Quentin from Huere-ano County, aren't you?" Smoke asked.

"Yes, sir. Santa Clara, to be exact."

"I've never been to Santa Clara," Smoke said.

"It's some south of Colorado Springs. It took me twenty-four hours to come up on the train," Lenny said. "I got into Big Rock at four o'clock this afternoon."

"I appreciate you making the long trip to tell us," Smoke said.

"Yes, sir, well, I gave Pearlie my word that I would come tell you, and I'm not one for going back on my word once I give it."

"You and Pearlie is good friends, are you?" Cal asked. There was almost a plaintive quality to Cal's question, as if fearing he might have been displaced as Pearlie's closest friend.

"Not so as you can say," Lenny replied. "I never even met him until after they took him to jail."

"How long had Pearlie been in town when this happened?" Smoke asked.

"That's just it. He hadn't been there any time at all. He said he was coming back home, but he stopped in town long enough to get him a beer and some supper when all this took place."

"Smoke, what are we going to do?" Sally asked. "We can't just leave him there to hang."

"We aren't going to," Smoke said. "Throw a few things together, Sally, and do it fast. We'll take the train down tonight."

"I'm going, too," Cal said.

"I wouldn't have it any other way," Smoke said. "Lenny, I know you just got here, but are you up to coming back with us?"

"Yes, sir, only . . ." Lenny paused in mid-sentence.

"Only what?"

"Only I don't have enough money for a ticket back."

"Don't worry about that," Smoke said. "I'll buy your ticket back." He pulled out his billfold, then drew out a twenty-dollar bill. "And this will pay for your trip up here."

Lenny held up his hand. "Oh, no, sir, why, the trip up here didn't cost me no more than two dollars."

"You had to eat, didn't you?"

Lenny smiled. "My ma runs a restaurant. It's a good restaurant, too, and she made me a lunch to carry along."

"Well, take the twenty dollars anyway," Smoke said.

Lenny's smile broadened. "Are you serious?"

"Yes."

"All right!" Lenny said, taking the money. "And thank you, Mr. Jensen."

It took Sally but a couple of minutes to pack some clothes, and half an hour later she, Smoke, Cal, and Lenny were in front of Sheriff Monte Carson's office in

Big Rock. Smoke dismounted, and handed the reins of his horse to Cal.

"Cal, how about you go with Lenny to get his horse turned back in at the livery, then get our horses boarded until we come back. I'm going to have a few words with the sheriff."

Sally also dismounted, and handed the reins of her horse to Cal.

"Sally, you get our tickets, and send a telegram to Pearlie to let him know we are coming," Smoke suggested.

"No, sir, don't do that," Lenny said quickly.

"Why not?"

"If you send a telegram directly to Pearlie, like as not, he'll never see it. The marshal will get it and keep it from him. What you ought to do, if you want to send him a telegram, is send it to my ma."

"You are right," Smoke agreed, nodding. "Yeah, that's probably a pretty good idea. All right, send it to Lenny's mom." Smoke took a piece of paper from his pocket. "And send this telegram to Mr. Murchison in Colorado Springs. I'm asking him to represent Pearlie, and to meet us when our train comes through Colorado Springs."

"I'm sure he will," Sally said. "He was such a nice man, and seemed so eager to help."

"Yes, well, there is a difference between what he did for us last time and what I'm asking him to do for us now," Smoke said. "I'm not sure how anxious he will be, but if he can't do it, perhaps he can recommend someone who can."

"I'll take care of it," Sally said.

As Sally, Cal, and Lenny set about their business, Smoke stepped into the sheriff's office, where he saw Sheriff Carson standing with his back to the door, pouring two cups of coffee.

"I saw you outside," Carson said without turning around, "and I figured you'd be coming in here for something. So we may as well talk about it over coffee." He handed the cup to Smoke.

"Thanks," Smoke said, taking the cup.

"What is it? What's up?"

"Do you know anything about the town of Santa Clara?" Smoke asked.

"I know a little bit about it," Carson replied. He took a sip of his coffee before he continued. "Why do you ask?"

"I'm afraid that Pearlie got himself into a bit of trouble over there."

"Oh? I didn't even know Pearlie was back."

"He's not, but from what I gather, he was coming back when he got into a shooting scrape."

"Tell me about it."

"According to Lenny York, the young man who brought us the news, Pearlie was just passing through. He stopped in town for a meal and a drink, and a friendly card game. Only, the card game wasn't all that friendly, and Pearlie got into an argument with one of the other players. A few moments later, that same man tried to shoot Pearlie in the back with a shotgun. Pearlie had no choice but to kill him."

Sheriff Carson's eyebrows raised and he lowered the cup of coffee. "If that's what happened, sounds pretty much like self-defense to me."

"Yes, you would think so, wouldn't you? But it turns out that the man Pearlie killed was Billy Ray Quentin, Pogue Quentin's son. Now I met the Quentins, both of them, at the cattle auction in Colorado Springs recently. And I must say, I didn't care much for either one of them."

"From what I've heard of the Quentins, I don't blame you for not liking them."

"Now, here is the problem," Smoke said. "Lenny York, the young man who brought us the news, says that the marshal of the town is pretty much in Pogue Quentin's camp."

Carson nodded. "You're friend is right, the marshal does work for him. His name is Clem Dawson."

"Do you know Dawson?"

"I've met him once or twice. He's from Kansas. From what I've heard, he was a pretty good sheriff at one time, but got into some trouble with bounty money while he was there. The story was that he had a private army of bounty hunters working for him. Supposedly, Dawson would give them leads on wanted men, and the bounty hunters would bring back bodies. There was never a live prisoner, mind you, just bodies. Dawson and his bounty hunters would then split the reward money. Of course, that was just the story that was going around about him. They were never able to prove anything, but the decent citizens of the county had the good sense to turn him out in the next election. Sometime after that, he turned up in Santa Clara as their town marshal."

"Did the townspeople Santa Clara not know about his past?"

"I doubt that they knew about him, at least not at first. They may know more about him now, but it doesn't make any difference," Sheriff Carson said. "Quentin not only owns the marshal, he owns most of the town, literally."

"Why doesn't the county do something about it?" Smoke asked.

Carson shook his head. "Smoke, you know how big a man you are around here?"

"I'm just a—" Smoke began, but Carson interrupted him.

"Don't give me that. You are the biggest man in these parts, and you know it. The whole county looks up to you, and would do anything you asked them to do. Well, sir, as big a man as you are here, that's how big Quentin is in Huereano County. But the difference is, the folks here who look up to you would do anything you ask of them because they like you and they know you are a good man.

"It's different with Quentin. As far as I can tell, nobody likes the son of a bitch, because he is an evil man. I don't know that he has done anything that the law can actually get him for, but he has certainly come close. And the reason everyone in Santa Clara will do anything he asks is because they are just flat out scared of him."

"I see."

"Marshal Dawson has Pearlie in jail, does he?" Carson asked.

"I'm afraid he does."

"Then my advice to you, my friend, is for you to get down there as quickly as you can. But unless I miss my guess, you don't need any advice from me. If I were a bettin' man, I would say you are on your way right now."

"Yes," Smoke said. "Sally is getting the tickets."

From the office, Smoke heard the whistle of the train as it approached from the north.

"I'd better get on my way," Smoke said. "Thanks for the information about Dawson." He held up the coffee cup. "And thanks for the coffee."

"Good luck, my friend," Carson said as Smoke stepped through the front door.

Sally was just returning from her errand when Smoke came out of the sheriff's office.

"Did you get the telegram sent off?"

"I did. And I asked him to send his reply to Denver."

"Good."

Santa Clara

"Let me get this straight," Walter Guthrie said. "The marshal wants me to build a gallows right in the middle of Front Street? Last time I built one, it was in the alley behind the jail. Are you sure the marshal wants this thing built in the middle of the street?"

"It doesn't make any difference where the marshal wants the gallows built. I'm the one paying for it," Quentin said. "And I want it built in the middle of Front Street. I want everyone in town to be able to watch when we hang the man that killed my boy."

"How do you know we are goin' to hang him?" Guthrie asked. "Accordin' to what I've read in the paper, and what I've heard said about it from some of those that was there, this here trial might not be all that clear a case. Fact is, they's some a' sayin' it was self-defense."

"It was murder, pure and simple," Quentin said. "For everyone who might say it was self-defense, I can get two who will be willing to say it was murder."

"Who can *actually* say it—or will just be *willing* to say it?" Guthrie asked.

"What difference does that make? One is as good as another. Now, are you going to build the gallows? Or am I going to have to get someone else to do it?"

"No need for you to get anyone else," Guthrie said. "You pay me the money, I'll build anything you want, anywhere you want."

Quentin took one hundred dollars from his billfold. "Is this enough to get it built?"

Guthrie smiled broadly, then picked up the money, folded it over, and stuck it in his pocket.

"Mr. Quentin, for this much money, I'll build a gallows that anyone would be proud to swing from."

"Get started on it," he said.

Guthrie got a significant part of the gallows built in one day, and when Kathleen York walked by it just before supper that evening, she was unable to suppress an involuntary shiver. Someone had already printed a sign, and the sign was prominently posted on the base of the gallows being built.

In one more week
On the 17th, *instant*
The Murderer of
Pogue Quinlin
will be hung on These Gallows.
The Public is invited.

"Check that there trapdoor, Jude," Guthrie called. "We need to make sure it don't hang up none."

The carpenter named Jude pulled a handle, and the trapdoor fell open with a loud clatter.

Kathleen jumped.

"Ha! Scare you did it, Miz York?" Jude called to the woman, who was headed toward the jail, carrying a cloth-covered tray.

Without answering, Kathleen stepped up onto the porch, then pushed the door open to step into the jailhouse.

"Miz York, you got no business bein' here," Marshal Dawson said as Kathleen York let herself in through the front door of the marshal's office.

"Your prisoner has to eat, Marshal Dawson," Kathleen said, holding up the tray to emphasize her comment.

"Yes, ma'am, I reckon so, but you didn't have to bring it over yourself. I could'a sent my deputy over to get the food."

"Yes, well, there is a little problem with you sending your deputy for the food."

"Really? And what problem would that be?" Dawson asked.

"It seems that not all the food makes it back to the jail when Mr. Wilson comes for it," Kathleen explained.

Dawson laughed out loud. "Well, now, you have to admit that that is your own fault there, Miz York," he said. "Truth to tell, if you wasn't such a good cook, Wilson wouldn't be pilferin' the food as he brings it over. What are you feedin' him tonight?"

Kathleen neither answered, nor offered to show him what she was bringing, so Dawson removed the cloth cover himself. When he did, he saw two pieces of fried chicken, mashed potatoes, gravy, corn, and biscuits. There was also a piece of apple pie, upon which had been melted a slice of cheese.

"Well, now, Miz York," Dawson said. "That is some dinner."

"This is leftovers from my special over at the café tonight," Kathleen said.

"That may be," Dawson said. "But I know damn well the town ain't payin' you enough meal money for a prisoner to eat like that. What are you plannin' on doin'? Stickin' us with a higher bill later on?"

"No need. The city pays ten cents for the meal, I won't charge you a penny more," Kathleen said.

"Then I don't understand. Why the feast?"

"From what I understand, the poor man is going to be hung when the judge arrives," Kathleen said.

"Yes, ma'am, you understand that right," he said. "Soon as Judge McCabe gets here, we'll hold the trial, then we'll hang him, prob'ly that same day." Marshal Dawson chuckled. "I reckon you seen that they are buildin' gallows out front."

"Yes, I saw it as I walked by," Kathleen replied. "I don't know why you decided to build it right in the middle of Front Street. That is a little gruesome, if you ask me."

"It may be, but that's where Mr. Quentin wanted it built."

"And you do everything Quentin tells you to do?"

"Well, let's be fair here, Miz York," Marshal Dawson replied. "After all, it was Quentin's boy who was murdered. And he's the one paying for the scaffold, not the town. So I reckon he can have the prisoner hung just about anywhere he wants to."

"Aren't you getting ahead of yourself? The jury hasn't found the young man guilty."

Dawson laughed out loud. "The jury ain't found him guilty, you say?"

"That's what I said."

"Well, the thing is, Miz York, that's just what you might call a technicality. I know you didn't come to Billy Ray's buryin', but iffen you had come, why, you would of heard Pogue warn ever'one that might serve on the jury that they better find this murder guilty."

"That isn't right," Kathleen said. "You can't order someone to find a person guilty. There has to be a trial, the jury has to listen to the case and weigh all the evidence, before they can decide guilt or innocence."

Dawson laughed. "You know all about juries, do you?"

"I know what is right and what is wrong," Kathleen replied.

"Yeah, well, don't worry about it. This fella is as guilty as sin and ever'one in town knows that, so there ain't no way the jury won't find him guilty, no matter whether Quentin ordered them to or not."

"I know two people who say that Billy Ray fired first."

"Oh, yeah? Who?"

"My son for one," Kathleen said. "And Mary Lou Culpepper for another."

Dawson laughed. "Mary Lou Culpepper? The whore? And you believe her?"

"I do. Especially when my son tells the same story."

"Yes, ma'am, well, that don't mean much, seein' as ever'one in town knows your son is stuck on that whore. But I reckon, when you get right down to it, we're goin' to have to go with the evidence, the other eyewitness accounts, and the prisoner's own confession."

"Confession?"

"Yes, ma'am. When I asked if he was the one that kilt him, why, he said, flat out, that he was. And there wasn't nobody in the saloon what didn't hear him say that."

"But that isn't an admission of guilt. Didn't he also say that Billy Ray shot first? That it was in self-defense?"

"He may have," Marshal Dawson admitted. "But the thing is, Miz York, that kind of thing ain't mine to decide. That's for the court to decide. All I got to go on is the man who said he kilt him, which is my prisoner, and Billy Ray's body, which is dead."

"Marshal Dawson reached for the biscuit, but Kathleen pulled it back.

"This food is for the prisoner," she said.

"Well, then, you better get it to him before it gets all cold," Dawson said.

Kathleen took the tray back to the cell.

"Lenny asked me to make certain you get enough to eat." As Lenny had before, she handed each dish through the bars to him before turning the tray on its side and sliding it through.

"Whoowee, I tell you the truth," Pearlie said as he first looked at, then smelled, the food. He took a bite of chicken, then smiled. "Yes, ma'am," he said. "It's almost worth bein' put in jail here if I'm goin' to get to eat like this."

Kathleen laughed nervously. "Don't be foolish, young man," she said. "I appreciate the compliment, but nothing is worth being in jail for."

"You must be Lenny's sister," Pearlie said.

Kathleen smiled, then blushed slightly. "I'm his mother," she said.

"You don't say," Pearlie said. "Well, all I can say is, you must'a had him when you was about twelve or somethin'. You sure don't look old enough to be his mother."

"That's very kind of you."

"Have you heard from Lenny?" Pearlie asked as he forked some mashed potatoes and gravy to his mouth.

"Indirectly," Kathleen said. She looked back over her shoulder to make certain Marshal Dawson wasn't watching her, and when she saw it was clear, she pulled a telegram from under the bodice of her dress.

Leaning a little closer to the cell, she spoke very quietly. "Your friend, Mr. Jensen, sent this telegram this afternoon."

"Why did he send it to you?" Pearlie responded, speaking as quietly as Kathleen.

"I expect he sent it to me so you would be sure and get it," Kathleen replied. "If he had sent it directly to the marshal, you might never even see it."

"Yeah," Pearlie agreed. "I don't know much about this marshal, but I think you might be right."

Kathleen pushed the telegram through the bars and, making sure he wasn't being watched, Pearlie took it.

LENNY YORK HAS TOLD US OF YOUR
TROUBLES PEARLIE STOP WE ARE ON
OUR WAY TO TAKE CARE OF IT STOP
KEEP UP YOUR SPIRITS STOP SMOKE

Chapter Sixteen

Tumbling Q

"Thank you, Pete," Quentin said as he took a paper from the telegrapher. "This telegram is from Smoke Jensen, you say?"

"Yes, sir, Mr. Quentin," the telegrapher said.

"Well, now, what do you know about that?" he said. "Smoke Jensen, huh?"

"Do you know Mr. Jensen?" Pete Hanson, the telegrapher, asked.

"Oh, yes, I know him," Quentin replied. "I met him in Colorado Springs during the cattle auction."

"I understand he is quite well known throughout the state," Pete said.

"So I have been led to believe," Quentin said. "I must say, he did not make a very good impression on me. What I am wonderig is, why would he be sending a telegram to the man who murdered my son?"

"Evidently, they are friends," Pete said. "As you will see when you read the telegram."

Quentin read the telegram, then looked up. "I wonder what he means by 'take care of it'?" Quentin asked.

"I beg your pardon?"

"His telegram says he is on his way to 'take care of it,' and I was just wondering what he meant by that."

"Oh, I couldn't hazard a guess as to what he might mean by that, Mr. Quentin," Pete said. "I just thought you might want to see the telegram, that's all."

"Yes, Pete, you were quite right in bringing it to me, and I thank you. If you get any more telegrams you think I might find interesting, please bring them to me as well."

Pete cleared his throat. "Of course I will, Mr. Quentin. I'm always glad to help out an outstanding citizen like yourself even though"—the telegrapher cleared his throat again—"even though I am taking a great personal risk in doing so. I am sure that you realize it is a violation of the law to show private telegrams to anyone other than the person to whom the telegram is addressed. And the punishment for violating that law is quite severe."

"Yes, yes, I understand," Quentin said as he withdrew a ten-dollar bill from his billfold and handed it to Pete. "The fact that you are sharing certain telegrams with me will never go beyond this point."

"Very good, sir," Pete said. He turned to leave but, before he left, he looked back toward Pogue Quentin. "You know, Mr. Quentin, I didn't mention it, but the telegram was not sent directly to the prisoner, nor even to the marshal."

"It wasn't? Who was it sent to?"

"It was sent to Kathleen York."

"Well, now, that is interesting," Quentin said. "Why would it be sent there?"

"I expect it's because young Lenny York spoke up for

this fella, Pearlie, right after the shooting. And later, he seemed to get real friendly with him while he was in jail."

"Yes, well, after I take care of the man who murdered my son, I'll take care of Lenny York."

"I'm sorry about your son, sir."

"Thank you," Quentin said.

Quentin followed Pete out onto the front porch of his large house, then watched as the thin, bespectacled telegrapher climbed into his surrey, picked up the reins, and drove away.

The truth was, Quentin had not been all that shocked over the fact that his son had been killed. Billy Ray was an unmitigated horse's ass, and Quentin knew it. The real surprise was that nobody had shot him before now.

But that didn't matter. Now it was a matter of power. If he did not make the killer of his son pay, it would be a sign of weakness.

He smiled. The fact that the one who killed his son was a friend of Smoke Jensen just made his play sweeter. He would be able to kill two birds with one stone. He laughed at that thought, and wished there was someone he could share the joke with.

Before Quentin went back into the house, he looked over toward the stable and saw his foreman talking to a couple of his hands.

"Cole," he called.

"Yes, sir, Mr. Quentin."

"Come over here."

Cole Mathers, a big bearded man with a wandering eye, walked over toward Quentin.

"I want you to run an errand for me."

"All right."

"I want you to go over to a place called La Vita. There, you will find a man named Cates. Tell him I want to hire him."

"Cates? Wait a minute. Are you talking about Snake Cates?" Cole asked.

"Some people might call him Snake Cates, but I wouldn't if I were you. Leastwise, not to his face. His real name is Bogardus."

"Bogardus?" Cole asked. He laughed. "Damn, if I wouldn't prefer to be called Snake."

"You will call him 'mister' if you know what's good for you."

"Oh, don't get me wrong, Mr. Quentin," Cole said, holding up his hand. "I may be dumb, but I ain't that dumb. No, sir, when I get around a fella like Snake Cates, I'll be callin' him mister for sure. He's got what, seventeen, eighteen men that he's kilt?"

"Something like that," Quentin agreed.

"And ever'one of 'em has been in a face-to-face shootout. I mean, he ain't got no easy kills in all them gunfights. No easy kills at all."

"Just find him, and bring him here."

"Uh, Mr. Quentin, he's goin' to ask for money."

"Give him one hundred dollars."

Cole cleared his throat.

"What is it?"

"Well, sir, for somebody like me, a hunnert dollars is a lot of money. I reckon I'd do pert' nigh anything for a hunnert dollars. But for somebody like Snake Cates, a hunnert dollars wouldn't be nothin'."

"The one hundred dollars is just to get him to come speak with me," Quentin said. "Tell him that I guarantee that we will come to an agreement that he will find satisfactory."

"All right," Cole said. Cole started toward the corral.

"Oh, and Cole?"

"Yes, sir?"

"If you can't find him, or if for some reason you can't persuade him to come back with you, don't bother to come back."

"I'll find him, Mr. Quentin. And I'll bring him back," Cole promised.

"What are you doing here?" Deputy Wilson asked when Mary Lou Culpepper came into the marshal's office.

"I've brought food for Mr. Pearlie," Mary Lou said.

"What the hell is it with this man?" Wilson asked. "Have the Yorks taken him to raise? First Lenny came by to feed him, then his mama, and now his whore."

Mary Lou didn't respond.

"You are Lenny's whore, aren't you?"

"I am his friend," Mary Lou said.

"His whore friend, you mean. All right, all right, go ahead. Take the food to him. Only, next time you come here, you better bring a little extra for me. Otherwise, I'll eat whatever you brung him. Go on, take his food to him. Only, don't you be givin' him anything more than food back there, if you know what I mean," Wilson added with a ribald laugh.

"Thank you," Mary Lou said, walking quickly to the cells at the back of the office, as much to get away from Wilson as for any other reason.

Because it was late in the day and the filtered light coming through the window was weak, the shadows reached into the three cells. For a moment, Mary Lou saw no one.

"Mr. Pearlie?" she called out.

"It's just Pearlie," a male voice replied. He moved out of the shadows so she could see him.

"I've brought you your supper," she said, pulling the cover off the tray.

Seeing the food brought a smile to Pearlie's face. "If I stay here long enough, I'm liable to get fat," he said. "That is, if I don't hang first."

"Oh, you mustn't say that," Mary Lou said quickly. "It's bad luck."

"You're Lenny's friend, aren't you?" Pearlie said. "I saw you in the saloon on the day it happened."

"Yes."

"Lenny is a very lucky man," Pearlie said as he bit into a ham and biscuit sandwich.

"Oh, we aren't that kind of friends," Mary Lou said. "Besides, someone as fine as Lenny, I mean, he plays the piano and all, could never really be that kind of friends with someone like me. Maybe you don't know it, but I'm a—uh—a whore."

"Like I said," Pearlie said. "Lenny is a very lucky man to have a friend like you."

Chapter Seventeen

La Vita, Colorado

The two young men stopped in front of the Ace High Saloon, dismounted, and looped the reins around the hitching rail. Both were wearing long trail dusters, and they brushed their hands against them, raising a cloud of dust.

"Whoa, hold it there, Jerry," one of the two said, coughing. "You're near'bout smotherin' me with all the trail dust you're a-raisin' there."

Jerry laughed. "Yeah, like you just stepped out of a washtub, I s'pose? Come on, Ken, let's get somethin' to wet down our gullets. Then we'll get us a bath, a bottle, and find us someplace to have a real good dinner."

"And a couple of women," Ken replied. "Let's don't forget to get us a couple of women."

"You wantin' to spend all that money we stole in one night, are you?" Jerry asked.

Ken chuckled. "Why not? As easy as that money was to get, we can always get some more. Did you see how that old fart shook when we told him we was robbin' him?"

"Come on, let's get us a couple of beers."

The two men stepped into the saloon, then stopped for a moment to have a look around. The saloon was busy, but not crowded. There were several empty tables, and several empty spots along the bar. One of the men standing at the bar was Cole Mathers, and he paid little attention to the two men as they came in.

"Want to stand at the bar or sit at a table?" Ken asked.

"Let's sit at a table," Jerry suggested, and the two men found one near the stove. Because it was summer, the stove was cold, and had been for several weeks now. But even though there was no fire in the stove at the present, the remnants of past fires were still present in the unmistakable aroma of old smoke and burnt wood.

"Oh, that ain't good," the bartender said when the two young men sat down.

"What ain't good?" Cole asked.

"That's Mr. Cates' table them two boys took. And Mr. Cates, he don't like nobody else sittin' at it."

Cole turned to look toward the two young men.

Shortly after they sat down, both Ken and Jerry noticed that the hum of normal conversation had ended and it grew quiet in the saloon. And the sudden quiet did not seem to be a mere coincidence, as it soon became evident that everyone in the house was looking directly at their table.

"Hey, you," Ken called toward Cole. "What is it you are a-lookin' at?"

"How do you know he's even a-lookin' at us?" Jerry asked with a mocking laugh. "Hell, one of his eyes looks one way and the other looks another. I'll bet he don't even know his ownself what he's lookin' at."

Cole turned away from the two.

"Oh, now," Ken said. "You done gone an' hurt his feelin's."

Jerry laughed, then looked around the saloon and saw that nearly everyone in the room was looking at them.

"What the hell are all you people a-lookin' at?" Jerry asked.

"Maybe they heard of us," Ken replied. "This here wasn't the first job we've pulled. Could be we're gettin' to be famous."

Jerry laughed. "Yeah, that's prob'ly it." He held up his hand as a signal to the bartender.

"Barkeep," he called to the bartender. "How about a couple of beers over here?"

"And I'll have the same," Ken added, laughing at the joke.

The bartender ignored the request.

"Hey, what the hell? Don't you want our business?" Trey asked.

"Not until you two galoots change tables, I don't," the bartender replied.

"Change tables? What do you mean, change tables? This here is the table we want."

"It ain't goin' to be the table you want when he comes in," the bartender said.

"When who comes in?"

"When *he* comes in," the bartender replied without specifics.

"Don't be a fool, mister," Jerry said. "If you know'd who it was you was talkin' to, you wouldn't be talkin' like that. Me and my friend here have kilt men for less than that. Now, if you don't want to make us mad, and believe me, barkeep, that ain't somethin' you want to do, you'll bring us them beers like we asked."

Before the bartender could respond, another patron pushed his way through the batwing doors of the saloon. He wasn't a very big man—in fact, he was quite small, no taller than five feet two inches, and weighing no more than 130 pounds. He was dressed in black, except for a tooled-leather pistol belt that bristled with filled cartridge loops. His eyes were small and dark, so dark that there was no delineation between the iris and pupils. He also wore a neatly trimmed mustache. He took a couple of steps toward the table, then stopped when he saw that it was occupied. He looked toward the bartender.

"It ain't my fault. I told 'em I wasn't goin' to serve 'em as long as they was sittin' at your table," the bartender said.

The small man's tongue darted out a couple of times before he spoke. "I would invite you gentlemen to find another table," the small man said. His voice was a quiet hiss.

"What's that you say? Damn, mister, are you so little you ain't got voice enough to speak up?" Ken held his hand to his ear. "You sound like a mouse pissing on a ball of cotton. How the hell is anyone s'posed to hear you?"

Ken laughed at his joke.

Jerry looked over at Ken. "Do you know what I think this little pissant just said? I think he invited us to find another table."

"Is that a fact? Well, we was here first, mister," Ken said. "So we *invite* you to find another table. Unless you want us to mop up the floor with your skinny little ass."

The small man smiled. "So, are you telling me you are willing to fight for that table?"

Jerry and Ken looked at each other, then broke out laughing. "You want to throw this litter feller out, or shall I?" Jerry asked.

"Oh, I don't believe in physical violence," the little man said. "That never settles anything."

"Ha! He don't believe in physical violence," Ken said. He looked back at the little man. "This ball has started. So either we finish this now, or you can just go get yourself another table and mind your own business."

"Oh, we are going to finish it," the little man said.

"We are, are we?" Ken chuckled and shook his head. "I tell you what, mister, since you are hell-bent on doing this, you can choose whichever one of us you want to fight."

"I intend to fight both of you."

"Both of us?"

"At the same time. Only, let's make it permanent."

"What do you mean by, 'let's make it permanent'?"

"What I mean is, leave that table right now, or stay where you are and draw your guns."

"Draw our guns? Mister, there are two of us and only one of you. And I don't mind tellin' you that we ain't exactly strangers when it comes to usin' guns. Either one of us can kill you where you stand, but you say you want to fight both of us at the same time. Now, are you sure you want to go through with this?"

"I'm sure."

Both Ken and Jerry stood; then they stepped away from each other. "Before we do this, I want ever'one in this here saloon to understand what is goin' on," Ken said. "Me an' my partner wasn't doin' nothin' but sittin' real peaceful at this table, when this little pissant come in here challengin' us to a gunfight. Do you all understand that? When the sheriff comes in after we kill this fella, I want to make sure ever'one knows we didn't start it."

"All right, mister, we'll all be willin' to testify that Mr.

Cates challenged you to a fight when you refused to move from his table," the bartender said.

"Mr. Cates?" Ken said, a look of confusion crossing his face. "What do you mean, Cates?" He turned back toward the little man, dressed in black. "Is your name Cates?"

"It is."

"Snake Cates?"

Cates's tongue darted out a couple of times before he responded. "I don't like that name," he said. "I prefer to be called Mr. Cates."

"Ken, what have you got us into?" Jerry asked.

"Look, Mr. Cates," Ken said, holding his left hand out in front of him, as if by that action he could hold Cates away. "We didn't mean nothin' by all this. If you want this table, you can have it. We was just—that is—well, we didn't have no idea that it was your table."

"It's too late for negotiations now," Cates said. "Like you said, you brought me to the ball, now I expect a dance."

"But I didn't know—"

"Ain't no use it tryin' to talk us out of it now, Ken," Jerry said. "This little feller is bound to go through with this. We don't have no choice in the matter. We are either goin' to have to kill him, or he is goin' to kill us."

For the next several seconds, there was a macabre tableau, a picture that would be frozen in time throughout the rest of the lives of all who were there to witness it. The witnesses fixed the scene in their mind, to be able to recall for future stories the picture of Snake Cates, poised and relaxed, standing in the middle of the saloon floor, facing two men, known then only as Jerry and Ken, who were standing about twenty feet away. The patrons of the saloon had moved to get out of harm's way, and they stood to one side, holding their beers, watching the scene unfold before them, building the memories that would be passed on to grandchildren and great-grandchildren of having once seen the great Snake Cates in action.

One would think that time itself had been suspended, except for the steady tick-tock of the large Regulator clock that sat against the wall just beside the piano, sending each measured tick into eternity.

A few even took particular notice of the time, the better for storytelling later on. It was exactly thirty seven minutes past six o'clock in the evening.

"Now!" Ken shouted, reaching quickly for his pistol. Jerry reacted at the same time.

Amazingly, Cates made no initial move toward his pistol. For just an instant, Ken and Jerry might have had the impression that they were going to beat him to the draw. What they didn't realize was that Cates was analyzing their draw to see which one of the two he should shoot first. Because Ken had his pistol all the way out of his holster before Jerry had cleared leather, Cates chose Ken as his first target.

Cates drew and fired twice, the two shots coming so close upon each other that to some of the witnesses the sounds ran together, making it appear as if he had shot only once. That mistaken impression was dispelled, however, when both Ken and Jerry went down, each one with a bullet in his heart.

Cates stood there for a moment longer, holding the smoking pistol in his hand, while a cloud of acrid gun smoke began drifting up, to gather just under the ceiling of the saloon. Not until he was absolutely certain that both men were dead did he return his pistol to his holster. Then, without any further regard for the two men he had just killed, he stepped over their bodies and walked over to his table.

For a long moment after the shooting, everyone in the saloon was quiet. A cloud of gun smoke drifted toward the ceiling and the smell of it burned the nostrils and irritated the eyes.

The bartender drew a mug of beer.

"Julio," he called.

"*Sí, Señor?*" Julio called. Julio had been sweeping the floor until the confrontation took place. Then he, like everyone else, had stopped all activity to watch.

"Take this beer over to Mr. Cates, then go get the sheriff and the undertaker."

"*Sí*, Señor Greer," Julio replied. Julio carried the beer over to Cates's table. Cates took the beer without any acknowledgment or thanks. It was, Cole noticed, as if Cates believed that being served a beer right after killing a couple of people was his just reward.

"Hey, Greer, how many does that make now?" one of the other patrons asked.

"Four," Greer said. Greer held up four fingers to illustrate his answer.

"Four? No, that can't be right. I know he's kilt a lot more than four," the patron replied. "Hell, they say he kilt at least ten down in New Mexico."

"I mean he has killed four men in this saloon," Greer said. Inexplicably, a broad smile spread across his face. "I'm going to have a sign made and hang it up outside." Greer waved his hand, as if exposing the sign. "It will read, 'The famous gunfighter Bogardus Cates kilt four men in this place.' Can you imagine how much business that will get for me?"

"You know what would get you a lot more business?" the patron asked.

"What?"

"Iffen you could put up a sign that says, 'The famous gunfighter Snake Cates was kilt here.'"

The patrons who were close enough to hear gasped, and several of them, including Cole, looked over toward Cates to see how he would react to it. Apparently, Cates was paying no attention whatever, because he was occupying himself with a game of solitaire.

"You want to put that sign up do you, Arnie?" Greer asked.

"Uh, no," Arnie replied quickly. He tossed the rest of his drink down, then wiped his mouth with the back of his hand, all the while looking toward the small but deadly gunman. "I have to go," he said, leaving quickly.

"Ole Arnie better watch that mouth of his, else one day he's goin' to say somethin' he shouldn't," Greer said to no one in particular.

"He shouldn't of said that," one of the saloon patrons said. "He's just lucky that Cates didn't hear him."

"I heard him," Cates said. He played another card without even bothering to look up from the game. "He just ain't worth my time."

Because the mortuary was just next door, the undertaker and his assistant were the first to arrive.

"Hello, Gene," Greer said.

"Who's going to pay for them?" the undertaker asked.

"I will, if you'll get me pictures of the bodies so I can put 'em up on the wall," Greer answered.

Gene nodded; then he grabbed the legs of one of the two bodies, and his assistant grabbed the legs of the other.

They began dragging the two bodies out just as the sheriff was arriving.

"Hold on, Gene," the sheriff said to the undertaker. He looked down at the two bodies. "Only one bullet hole in each of them?"

"Yes," the undertaker replied.

The sheriff looked over at Cates, who was still playing solitaire. "With shooting like that, I don't suppose I have to ask who did it, do I?"

No one responded.

"Anyone know these two boys?"

"I never saw either one of them before today," Greer said. "Do you know them?"

"No, I don't," the sheriff replied.

"Can we take them now, Sheriff?" Gene asked.

The sheriff nodded. "Yeah, go ahead." He looked out over the saloon. "Anybody see what happened?"

Nobody responded.

"Come on, there are what—ten of you here? Ten of you in a room no bigger than this, but not one of you saw anything?"

"I saw it," Cole said, speaking up.

Cole glanced over toward Cates, and saw that the gunman had interrupted his game of solitaire and was now staring at him with his small, dark, obsidian eyes.

"Well, finally I get someone who isn't blind," the sheriff said. "All right, mister, tell me. What did you see?"

"It looked to me like the two men Mr. Cates killed had something they wanted to prove," Cole said.

"Something to prove? What do you mean by that?"

"I don't know. Maybe they wanted to prove that they weren't scared of Mr. Cates or something. I mean, I can't think of any other reason why they would have wanted to goad him into a gunfight."

"Wait a minute," the sheriff said. "Are you telling me that these two men goaded Cates?"

"That's what I'm saying."

"How did they do that?"

"Well, first, they sat at his table, and when they were asked, real friendly like by the bartender here, to change tables, they didn't do it."

"That's right, Sheriff, I asked them, real nice, if they would please change tables," Greer said.

"Go on," the sheriff said to Cole.

"And then, when Mr. Cates asked them if they would mind changin' tables, and he asked them just as friendly as the bartender did, well, they challenged him to a fight."

"The two men challenged Cates?"

"That's right. I reckon they thought that, bein' as there was two of 'em, they could beat him," Cole said.

"Anyone in here see it any different than that?" the sheriff asked.

"No, Sheriff, if you ask me, I'd say that's just the way it happened," Greer said.

"Looked that way to me, too," one of the other patrons said.

The sheriff shook his head. "If that's so, how come none of you spoke up when I asked you?"

"I was just fixin' to speak up when this feller did," the saloon patron said.

"Yeah, me, too," Greer added. "I was fixin' to tell you the same thing that this here fella said."

The sheriff looked at Cates. "Mr. Cates, I don't know

how much longer you're planning on staying in La Vita, but I'll be one happy fella when you leave."

Cates took a drink of his beer and stared at the sheriff, but he said nothing.

The sheriff left then, and the moment he left, the others in the saloon started talking, nearly every one of them at once, replaying the exciting event they had witnessed.

"Boom, boom," one of the patrons said, making a pistol with his hand as he demonstrated. "They were that fast that I thought he'd only shot one time."

"And he hit both of them, right square in the heart," one of the others said.

"I wonder what them two boys was doin', challengin' Cates like they done?"

Cole did not join in any of the conversations, but waited for a few minutes before he walked over to Cates's table. He stood there for a moment, expecting Cates to look up, but Cates didn't look up.

"If you're thinkin' I owe you somethin' for what you said to the sheriff, you are wrong," Cates said. "I don't owe you nothin'." Cates continued to study the cards.

"Red eight on the black nine," Cole suggested.

Cates made the move. "I don't owe you nothin' for that either," he said.

Cole put a one-hundred-dollar bill on the table in front of him.

Cates picked the bill up, examined it for a moment, then, for the first time since Cole approached the table, looked up at him.

"What is this for?" he asked.

"To get your attention," Cole replied.

Cates took a swallow of his beer, then wiped the foam from his moustache.

"All right," he replied. "You got my attention. What do you want?"

"The man I work for would like to hire you," Cole replied.

"For one hundred dollars? I don't do much for one hundred dollars."

"No, sir. Like I said, the one hundred dollars is just to get your attention. Mr. Quentin guarantees that the two of you will come to an agreement that you will find satisfactory."

"How satisfactory?"

Cole shook his head. "I don't know," he said. "I'm only telllin' you what Mr. Quentin told me to tell you."

"Is Quentin rich? Because I don't come cheap."

"Mr.Quentin is very rich."

With his leg under the table, Cates pushed one of the chairs out. "Have a seat," he said. "Tell me about this man Quentin."

Chapter Eighteen

Smoke, Sally, Cal, and Lenny had a one-hour layover in Denver where they were to change trains. As they waited in the depot, Smoke walked over to a window under a sign that read WESTERN UNION. Not seeing anyone when he looked through the vertical bars, he slapped the palm of his hand on the little desk bell. The ring reverberated through the room.

At the back of the room the door opened, and someone stuck his head in. He was wearing a billed cap with the words WESTERN UNION written on the front, and looking toward the window, he saw Smoke.

"Yes, sir," he called to Smoke. "Do you wish to send a telegram?"

"No. I hope I have one here waiting for me," Smoke replied. "Would you check your 'will call' box?"

"I'll do that. And you would be?"

"Jensen. Smoke Jensen."

The telegrapher smiled. "Ah, yes, indeed, Mr. Jensen, you do have a telegram waiting for you," he said. "I recall getting it last night."

Walking back over to the table on which the telegraph instrument sat, the Western Union clerk rifled through a pile of papers and envelopes before coming up with one. He checked the name on the outside, then brought the envelope back up to the front window and passed it through the opening it to Smoke.

"What do I owe you?" Smoke asked.

"Not a thing, sir. It has already been paid for," the telegrapher replied.

"For your trouble," Smoke said, handing the telegrapher a quarter.

"Why, thank you, sir," the telegrapher replied.

This was a response to the telegram Sally had sent before they left Big Rock. In the telegram, he had not only asked Murchison to represent Pearlie, he had also asked Murchison to respond by telegram to the Denver and Rio Grande Railroad depot in Denver, with instructions to the telegraph office to hold the telegram in the "will call" box.

Smoke took the envelope back over to where Sally and the others were waiting.

"What does he say?" Sally asked.

"I don't know, I haven't read it yet."

"Smoke, what if he won't do it? What will we do?"

"If Murchison can't, or won't, we'll just have to find a lawyer who will do it," Smoke replied.

Smoke opened the envelope, removed the telegram, read it, smiled, then handed it to Sally.

FOR WHATEVER VALUE YOU PLACE UPON
MY ABILITY TO HELP I HEREBY PLACE MY
HUMBLE SKILLS IN YOUR SERVICE STOP
I WILL MEET YOU AT THE DEPOT IN
COLORADO SPRINGS STOP

* * *

It was eight o'clock in the morning when the train approached the outer environs of Colorado Springs. Sally was looking through the window as they passed through a residential area, and she smiled when she saw a young boy and girl who had come down from their house to stand beside the track and wave at the passengers on the arriving train.

Sally waved back.

The train passed through the residential section, then a section of warehouses and businesses, then the rail yard itself, before finally coming to a stop at the depot.

"Do you see him?" she asked.

"Yes, there he is," Smoke said, pointing to the lawyer, who was standing on the platform. His suitcase was sitting on the ground beside him.

"It looks like he is ready to go," Sally said. "He has his suitcase."

The conductor passed through the car, calling out. "Colorado Springs, folks. This is Colorado Springs. For those of you going on through, we'll be here for half an hour. Colorado Springs."

"I'll go out and get him," Smoke said.

"If the train is going to be here for half an hour, why don't we all go out?" Sally suggested. "We can stretch our legs, and get a breath of fresh air. After a night of trying to sleep on those hard seats, it will feel good."

"Cal, Lenny, you two want to stretch your legs a bit?" Smoke asked.

The two young men agreed, so all four got up and started toward the end of the car. Smoke glanced through the windows as they walked toward the exit, and he could see Murchison, anxiously watching each of the detraining passengers. Murchison saw Smoke and Sally as soon as they stepped down from the train, and he smiled at them as he waited for them to approach him.

"Hello, Tom," Smoke said, extending his hand in greeting to the lawyer who had worked with him during the recent auction. "I want to thank you for answering my telegram," Smoke said.

"I am glad to do it," Murchison replied. "And as I said in my telegram—did you get my telegram by the way?"

"Yes, I picked it up in Denver."

"Good. As I said in my telegram, I am willing to do anything you want. But listen, Smoke, are you sure you want me for this? I'm not sure I'm the best one for the job. After all, this is a criminal case."

"Pearlie ain't no criminal," Cal said quickly.

"This is Pearlie's friend, Cal," Smoke said. He smiled. "Of course, he is our friend, too."

"Cal, the fact that someone's case is a criminal case doesn't necessarily mean the person being tried is a criminal," Murchison explained. "It is just a means of differentiating civil from criminal court proceedings. But I'm sure you know that under our system of jurisprudence, the accused is presumed to be innocent."

"Innocent, yeah, that's what Pearlie is all right," Cal said.

"Why do you seem so hesitant, Tom?" Smoke asked.

"Because I am not what you would call a criminal lawyer."

"Have you ever tried a criminal case?"

"Yes, of course I have, but it has been a long time since I did so," Murchison replied. "I just wanted you to be aware of that so that, if you want to, you would have time to find another lawyer."

"Are you willing to take the case?" Smoke asked.

"Am I willing? Well, yes, I'm more than willing. To be honest, I must say that I find the idea of trying such a case again intriguing. But the fact that I consider you a friend, and this case involves a friend of yours, does make it a bit intimidating."

"Let me put it another way," Smoke said. "If Pearlie is innocent, and I take Lenny's word that he is, do you feel confident that you can do a good job for him?"

"Lenny's word?"

"This is Lenny," Smoke said, indicating the young man, who had initially hung back. "Lenny was there when it happened, and he saw everything. He is going to be your star witness," Smoke said.

Murchison nodded. "Well, it helps to have a witness," he said. "But to answer your question, yes, I am confident I can do a good job for him."

"You are going to get him off?" Cal asked.

"I certainly intend to make every effort to get him off," Murchison replied He turned his attention toward Lenny. "Tell me, Lenny, how did you happen to see this? Were you with Pearlie when this happened?"

"No, sir, I wasn't exactly what you would call with him," Lenny replied. "To be honest, I didn't even know who he was then. I just happened to be in the saloon when it happened, and I saw it all."

"You don't know Pearlie?"

"No, sir. Well, I know him now, because I talked to him after they put him in jail. But I didn't know him before all this happened."

"Is that a problem, Mr. Murchison?" Cal asked. "I mean, is it a problem that Lenny didn't know Pearlie?"

"No," Murchison replied. "Quite the contrary, it is good. The fact that they didn't know each other before will give more weight to Lenny's statement. If they had known each other, the prosecutor could taint Lenny's testimony by suggesting that it was being given to help his friend."

They talked a bit longer; then the conductor stepped down from the train.

"Board!" he shouted loudly, and after a wave toward the front of the train, the engineer blew his whistle twice.

Murchison reached for his suitcase, but Lenny hurried over to pick it up. "I'll carry this for you, sir."

"Why, thank you, Lenny."

Smoke and the others reboarded train, then returned to their original seats. Smoke and Sally sat facing forward, while Murchison and Lenny sat in the rear-facing seat across from them. Cal found an empty seat just on the opposite side of the aisle from Smoke and Sally.

As they started rolling out of the station, the conductor came through the car punching tickets. Murchison waited until the train was well under way before he turned to Lenny.

"Now, Lenny, as best as you can remember, I want you to tell me exactly what you saw," Murchison said.

"I saw Billy Ray Quentin come busting in to the saloon with a shotgun. He shot at Pearlie, and even though Pearlie managed to jump to one side just before Billy Ray fired, he got hit by some of the shotgun pellets anyway."

"Pearlie got hit? You didn't tell us that," Sally said, clearly disturbed by the news.

"Oh, there ain't really nothin' to worry about on that score, ma'am," Lenny said. "He wasn't hurt hardly none at all. Doc Urban, he's a friend of mine, well, actually he's a friend of my ma's, he took the shot out and fixed Pearlie up real good."

"So, Pearlie saw Billy Ray coming after him with the shotgun, and managed to jump out of the way in time to avoid getting killed. Is that what you are saying?" Murchison asked.

"Yes, sir. But Billy Ray, he raised up his shotgun and was about shoot again. That's when Pearlie shot him."

"As you can see, Tom, it sounds like a clear case of self-defense," Smoke said.

Murchison chuckled. "If there is one thing I've learned in all the years I have been a lawyer, Smoke, it is that there is no such thing as a clear case of anything."

"Well, you know what I mean," Smoke said.

"Yeah, I know what you mean. I don't mean to be too hard on you," Murchison said. "I'm just trying to fill you in on some facts. Where did this take place?"

"In the New York."

"What? In New York?"

"The New York is a saloon in Santa Clara," Lenny said. "I play the piano there."

"Why, Lenny, do you play the piano?" Sally asked.

"Yes, ma'am."

"How wonderful! I love music. I shall look forward to hearing you play."

"Yes, ma'am, I'd like to play for you sometime."

"You say the New York is a saloon," Murchison said, continuing his questioning. "Did the shooting take place inside the saloon?"

"Yes."

"How many others were in the saloon at the time?"

"I'm not sure exactly," Lenny replied. "I'd say about twenty."

"Twenty people saw the shooting?"

"Yes, sir."

Murchison turned toward Smoke, with a big smile spreading across his face. "Maybe I was wrong," he said. "With twenty eyewitnesses, this very well could be a clear-cut case."

"There won't none of the others testify," Lenny said.

"I won't be able to get anyone else to testify? Why not?"

"Like I said, the name of the man that got killed was Billy Ray Quentin. He is—that is, he was—Pogue Quentin's son, and I don't reckon there are many people in town who would be willing to go up against Pogue Quentin."

"I have met Pogue Quentin," Murchison said. "And I find it hard to believe that someone like Pogue Quentin would actually have that many friends down in Santa Clara."

Lenny choked back a chuckle. "Oh, don't get me wrong, Mr. Murchison. It's not because they are his friends that they won't testify," he said. "It's because they are afraid of him."

Murchison nodded. "Yes, I must say, that sounds more like the Pogue Quentin I met. He struck me then as someone who would attempt to get his way by intimidation."

"Intimidation—does that mean scarin' people?" Lenny asked.

"Yes."

"Well, he doesn't scare me. I will testify."

"Are you the only one?"

"Oh, I'm pretty sure you can get Mary Lou Culpepper to testify, but I don't know whether the jury will pay much attention to her."

"Why is that?"

"Because, like me, she works in the saloon."

"Exactly what kind of work does she do in the saloon? Is she a—"

"She's a whore, if that's what you are asking," Lenny said, answering the question before Murchison had completed asking it. "But she's a good, honest woman."

Murchison shook his head. "It doesn't really make that much difference how good and honest a woman she is," he said. "I'm afraid you are right. The very fact that she is a whore will, more than likely, cause the jury to give little weight to her testimony. We are going to have to find someone else."

Lenny shook his head. "There isn't anyone else."

Murchison stroked his chin, then, with a sigh, leaned back in his seat. "I should have stuck with my first premise. I've been around long enough to know that, no matter what you might think, there really is no such thing as a clear-cut case."

Santa Clara

Deputy Wilson looked up from his desk as the four men and one woman came through the front door of the jail.

"Here, what's goin' on here?" he asked. "You can't come bargin' in like this! What do you think you are doin'?"

"Pearlie!" Cal shouted, seeing his friend in the cell at the back of the jail.

"Cal, Smoke, Sally, I knew you would come!" Pearlie said.

"You can thank Lenny here, he's the one that told us," Cal said.

"I do thank you, Lenny. I haven't known you long, but you are a true friend."

"I told you, you can't be in here," Wilson said. "They's only certain times you can visit a prisoner, and this here ain't one of those times."

"You are wrong, Deputy," Murchison said. "As this young man's lawyer, I can visit him anytime I want in order to establish his defense."

"All right, maybe you can, but who are all these people? They can't be here," Wilson insisted.

"You are wrong about that as well," Murchison said. "They are all helping me construct a case for the defense."

Wilson was clearly agitated, and obviously unsure as to what everyone's rights were. Finally, he acquiesced, then returned to his desk and sat down. "All right," he said. "Go ahead and have your visit. But I'll be keeping an eye on you."

As soon as they reached the cell in the back, Sally stuck her hand through the bars and ran her fingers over the entry wound scars that were left on Pearlie's cheek by the shot. "Oh, Pearlie," she said. "Lenny told us you had been shot. Do the wounds hurt?" she asked.

"To tell the truth, I didn't even feel 'em when they first hit me. But after a while, they commenced to stingin' a bit. Now, though, they don't hurt none at all."

"How did you wind up here in Santa Clara, of all places?" Smoke asked.

"Well, sir, I was comin' back home, is what I was doin'," Pearlie said. "I was comin' back to my old job. That is, if you would have been willin' to take me back."

"Of course we would take you back," Sally said. "We would have taken you back five minutes after you left."

"Yes, ma'am, well, five minutes after I left, I almost turned around and come back," Pearlie said. He was silent for a moment before speaking again. "It would have been better if I had done that. 'Cause if I had, I wouldn't be in all this trouble now."

"Don't worry about it, Pearlie," Smoke said. "We'll get you out of here, I promise."

"Really? I wish I could be that sure about it. Perhaps you didn't see the scaffold they are building," Pearlie said.

"I saw it. It's practically in the center of town. You can't miss it."

"I don't figure they would waste their time buildin' somethin' like that if they didn't have no intention of usin' it."

"They can have all the intention of using it they want," Smoke said. "I'm telling you right now, that scaffold is not going to be used. At least, not for your necktie party."

Pearlie smiled. "I figured if I could just get you here in time, ever'thing would all work out," he said.

"This is Tom Murchison," Smoke said. "He's going to be your lawyer."

"Well, now, my own lawyer," Pearlie said. "How about that? That makes me feel like a big shot."

"When is the trial?" Murchison asked.

"Tomorrow."

"Tomorrow? Impossible," Murchison said. "I can't possibly prepare a defense by tomorrow."

"You damn well better," Deputy Wilson said, overhearing the conversation. "Judge McCabe will be comin' in tonight, and he don't like waitin' around." Wilson laughed. "Yes, sir, we'll have your friend tried, convicted, and hung by sundown tomorrow."

"You had better hope he isn't found guilty," Smoke said.

"What do you mean I had better hope he isn't found guilty? Hell, I want the son of a bitch to be found guilty. I like hangin's, and I can't think of anything I'd rather see than your friend here dancin' from the end of a rope."

"If it happens, you won't see it," Smoke said.

"The hell I won't. I'll be a' standin' right there in the front row," Wilson said.

"You won't be standing anywhere," Smoke said.

"Why do you say that?"

"Because if Pearlie is found guilty, I'll kill you."

"What?" Wilson gasped. "Did you just threaten me?"

"That was not a threat," Smoke said. "That was a promise."

"Deputy, by law, we are entitled to a private visit with my client," Murchison said. "Would you please excuse us?"

"What?"

"Go away," Smoke said. He pointed to the desk. "Go over there and sit down and let us conduct our business."

"Look here, I'm the law," Wilson said. "You can't talk to me like that."

"Smoke, let's don't wait," Cal said. "Let me kill him now."

"I—uh—you are going to hear about this!" Wilson said, sputtering. But faced with a concerted glare from both Smoke and Cal, he returned meekly to his desk.

Not until he was out of earshot did they resume their visit with Pearlie.

"Pearlie, have you been eating all right?" Sally asked.

"Yes, ma'am!" Pearlie said. "You can't believe how good I've been eating!"

"Really? The jail feeds you that well?" Sally asked, surprised by Pearlie's response.

"Oh, no, ma'am, the jail don't have nothin' to do with it," Pearlie said.

Sally winced at the grammar, but said nothing.

"No, ma'am. The reason I'm eatin' good is because of Lenny's ma, Mrs. York. Mrs. York, and Lenny's friend, Mary Lou. Both of them have been bringin' me food for near'bout ever' meal. Good food, too. Smoke, have you met Mrs. York yet?"

"Not yet," Smoke answered.

"We're goin' over there from here, and I'm going to introduce them then," Lenny said. "We thought you might be worryin' about whether or not we would get here in time, so we came here first."

"You damn near didn't get here in time," Pearlie said. "One more day and I would'a been a goner."

"Don't lose faith, Pearlie," Sally said. "We will get you out of here."

Pearlie flashed a big smile. "Oh, I ain't worried about it now," he said. "I got no doubt but what this will all be behind me soon. Though I confess that bein' able to see that scaffold, just by lookin' out the window, was a bit, well, let's just say it was puttin' me off a mite."

When Smoke, Sally, Cal, Murchison, and Lenny left the jail, they went directly to Kathleen's Kitchen and Boarding House, where the young man's mother greeted her son with a welcoming hug.

"Ma, I want you to meet these folks," Lenny said. "They are all Pearlie's friends. This here is Mr. and Mrs. Jensen. And this is Mr. Murchison. He's the lawyer who is going to get Pearlie out of jail."

"How nice to meet you," Kathleen said. "I can see how Pearlie would have a lot of friends. In the short time I've known him, I've found him to be one of the nicest and most gracious young men I've ever met."

"Thank you, we think so as well," Sally said.

"I told you you would like him, Ma," Lenny said.

"So you did," Kathleen agreed. She smiled at Cal. "And you must be Cal," she said.

"Yes, ma'am, I am," Cal replied, confused at hearing her call his name. "How come you to know that? Lenny didn't say my name."

"He didn't have to. Pearlie has spoken well of you. He considers you his special friend," Kathleen said. She pointed to the low-crowned black hat Cal was wearing. "And he told me all about your silver hatband."

Cal took his hat off and fingered the silver band. "Yes, ma'am, well, I loaned it to him is what I done, 'cause I know'd he would bring it back to me and that way, he wouldn't stay gone forever. Course, I didn't count on him windin' up in jail or nothin'."

"Ma, none of us have eaten yet, and we are very hungry," Lenny said.

"Oh, forgive me for not asking you earlier. Please, please, sit down and I'll have your lunch out here right away."

"I want to thank you, Mrs. York, for taking such good care of Pearlie," Sally said.

"Please, call me Kathleen."

"Only if you call me Sally. Pearlie told us about the food you have been taking to him. From the way he described it, I am very much looking forward to the meal."

"I hope you aren't disappointed."

"I'm sure we won't be."

"Did you make chicken and dumplin's today?" Lenny asked.

"Yes, we did."

"I figured you would, this being Wednesday. You always make chicken and dumplin's on—" Lenny paused in mid-sentence, then said, "We?"

"What?"

"You said, yes, *we* did," Lenny said. "What do you mean, we?"

"I've hired some help."

"Really? Well, I'm real glad you did that. You work too hard. You don't need to work as hard as you do."

Kathleen smiled as she went into the kitchen. A moment later, she came out carrying a tray filled with plates. Behind her, also carrying a tray, was Mary Lou Culpepper.

"Mary Lou!" Lenny said, standing up quickly. "You're workin' here now?"

Smiling, Mary Lou nodded. "Your ma hired me," she said.

"How—uh—how is it going?"

Kathleen put her arm around Mary Lou's shoulders. "It's going really well," she said. "Mary Lou and I are getting along just famously, aren't we, dear?"

"Yes, ma'am," Mary Lou said.

"Kathleen, I see that this is a boardinghouse as well as a restaurant," Sally said. "Is it for longtime borders only? Should we go to the hotel?"

"You don't want to go to the hotel," Kathleen said. "That is, unless you want to do business with Pogue Quentin. He owns the hotel. You can stay right here. I have two very nice rooms, one for you and Mr. Jensen, and one for Cal and Mr. Murchison. That is, if the two of you don't mind sharing a room," she added, looking toward Cal and Murchison. "And we have a very nice drawing room where you can relax," she added.

"I don't mind sharing a room if Cal doesn't," Murchison said.

After supper, Kathleen showed them to their rooms. As they passed through the drawing room, Sally saw an upright piano, similar to many of the instruments she had seen in private homes, schools, churches, and even saloons throughout the West. The only difference was this piano was obviously loved and very well cared for, because it was in much better condition than almost any other piano she had seen since she left New Hampshire. She walked over to it, then ran her hand across the smooth, polished surface.

"Oh, what a beautiful piano," she said.

"You should hear Lenny play it," Kathleen said, proudly. "It has a beautiful tone."

"Lenny, I would love to hear you play something. Would you play for us?" Sally asked.

"Oh, Mrs. Jensen, you don't want to hear a saloon piano player," Lenny said.

"No, and I don't want to hear a saloon piano player either," Kathleen said.

Sally looked at Kathleen in surprise, but before she could say anything, Kathleen continued.

"What I want to hear, and what I am sure these fine people would like to hear, is a pianist, not a saloon piano player. Play something, Lenny. Play something beautiful," Kathleen said.

"You mean concert music?" Lenny asked.

"I mean something beautiful," Kathleen said.

"All right," Lenny said. He sat down, opened the lid over the keyboard, and for a few seconds, did nothing. Then the melodic phrasing of Beethoven's Piano Sonata no. 14 poured forth from the piano, filling the parlor with its repeating theme and beautiful melody. This was not "Buffalo Gals," or "Cowboy Joe," or one of the other songs so often heard in saloons. This was something one might hear on the stage in New York, Boston, London, or Paris.

Lenny played through to the finale. Then he let his arms drop to his side as the last melodic notes hung in the air. Looking up, he saw tears in Mary Lou's eyes.

"Mary Lou, what is it?" Lenny asked. "What's wrong?"

"Nothing is wrong," Mary Lou answered. "I've only heard you play in the saloon—I had no idea you could play like this. I've never heard such music. I never knew anything could be so beautiful."

Chapter Nineteen

Sally stayed back to visit with Kathleen and Mary Lou, while Smoke, Cal, Lenny, and Tom Murchison walked down to the New York Saloon.

"Hey, Lenny, it's good to see you back," Rodney Gibson said when Lenny and the others stepped inside.

"Hi, Mr. Gibson. I suppose Mr. Evans told you where I went. I hope you didn't mind."

"He said you went to tell Pearlie's friends about his trouble."

"Yes, sir, I did. These are Pearlie's friends, Smoke Jensen and Calvin Woods. And this is his lawyer, Tom Murchison."

"Pleased to meet you," Gibson said, shaking hands with the three men.

Also present in the bar were Lloyd Evans, Elmer Brandon, Doc Patterson, and Deckert. Lenny introduced them as well.

"I suppose you know that Mary Lou isn't working here anymore," Gibson said.

"Yes, sir, she's working for my ma now."

"I ought to be angry with your mother for taking her

away from me, but I'm not. Mary Lou is a good girl who fell on some hard times. I hope things work out for her."

"I do, too," Lenny said.

"So Pearlie has a lawyer, does he?" Doc Patterson asked. He chuckled. "I don't reckon that's going to make Pogue Quentin all that happy."

"Oh? Does Pogue Quentin not believe in the right of the accused to have counsel?" Murchison asked.

"Oh, I reckon he is all right with it in principle," Doc Patterson said. "He's just not that happy with it in fact, when the lawyer is defending the man who killed his son. Especially if the lawyer is from out of town, and not controlled by Quentin."

"Are all the lawyers in town controlled by Quentin?"

"The lawyers and the law."

"Why does the town put up with it?" Cal asked.

"I reckon because he owns everything in town," Deckert said.

"He doesn't own my saloon," Gibson said.

"And he damn sure doesn't own my newspaper," Brandon said.

Doc Patterson chuckled. "He doesn't like that either. Sometimes your articles get him pretty upset."

"Freedom of the press, gentlemen," Brandon said, holding up his finger to make a point. "It is the most precious of all our rights and as long as I own this newspaper, and that will be as long as there is breath in my body, I will be a voice crying out in the wilderness against the evil oppressor."

Doc laughed, and applauded quietly. "Spoken like a noble patriot," he said.

"There he is!" a loud voice called then, and looking toward the swinging bat wing doors, they saw Marshal

Dawson and Deputy Wilson. Wilson was pointing at Smoke. "That's the one who said he was going to kill me."

"What's your name, mister?" Dawson asked, his face scowling in anger and intimidation.

"Jensen. Smoke Jensen."

The hard set of Dawson's face drained away, his pupils narrowed, and he took a quick, short breath.

"*The* Smoke Jensen?"

"That's an interesting question," Smoke replied. "I'm the only Smoke Jensen I know, so I suppose you could say that I am 'the' Smoke Jensen, but I don't know for sure."

"What difference does it make who he is?" Wilson asked angrily. "I told you, he said he would kill me if we hung Pearlie."

Dawson said nothing.

"Well, there he is, just standing there," Wilson said. "You ain't goin' to let him get away with that, are you? I'm an officer of the law. He can't talk to me like that."

Dawson still said nothing.

"Ask him," Wilson said. "Ask him if he said he was goin' to kill me if Pearlie got hung."

When Dawson remained quiet, Wilson spoke again.

"Ask him," he demanded again.

"Do you really want to ask that question?" Smoke asked, not answering directly.

"No," Dawson said, speaking for the first time. "I don't intend to ask the question. Let's go, Wilson."

"What?" Wilson asked, growing even angrier now. "We're just goin' to leave and do nothing?"

"Yeah," Dawson replied. "We are just going to leave and do nothing."

"I'll be damned," Gibson said. "I never thought I would see anything like what just happened. As a matter of fact,

I'm not sure what just happened. Mr. Jensen, step up to the bar. You and your friends can have a drink on the house."

"Hell, Rodney, does that include us?" Brandon asked. "We just made friends with Mr. Jensen."

Gibson laughed. "Yes," he said. "That includes everyone."

As the men stood along the bar waiting for the drinks to be served, Lenny spoke up.

"Doc Patterson, Mr. Brandon, and Mr. Deckert were playing cards with Pearlie and Billy Ray when everything started," Lenny said.

"Good, good, maybe I can convince you to be a witness for the defense," Murchison said.

Brandon shook his head. "It won't do you any good," he said. "Doc and I left before the shooting. We didn't see a thing."

"What about you, Mr. Deckert?" Murchison asked.

"I wasn't actually playing cards then," Deckert replied.

"No, but you were sitting at the table, watching us play," Brandon said.

"You saw it, didn't you?" Murchison said. "You saw everything."

"I ain't goin' to testify," Deckert said.

"Why not?"

"You don't understand," Deckert said. "You don't live here. None of you do. You think this is just a trial like any trial in any other town, but it ain't. This trial has already been held, and Pearlie has already been found guilty. Don't you understand that? He has already been found guilty. The jury, the judge, even the court, they don't mean a thing. The only thing that means anything in this town is Pogue Quentin."

"Mr. Deckert, I know you have seen the gallows in the middle of the street down there," Smoke said.

"How can I not see it?" Deckert replied. "The whole town has seen it."

"Are you willing to watch an innocent man hang, just because you are afraid to testify?"

"I'm not afraid to testify."

"Oh?"

Deckert stroked his chin. "All right, maybe I am afraid. But if I thought it would do any good, I would testify anyway. It just won't do any good, that's all."

"I'll be a witness for you, Mr. Murchison," Lloyd Evans said.

"You saw it?"

"I didn't see what started it all," the bartender said. "But I did see the end of it. I saw Billy Ray come in here, blazing away with his shotgun."

Murchison smiled, and lifted his beer to the bartender. "That's a start," he said.

"Wait a minute, maybe my testimony would do you some good after all," Brandon suggested. "I mean, Evans saw how it all ended, Doc and I saw how it started. I guess we could testify about that."

"Hold it, Elmer, don't count me in on that," Doc said.

"Doc, you saw how it all began, same as I did. You could be a witness."

"If I don't know any more than you do about it, what good would my testimony be?"

"You afraid to testify, Doc?" Cal asked.

Doc shook his head. "It's not that I'm afraid," he said. "But I'm a veterinarian. I see maybe ten or twelve dogs and a couple of cats that are pets in this town. And I see thirty thousand head of cattle that belong to Quentin. I can't make a livin' just by tendin' to people's pets."

"I see your point," Brandon said. Brandon looked back

at the lawyer. "He's right, Mr. Murchison. Even if he does testify, he won't be able to add to anything I might say. And testifying could cost him his livelihood."

"All right," Murchison said. "I guess we can get along without your testimony."

"Thanks," Doc said, the relief on his face obvious.

"Damn, I wish the trial was a couple of days from now," Brandon said.

"Why is that?"

"I could write an article about it," Brandon said. "I could write an article and remind people of their civic duty."

Half an hour later, Brandon stood in his newspaper office, looking at the Washington Hand Press that loomed in the shadows. Walking over to it, he ran his hand across the top arc of the press, the metal feeling cool to his touch. He looked over at his type trays, then smiled.

"Why the hell not?" he asked, saying the words aloud, even though he was alone in the room. "What do you think, Emma?" he asked, looking up as if speaking to his late wife. "I'll put out an extra. I've never done it before, but I can't think of a time when there's ever been more of a reason for one than now. Yes, sir, an extra edition."

Holding a lit match to the wick of a nearby kerosene lantern, Brandon turned up the light, then started setting the type.

Half an hour later, he took the first sheet off the press, then held it up for a closer examination.

"Here it is, Emma," he said. "Yes, sir, this will shake them up."

Tumbling Q

The sun was not even up the next morning when Marshal Dawson showed up on Quentin's front porch. He banged on the door until, finally, he saw the moving gleam of a candle as someone inside came down the stairs to answer the door. It was Quentin, wearing a sleeping gown and carrying a candle.

"Dawson," Quentin said grumpily. "What are you doing here? What time is it?" Quentin looked around toward the big grandfather clock that stood in the foyer, just at the foot of the stairs. "It's not even five o'clock yet."

"I thought you might want to see this," Dawson suggested, holding out a copy of the newspaper.

"A newspaper? Why the hell would I want to read a newspaper at this time of morning?"

"Just read it," Dawson said. "You'll see why."

Quentin gave Dawson the candle to hold, then using the small bubble of golden light cast by the candle, he read the paper. Not until he was finished did he talk again.

"Where did this come from?" he asked.

"It was pushed under the door at the jail," Marshal Dawson said. "It must've been around midnight last night. I never saw it until this mornin'. What I don't understand is how it got there. This isn't the day the paper comes out."

"This isn't a regular issue," Quentin said. He pointed to the banner across the top. "It says here that this is an 'extra.' That means a special paper printed at a time that isn't normal. I wonder how many copies he printed."

"Looks to me like he might have printed enough so that ever' man, woman, and child could have his own copy," Dawson said. "As I was ridin' out here this mornin', I seen 'em lyin' all over the place, on porches, in wagons. They was a pile of 'em down at the train station and another bunch at the stage depot."

"And you didn't think to go gather them up, did you?"

"Uh, no, I didn't think about doin' nothin' like that. I reckon I could do that when I go back."

"It's too late. By the time you get back, the people in town will be waking up'," Dawson said. "Within an hour, I expect just about everyone in town will have read it."

"I expect so," Dawson agreed.

"Why did you let him do it?"

"Well, in the first place, Mr. Quentin, I didn't know he was goin' to print the thing. And in the second place, how was I goin' to stop it anyway? I mean, it ain't against the law to print a newspaper."

"In Santa Clara, the law is what I say it is."

"Well, yes, but—"

"There are no buts," Quentin said. "I own the law and I own you, bought and paid for. And I intend to get my money's worth."

"All right, what do you want me to do about the paper?" Dawson asked.

"Nothing. It's too late, the paper is out already. What I intend you to do is make certain the man that killed my son gets what's comin' to him."

"You don't have to worry none about that. That's goin' to happen," the marshal said.

"Did you get Gilmore appointed prosecuting attorney?"

"Yes, sir, we done that all right," Dawson said. "Judge McCabe got in on the evenin' train last night, and me 'n Gilmore met him."

"Well, it's good to see that you aren't totally incompetent. What time does the trial start?"

"The judge said he'll start the trial at one o'clock this afternoon." Dawson chuckled. "I figure he'll have the trial over by three, and we'll have that fella hung by four."

"I want you to go back into town now and make certain nothin' happens to get in the way."

"What could possibly get in the way?"

"That's what you said the other day. I didn't have anything to worry about, you told me," Quentin said. He held up the broadsheet. "Then Brandon published his extra."

"Well, what is that goin' to do? It's just a paper."

"Have you ever heard the expression the pen is mightier than the sword?" Quentin asked.

"No. I don't know what that means."

"I wouldn't expect you to know," Quentin said.

"Look, I know you're mad, Mr. Quentin, but I didn't know Brandon was goin' to put out a paper like this. I mean, I never heard of an extra. I didn't think you could put out a paper except on the day they're supposed to come out."

"That's just it, Dawson. You didn't think."

"You want me to put Brandon in jail or something?"

"No," Quentin said. "I don't want you to do anything about him. I'll take care of the situation."

"All right," Dawson said.

Quentin stood on his front porch until Dawson mounted his horse, then started the five-mile ride back to town. After that, Quentin walked across the yard to the bunkhouse. Cole Mathers, his foreman, had a small, private room at the end of the bunkhouse. Quentin, still carrying the candle, opened the door.

"Cole," he said.

Cole snorted and sniffed, then rolled over in his bunk.

"Cole," Quentin said again.

Cole opened his eyes and seeing Quentin standing over him, holding a candle, sat up in his bunk. "Yes, sir?"

"You were in town last night, weren't you?"

"Yes, sir."

"What time did you get back to the ranch?"

"About eleven or so."

"Did you know about this?" Quentin asked. He held out the newspaper and Cole looked at it. He read a few lines, then shook his head.

"First time I've seen it," he said.

"It was published last night. I thought maybe you saw it." Cole shook his head.

"Where is Cates?"

"He's staying over at Gillespie's house."

"You mean my house," Quentin said.

"Yes, sir, well, it's your house now. What I meant was, he's over at the house that used to be Mr. Gillespie's house before he left."

"Go get him, tell him I want to see him."

"All right," Cole said. He got out of bed and started getting dressed. "Mr. Quentin, you sure you want Cates workin' for you?"

"Yes, I'm sure. Why do you ask?"

"Because I don't mind tellin' you, that creepy little son of a bitch makes me nervous."

Quentin laughed. "Good. That's why I hired him. I want him to make people nervous."

"Even his friends?"

This time, Quentin's laugh was louder than before. "People like Cates don't have friends, Cole, you ought to know that," he said. "They just have a few people whose name they might happen to know."

Chapter Twenty

Elmer Brandon's morning routine never varied. As always, he was Kathleen York's first customer of the day. His breakfast this morning was the same as it was every morning, one hardboiled egg, one strip of bacon, one biscuit with butter and jam, and coffee.

"Mr. Brandon, I read the editorial in your extra edition," Mary Lou said as she waited on his table. "I thought it was very good."

"Why, thank you, Mary Lou, it is nice of you to say so."

Two other early diners spoke up as well, and their comments were as complimentary as Mary Lou's.

Kathleen came over to Brandon's table and poured a second cup of coffee for him.

"What are you having for lunch?" Brandon asked.

"I've got a good vegetable soup on," she said. "But lunch is going to be an hour earlier today. I intend to close the restaurant so I can watch the trial."

"Oh, good idea," Brandon said. "And since I'm going to be one of Mr. Murchison's witnesses, I need to eat an early lunch anyway."

Just as Brandon finished his second cup of coffee, he saw Smoke, Sally, Cal, and Murchison coming in for breakfast. He stopped by their table on his way out.

"Mr. Brandon," Smoke said. "I read your article. It was a great piece. No doubt it will be the talk of the town today."

Brandon chuckled. "Oh, I've no doubt it will be the talk of the town," he said. "But there are a lot of people who aren't going to be all that pleased with it."

"Anyone with a sense of justice and fair play will like it," Murchison said. "The truth is, Mr. Brandon, I believe your article may just guarantee us an impartial jury and a fair trial."

"I hope so," Brandon replied. "And I know that I'm looking forward to being a witness for you. Do we need to talk about it before I testify?"

Murchison shook his head. "That won't be necessary," he said. "As I understand it, your testimony is going to tell how the trouble began, but you have no knowledge of the actual shooting. Is that right?"

"That's right."

"That will be a big help. Court convenes at one o'clock this afternoon. Just make certain you are there in time."

"I'll be there bright-eyed and bushy-tailed," Brandon teased.

Saying good-bye to the others in the restaurant, Brandon stepped outside. He was feeling particularly good about himself today. He had gotten into the newspaper business to do good, but somewhere along the line it had become much easier just to go along without making any waves.

"Emma," he said. "I hope you are looking down on me now. And I hope I have made you proud."

Emma, his wife of nineteen years, had died two years earlier.

"Hello there, Elmer," Donovan called, as Brandon walked by Donovan's Leather Goods Shop. "That was a great article you wrote. It's about time someone said something like that."

"I was just doing my duty," Brandon replied.

Poindexter, who managed Quentin's General Store, was less than complimentary. He was out sweeping the front porch when Brandon walked by, and he made an effort to sweep the dirt onto the editor.

"Here! What are you doing?" Brandon asked, stepping lively to get out of the way.

"You had no right to say the things you said about Mr. Quentin," Poindexter said. "He's done a lot of good for this town."

"You mean he's done a lot of good for you," Brandon replied. "Most of us remember when Mr. Collins owned this store. This used to be a very nice store. But that was before Quentin ran him out of business, then hired you to run it for him. I don't know how you could have done that, Poindexter. You used to work for Collins. So much for loyalty."

"A man has to make a living," Poindexter said.

"Yes, but not everyone has to betray their friends," Brandon replied, walking away without engaging the Quentin man in any further conversation.

As was his daily custom, Brandon stopped in the vet's office for a moment or two before going back to the print shop, where he not only published the newspaper, but did custom printing.

Doc Patterson was looking at a small dog.

"What's wrong with the puppy?" Brandon asked.

"Nothing really," Doc said. "Mrs. Peabody thought maybe it had the mange, but he just had a flea bite and the dog scraped away some its fur getting to it."

"Did you read my extra?" Brandon asked.

"Yeah, I read it. Is that the only reason you stopped by this morning, to get my comment on your article?"

Brandon chuckled. "Yeah, it is," he said. "Every other morning, I just stop by to make a pest of myself. But this morning I stopped by because I wanted to see what you thought of my editorial."

Doc smiled, then nodded. "Well, you do make a pest of yourself most of the time," he said. "But to answer your question, I thought your editorial was brilliant. But—"

He let the word "but" hang.

"But what?" Brandon asked.

"Aren't you taking a big risk? We both know what kind of a person Quentin is."

"Sir, I will have you know that I am a member of the most noble, honest, and trustworthy profession in America. I am a newspaperman, and I will not let someone like Pogue Quentin frighten me away from doing my duty."

"You are to be praised, sir," Doc said. Walking over to the coffeepot, he poured a cup, then held it out toward Brandon.

Brandon declined. "No, thanks, I had a second cup down at Kathleen's this morning."

"No doubt milking as many accolades as you could from the other diners who read your article," Doc suggested.

"Alas, Doctor, you know me too well," Brandon replied with a little chuckle.

"It was a good article, Elmer, perhaps the best I have ever seen you write. But I am afraid it is all for nothing," Doc said as he took the first swallow of his coffee.

"All for nothing? Why do you say that?"

"Because you are not going to get enough men with the courage and honor who will serve fairly on the jury."

"What about you, Doc?"

"What about me?"

"You are one of the most likely to be selected for jury duty. Will you serve honorably?"

"I very much hope that I am not selected for jury duty," Doc said.

"That's not an answer, Doc. The question is, if you are selected, will you serve honorably?"

"Like I said," he repeated. "I very much hope that I am not selected for jury duty."

"Doc, I am disappointed in you. I can understand your reluctance to be a witness, but not your reluctance to be a juror. If not for the fact that I am going to be a witness, I would very much want to serve on the jury."

"For crying out loud, Elmer, why would anyone actually want to serve on a jury?" Doc asked.

"Civic duty perhaps?" Brandon replied. "And just to see that for once, in this town, justice is done."

"I guess that's reason enough."

"Also, I very much would like to irritate the hell out of Pogue Quentin," Brandon added.

Doc laughed out loud. "Now that," he said, "I can believe."

Brandon started toward the door. "I would love to stay long enough for you to continue to heap praise on me for my brilliant article, but, alas, I must get to work. I have some posters to print for Milo's Emporium," he said. "I need to get them out of the way so I can go to the trial this afternoon to give testimony. Are you going to be there?"

"We've already been through all this, Elmer," Doc said. "I'm not going to be a witness."

"I'm not talking about you being a witness. I'm just talking about you being there to give me some moral support."

Doc chuckled, quietly. "Moral support?" he said. He nodded. "Yes, moral support I can do. I'll be there."

"I'll see you then."

With a final wave to his friend, Brandon walked on down to the street another block and a half until he reached the newspaper office. Unlocking the doors, he stepped inside, shut the door, and walked over to open the curtains.

"Leave them closed," a voice said. The voice was low and had a snakelike hissing quality to it.

Brandon felt the hairs stand up on the back of his neck, a hollowness in the pit of his stomach, and a weakness in his knees. Turning, he searched the shadows of his office for the origin of the voice. But because the curtains blocked the morning sunlight, the office was so dimly lit that he saw no one.

"Who is there?" he asked. "Who are you? What do you want?"

He saw something move deep within the shadows. Whoever it was, he was very short, so short that Brandon thought it might be a young boy. The quick fear he had felt was now replaced by a sense of irritation.

"What are you doing in my office, boy?" he asked angrily. "Does your mama know you are here? Get out—get on home with you."

The figure stepped out of the shadows. He was small, but he was no boy. He was dressed all in black and was wearing a pistol belt that bristled with filled bullet loops.

He wore a mustache, and even though his eyes were as dark as coal, they somehow seemed to catch the ambient light so that they were shining in the darkness. Brandon had seen this person only once before in his life, but he recognized him immediately.

"Cates!" Brandon gasped. "You are the one they call Snake Cates." The fear returned. This time it was much more than a hollow stomach, weak knees, and raised hair on the back of his neck. This time it was a numbing paralysis that made it difficult for Brandon to stand, and even harder to breathe. He could feel his heart pounding

The small figure took a deep, hissing breath. Then his tongue darted out just before he spoke, adding to his snakelike demeanor.

"Mr. Quentin is very upset with you," the small man said. "He has sent me to let you know just how upset he is. He wants you to put out another edition. "

"Another edition?"

"He wants you to tell the people of Santa Clara that you have been thinking about what you wrote earlier, and now you have changed your mind. He wants you to apologize in print."

"I—I couldn't do anything like that," he said. "Why, I would be discredited for the rest of my life. I may as well not be a newspaperman anymore."

"That's the other thing," Cates said. "After you apologize, he wants you to leave town. Forever."

"No, I can't do that. My Emma is buried in this cemetery. I intend to lie alongside her."

"If you don't agree to Mr. Quentin's terms, you will be lying alongside her sooner than you thought."

At that moment, Brandon knew that, no matter what he did, he was about to die. And from somewhere, deep inside him, he found a courage he didn't know he possessed.

"You tell Quentin I said to go to hell."

Doc Patterson was making an entry in his ledger about the puppy he had just examined when he heard the gunshot. Gunshots were not all that unusual in Santa Clara. Sometimes someone would get a little drunk, then shoot his gun out in the street. But it was too early in the day for that kind of gunshot.

Suddenly, Doc had an overwhelming sense of foreboding, and he stepped out onto the porch in front of his office. He saw Donovan standing just outside his leather goods store.

"Donovan, what was that?" Doc asked.

"Sounded like a gunshot."

"Yes, but from where? And who was it?"

"Help!" a young boy shouted, running up the street in full stride.

"Johnny, what is it?" Doc called to the boy.

The boy stopped running. "It's Mr. Brandon, Dr. Patterson."

"What about Mr. Brandon?"

"He has been shot!"

"Show me!"

Johnny started running back toward the newspaper office, and despite his age and relative girth, Doc ran alongside, his boots making loud clumps on the boardwalk as kept pace with the boy.

"Where is he?" Doc asked the boy when they reached the newspaper office.

"He's inside," the boy replied. "I was comin' to collect

my pay for the newspapers I delivered last night and I heard the gunshot. When I ran inside, I seen Mr. Brandon lyin' on the floor over by the press. I was too scared to go over any closer."

Doc went inside and looked around, but because the drapes were pulled shut, it was too dark to see. By now a few others had come in as well.

"Open the curtains!" Doc ordered.

When the curtains were drawn, the morning sun spilled in through the windows, lighting up the room. That was when Doc saw Brandon lying facedown on the floor.

"Elmer!" Doc shouted. Kneeling beside him, he put his hand on Brandon's neck to check for a pulse.

There was none.

"Johnny, when you came down here, did you see anyone else?" Doc asked.

"No sir, I didn't see no one else," Johnny replied. "Is— is Mr. Brandon dead?"

Doc nodded. "I'm afraid so."

"I don't reckon I've ever been this close to a dead man before," Johnny said. "Well, I've seen 'em laid out in funerals and all, but I ain't never seen one what has just been kilt." Johnny came closer to look down in young but macabre curiosity.

Looking toward the back of the shop, Doc saw that the back door was standing wide open. Moving quickly toward it, he looked outside, glancing up and down the alley. He saw no one.

"What is it? What's going on here?" a voice asked.

Stepping back inside the newspaper office, Doc saw Marshal Dawson just coming in off the street.

"Mr. Brandon's been shot," the newspaper boy said.

"Is he dead?"

Doc nodded. "Yeah," he said in a choked voice. "He's dead."

"Did you do this, Patterson? Did you kill Brandon?" Dawson asked, snapping his words out in accusation.

"For crying out loud, Dawson, you know better than that," Doc said. "Elmer Brandon was my best friend."

"Friends has been known to get into arguments before," Marshal Dawson said.

"Doc Patterson couldn't of done it, Marshal," Johnny said.

"How do you know he couldn't have done it?"

"'Cause when I heard the gunshot, I run into the shop just long enough to see Mr. Brandon lyin' there. Then I run back down the street where I seen Doc Patterson standin' in front of his office. He couldn't of got there that fast."

"I suppose you are right," Dawson replied. He walked over to look down at Brandon's body. "Maybe it was a suicide, or an accident or something," he suggested.

"Do you see a pistol anywhere, Marshal?"

Dawson looked around the room. "No."

"Then that should prove that it was no suicide or accident," Doc said. "He was murdered."

"Well, if he was, it was his own fault."

"What? His own fault? How can you say something like that?"

"Come on, Doc, you read his article, I'm sure," Dawson said.

"I'll be damned," Doc said. "You're right, I think Quentin killed him, but I never thought I'd hear you say that."

"What? Who said anything about Quentin killin' him?"

"You did. You said it was because of his article."

Marshal Dawson shook his head. "I didn't say nothin' about Quentin doin' the killin'. There's no doubt in my mind but that the article made a lot of people in this town very mad. More than likely it was one of them, I just don't know who."

"I don't see how it could make anyone but Quentin mad," Doc said.

"Are you accusing Quentin?"

"Yes."

"Then you are a fool. I was out at the Tumbling Q this morning, and Quentin was there. He probably has twenty witnesses who will say he was there all morning. Quentin didn't do it."

"If Quentin didn't do it, then who did?"

"I told you. I don't know who did it. I just know who didn't do it. But don't worry, I'll find out."

"Yeah, I'm sure you will," Doc said dryly.

By now there were at least twenty or more people who had gathered in and in front of the newspaper office, crowding in closer, trying to find out what was going on.

At the far end of the street, in Quentin's General Store, Hoyt Poindexter saw someone looking at the display of bandannas he had just put out on a table this morning. The customer was so short that only his head and shoulders reached above the table.

"Yes, sir, can I help you?" Poindexter asked.

The little man's tongue darted out a couple of times before he spoke. "I want the red one," he said, his voice little more than a hiss.

"I'll get it for you," Poindexter said, reaching for the red

bandanna. As he moved closer to the table, he could see
out the window, and noticed that, down at the other end
of the street, a crowd was beginning to gather around the
newspaper office. He paused for a moment as he looked
toward the gathering.

"That one," the little man said again.

"Oh, I'm sorry," Poindexter said, getting the bandanna
and handing it to the little man. "That will be ten cents."

The short man reached into his pocket.

"I wonder if he is putting out another extra," Poindexter asked.

"Who?"

"Mr. Brandon, the newspaper editor. He put out an
extra edition about the trial last night, first time he's ever
done anything like that. And now there seems to be something going on down there."

"I wouldn't know," the little man said as he handed a
dime to Poindexter.

"Thank you for your business, sir," Poindexter said.

With the transaction completed, and no more customers in the store, Poindexter walked out onto his
front porch and looked down toward the newspaper
office, wondering just what was going on.

The little man with the new red bandanna rode out
of town.

When Doc stepped into Kathleen's Kitchen a few
minutes later, he saw Pearlie's friends having breakfast
and talking animatedly about the special edition of the
newspaper.

"It is an exceptionally well-written piece," Murchison

said. "I just hope the good people of Santa Clara realize what a talented journalist they have in Mr. Brandon."

"Hello, Doc," Smoke said, seeing the veterinarian standing just inside the door. "Come join us. We are talking about the newspaper article your friend wrote."

"Elmer is dead," Doc said in a flat, somber voice.

"Who is dead?" Cal asked.

"Elmer Brandon."

Sally gasped. "You mean the newspaper editor?"

Doc nodded.

"He just left here no more than half an hour ago," Murchison said.

I know," Doc said. "He left here, then he stopped my office for a few minutes, the way he does every morning, then he walked on down to his office. Someone must have been waiting for him there, because no more than two minutes after he left me, he was dead."

Smoke picked up the newspaper and looked at the article again. "I guess he was more courageous than we thought."

"Mr. Murchison, Elmer was going to testify for you, wasn't he?" Doc Patterson said.

"Yes, sir, he was."

"Well, now, I'm going to."

"I appreciate that, Dr. Patterson, I truly do," Murchison said.

Chapter Twenty-one

Because the New York Saloon was the only building large enough to hold the number of people expected to attend the trial, the hearing was held there. Gibson had been told that no liquor could be sold during the time of the trial, but the trial generated enough early business to compensate him for it, so he willingly closed the bar at twelve thirty.

More than half the population of the town made plans to attend the trial. This included several women and the parson of the local church, none of whom who had never seen the inside of the saloon before. Earlier today, out of deference to the ladies who would be attending the trial, Gibson hung a white silk cloth over the nude painting, *Note From Cupid*.

It was obvious that many of the women had heard of the painting, because several of them looked for it as soon as they came in, and a few even expressed their disappointment over the fact that the painting had been covered.

Smoke, Sally, Cal, Lenny, Mary Lou, and Kathleen were sitting in the front row, immediately behind the defense table. They had arrived early so that they were there when Pearlie was brought into the improvised courtroom, his hands shackled behind him. Deputy Wilson was the escorting officer, and he strutted importantly alongside Pearlie, guiding him by way of his hand gripping Pearlie's elbow.

"Hello, Smoke, Miz Sally, Cal," Pearlie said, smiling at his friends as he walked by them. "Hi, Lenny, Miz York, Miss Culpepper."

They all responded.

"Don't you worry none, Pearlie," Cal added encouragingly. "Everything is going to be just fine. Mr. Murchison is the smartest lawyer I know."

Pearlie laughed. "Cal, that would give me a lot of comfort if I thought you knew a lot of lawyers."

Murchison chuckled.

"Now you sit there, and you don't give me any trouble," Wilson said authoritatively as he unlocked the shackles. "'Cause I'm goin' to be sittin' right over there and I'll be keepin' my eyes on you for the whole time."

Pearlie rubbed his wrists as he sat down.

The saloon was buzzing with the conversation of well over one hundred spectators, but suddenly the conversation grew quiet. Curious as to why the conversation had suddenly stilled, Smoke turned in his chair and looked back toward the front door. There, standing just inside the batwings, he saw Pogue Quentin, accompanied by a small, evil-looking man.

"Smoke, that fella with Quentin. That's—" Cal started to say, but Smoke interrupted him.

"Borgardus Cates," he said.

"Yes, they call him Snake Cates. He's one of the deadliest killers in the country," Cal went on, anxious to show that he knew something about Cates.

"I wonder what he's doing here," Sally said.

"I'm sure Quentin hired him," Smoke said.

"Smoke, do you think he is the one who killed Mr. Brandon?"

"I would bet on it," Smoke replied.

"You have to know that Marshal Dawson would suspect that, yet here he is, just as bold as life."

"The mistake you are making, Sally, is in thinking that Dawson is a real law officer," Smoke said. "He isn't. He is Quentin's man."

Quentin and Cates walked to the front of the room. There were no empty seats in the front row, but when Quentin glared at two men who were sitting there, they got up quickly and went to the back of the room, thus enabling Quentin and Cates to sit behind the prosecutor's table.

Murchison had already met the prosecutor, having talked with him for a few minutes about half an hour ago. Santa Clara did not have a full-time prosecuting attorney, nor did Huereano County. It was normally the responsibility of the presiding judge to appoint one, but in this case, he didn't have to. When Marshall Dawson and Percy Gilmore met the judge at the depot last night with the request that Gilmore be assigned the position of prosecutor, it had surprised Judge McCabe.

Appointing someone who actually wanted to be the prosecutor was a rare break from the routine. Most of the time, Judge McCabe would encounter resistance from those he appointed as prosecutor, so he welcomed this turn of events and appointed Gilmore to the position, even before he left the depot.

As Quentin and Cates took their seats behind the prosecutor's table, Gilmore turned to engage them in conversation. They spoke so quietly that nobody near them could hear what was being said.

"You did what?" Gilmore gasped aloud.

"You don't have to worry about it none," Quentin said. "You didn't have nothin' to do with it. It was—"

Gilmore held up his hand and shook his head. "No," he said. "Don't say another word. I can't know anything about it, do you understand? Say nothing more to me about this." Gilmore turned his back to them.

Lenny chuckled. "Mr. Gilmore seemed upset with Quentin. I wonder what that was all about," he said.

Before anyone could respond to Lenny's question, Marshal Dawson stepped up to the front of the room and cleared his throat a few time until he had everyone's attention.

"Oyez, oyez, oyez, this here Court of Huereano County, Santa Clara, Colorado, is now in session. Everyone will come to order, the Honorable Judge Cleetus McCabe presiding. All rise."

Smoke, Sally, Cal, Lenny, Mary Lou, and Kathleen stood with the others. Conversations were cut off in midsentence, and there was a scrape of chairs and rustle of clothing as those in the gallery stood. A spittoon rang, then rocked on the floor as someone made an accurate expectoration of his tobacco quid.

Judge McCabe was a rather large man, with cheeky jowls, piercing blue eyes, and a bald head. He ambled to the bench, then sat down.

"Be seated," he said.

There was another scrape of chairs as those present took their seats. McCabe picked up the piece of paper that was lying on the table that served as his desk.

"Comes now before this court, in the case of The

People versus—" He paused for a moment, then looked up. "Pearlie? Pearlie what?"

"Just Pearlie, Your Honor," Pearlie replied.

Judge McCabe shook his head. "No," he said. "That won't do. I'm going to need your entire name."

"Please the court, Your Honor," Murchison said. "As the person named in the indictment is identified only as Pearlie, and as my defendant readily agrees that he is the Pearlie so named, there is no legal requirement that any other name be used. I'm sure Your Honor is aware there have been cases tried and adjudicated for persons known only as John Doe."

Judge McCabe stroked his chin for a moment as he studied the document before him. Clearing his throat, he looked up at Pearlie.

"Do you hereby state before this court that you are the person identified in this indictment as Pearlie?"

"I do, Your Honor," Pearlie replied.

"Then Pearlie it shall be," McCabe said. He turned back to the document and continued to read. "In the case of The People verses Pearlie, the charge is murder, and murder in the first degree."

This time, McCabe looked over at the prosecutor's table. "Murder in the first degree? Are you sure you wouldn't like to amend this charge? I was under the impression that it was a spur-of-the-moment killing. Murder in the first degree requires premeditation. That's going to be a hard case to make, don't you think?"

"First degree, Judge," Quentin called out. "I want this son of a bitch to hang."

Angrily, McCabe picked up his gavel and brought it down sharply on the table. "Order in the court!" he said.

"Any more outbursts like that, Mr. Quentin, and I will have you escorted from this court. Do you understand?"

Quentin glared at the judge, but said nothing.

"Do you understand, sir?" McCabe asked, the tone of his voice even sharper than before.

"Yeah, I understand," Quentin replied.

Gilmore turned toward Quentin. "This is going to be hard enough as it is," he said quietly. "Please don't make it any harder."

"Mr. Prosecutor, do you wish to amend the charge?" McCabe asked again.

"No, Your Honor. There is no set time limit for premedication. It can be as little as a second."

"Very well, the charge shall be prosecuted as entered. With lawyer for the defense present, and with the prosecutor present, we shall now proceed with voir dire of the impaneled jury."

The first juror questioned by Murchison was James Colby. "Mr. Colby, what is your occupation?"

"I'm a rancher—sort of," Colby replied.

"Sort of?"

"I'm still running longhorns when everyone else is switching to Herefords. It's getting harder to hang on."

"Did you know Billy Ray Quentin?"

"Yeah, I knew him," Colby replied.

"How well did you know him?"

"In a town this size, and with someone like Billy Ray, almost every one knew him."

"What do you mean, someone like Billy Ray?"

"He was the son of the wealthiest man in the county. And he could be quite unpleasant. Like I said, everyone knew him."

"Do you have any financial obligation or business relationship with Pogue Quentin?"

"No," Colby answered resolutely.

"Do you think you could render an honest verdict, based entirely upon the evidence presented in this case?"

"I do."

"The defense accepts the juror, Your Honor," Murchison said, returning to his seat.

"Voir dire, Mr. Prosecutor?" McCabe said.

Gilmore stood up, but did not walk away from the prosecutor's table. "Mr. Colby, you said that Billy Ray could be unpleasant. What did you mean by that?"

"You knew him as well as I did, Percy," Colby answered. "Why would you even have to ask such a thing?"

"Did you like Billy Ray?"

"I don't know if anyone liked him," Colby replied. "But that doesn't mean I can't be fair."

"I see. Let's change directions, Mr. Colby. Were you present at a meeting in Pogue Quentin's home several months ago, when several ranchers from the area made the decision to pool their livestock and property into one larger cooperative ranch?"

"You know I was. You were there, too."

"Yes, I was. And I know the answer to this question as well, but I want you to answer it for sake of the court. Did you join with the others?"

"No. I did not."

"Why didn't you join, Mr. Colby?"

Colby looked over toward Quentin with a disapproving expression on his face.

"Because I thought he was just settin' everything up so as to cheat us out of our land," Colby said. "And it turns out that I was right. Gillespie, Peters, Baker, and the others—they are all gone now. Gone without so much as one cow or one acre to their name. Quentin owns it all."

"Do you find fault with Mr. Quentin for that?"

"Beg your pardon?"

"Do you blame Mr. Quentin for the fact that these other gentlemen you mentioned lost their property?"

"You damn right I do," Colby said resolutely. "He stole that land from them as sure as if he had done it with a gun."

Gilmore turned toward the judge. "Your Honor, dismiss for cause. It is clear that there is some animosity between this juror and the father of the victim."

"You may step down, Mr. Colby," McCabe said. "You are dismissed from this jury."

Gilmore dismissed two more of the potential jurors, both of whom had had run-ins with Billy Ray, and Murchison dismissed two of the jurors who were currently cowboys working for the Tumbling Q. They finally ended up with a panel of twelve.

"Those jurors who have been dismissed may stay as spectators, but you are to have no contact with the remaining jurors," McCabe said. He looked over toward Gilmore. "Mr. Prosecutor, you may give your opening statement now. Make your case."

Gilmore walked over to the jury. "Hello, Greg," he said to the first juror. "Is your wife going to enter her plum jam in the county fair this year?"

The juror smiled. "Yes, sir, she sure is. You know Alice. Her plum jam has won a blue ribbon for the last three years running."

"As it should have. I know it's certainly the best I've ever eaten." Gilmore smiled. "In fact, I had it on a biscuit for breakfast this morning. I'm sure she'll do well again this year."

Gilmore turned to the next man. "Good afternoon, Adam, how is little Sterling doing? I know he broke his arm. Is it healing up all right?"

"His arm is coming along just fine," Adam replied. "He complains that the cast makes it itch all the time."

Gilmore chuckled. "Oh, indeed, it will certainly do that. I remember that I broke my arm when I was about the same age as young Sterling is now. I fell off the roof of the barn. But you just remind him how good it will feel when he can finally get the cast off and scratch."

"Yes, sir, I'll do that," Adam said.

Gilmore went on down the line, speaking to every other member of the jury in the same way, calling each of them by name and making some personal comment, either about them, or about someone in their family.

"Now, fellas," he said, after he had spoken to each one of them individually, "in a few minutes, that man sitting behind the table over there"—Gilmore pointed to Murchison—"the counsel for the defense, is going to give you his opening statement. No doubt, he is going to begin by addressing you as 'gentlemen of the jury.'

"He has to do that, you understand, because he doesn't know you. He is a stranger to our town, and it will be a stranger who addresses you."

Gilmore pointed to Pearlie.

"A few days ago, the defendant was also a stranger to our town. None of us had ever heard of him. But he is certainly not a stranger any more. By now, everyone in town knows him, and knows the evil deed he did. You see, nine days ago the defendant, this—spawn of Cain—came into town, had a few drinks, got into a card game, and became so enraged over what was happening in that game that he killed—no—he murdered Billy Ray Quentin.

"I knew Billy Ray. All of you knew Billy Ray. In fact, I would go so far as to say that everyone in town either knew him or knew of him. We knew him because he was the son of Mr. Pogue Quentin, who is, arguably, the wealthiest man and the leading citizen of our fair city."

Gilmore paused in his presentation and looked pointedly toward Quentin, inviting everyone else to look as well.

"More importantly, my fellow citizens of Santa Clara, we knew him because Billy Ray was one of us. He was full of life, and I dare say that at one time or another his antics gave all of you something to laugh about, either with him—or at him. Oh, don't misunderstand; I know Billy Ray wasn't always a 'hail fellow well met' type person. I would be the first to admit that Billy Ray could be a bit of a rascal on occasion. He liked to drink, and when he was drunk, he could sometimes be somewhat overly rambunctious. And just as all of us laughed at and with him from time to time, I'm sure that all of us became angry with him just as often.

"But none of us ever got so angry at Billy Ray that we killed him."

Gilmore pointed to Pearlie.

"No, sir. That bit of malevolence was left to be perpetrated by a stranger."

Gilmore was quiet for a moment. Then he shouted the next sentence so loudly that it made some of the people in the jury jump. "This man!" he shouted. "This man, who will admit only to the name of Pearlie, came into our town and took one of our own from us!"

Again, he was quiet for a long moment. When he

resumed speaking, his voice was much quieter and well modulated.

"Today, each one of you has been called upon to perform a solemn task. You are being asked to decide the fate of another human being. The decision you make here could mean that this man will be required to forfeit his life, and no decision you will ever make in your life will be graver or more awesome than this.

"But when you render your decision, I want you to consider something. You are not doing it alone. This murderer will have a lawyer to plead for him. This murder will have a jury to hear and weigh all the facts. And this murderer will have his sentence imposed by a judge, duly recognized by the state of Colorado. Compare this to the rash decision Pearlie made in the blink of an eye, which was all the time left to Billy Ray Quentin, after the defendant decided to kill him.

"After you hear this case, I am sure that you will bring in a verdict of guilty, and we will have justice when the town gathers around the gallows on Front Street to watch this murderer be hanged by the neck until he is dead."

Gilmore stood silently before the jury for a long moment, letting the word "dead" hang in the air. Then, with a final nod toward the gentlemen of the jury, he returned to his table.

"Damn, he is good," someone said from behind Smoke. "I had no idea Gilmore was that good."

Murchison sat at his table for a long moment until, finally, the judge called upon him.

"Counselor for the defense, do you waive your opening remarks?"

"No, Your Honor, I will speak to the jury," Murchison said.

Standing, he looked toward the jury.

"Mr. Gilmore was correct in saying that I would begin my remarks by addressing you as 'gentlemen of the jury.' I do so, with the highest respect for those of you who have been called upon to—as the prosecutor was also correct in saying—make the most awesome and the gravest decision of your lives.

"He was wrong, however, in saying that you would be addressed by a stranger. On the contrary, you are going to be addressed by someone you all knew, respected, and, I think I am safe in saying, someone you could call your friend. I will be mouthing the words, but the words will not be mine. The words will be those of Elmer Brandon, as he wrote them in his extra edition of the *Santa Clara Chronicle,* which he published last night.

"Ironically, they are the last words he ever wrote because as I'm sure most, if not all of you, know, this talented and courageous newspaper editor was murdered this morning."

There were some in the gallery who did not yet know that Brandon had been murdered, and upon Murchison's announcement, there were a few shocked responses.

Judge McCabe picked up his gavel, but rather than bring it down sharply, he gave the gallery a moment to let the shock sink in.

"I have no doubt but that he was murdered because he had the courage, and the sense of obligation, to write these very words I'm about to read to you."

Murchison picked up the extra broadsheet, and began to read.

"For the first time in this newspaper's history, the *Chronicle* has issued an extra edition to inform the citizens of Santa Clara of a true and unique opportunity. Tomorrow, the 17th of September, a young man, a visitor to our community who we know only as Pearlie, will be put on trial for his life.

"The opportunity that trial offers the citizens of Santa Clara is the prospect of resurrecting something that beats deep within the breast of all Americans, something which sets our nation apart from all the nations of Europe and the rest of the world, something that many in this town abandoned long ago, upon the altar of economic security. That something is Democracy.

"Though no one has yet spoken the words aloud, it is no secret to anyone that this town has, for many years now, been in the clutches of a true despot. That despot is Pogue Quentin, who, by skillful and perfidious, if not illegal manipulation, has managed to gain control of nearly all the ranch land surrounding our fair city. He has used that same means to acquire many of the businesses in town so that, by now a majority of our citizens are dependent upon him for their very existence. We may owe Pogue Quentin our livelihoods, but we do not owe him our souls, and by the words here written, your humble scribe is calling upon all to reclaim those souls, so nearly lost.

"How can you do that?

"By making certain that the inalienable rights of trial by jury and innocent until proven guilty are accorded the young man who now stands in peril of his life, due to the trial upcoming.

"Recently, Pogue Quentin's son, Billy Ray, was killed in a shooting that occurred at the New York Saloon. Though some off-the-record testimony says that the shooting was justifiable, we, the citizens of Santa Clara, have, for the last week, had to suffer the unpleasant sight of a terrible instrument of death, a gallows, constructed in the middle of Front Street. This gallows was constructed, not by the city, or the county, or the state. It was a private construction, paid for by Pogue Quentin. It was constructed to facilitate the execution, by hanging, of a young man who has not yet had his day in court.

"I can also reliably report, having attended the cemetery interment of Billy Ray Quentin and been a witness to the outrageous actions of Pogue Quentin, that he interrupted the sacred burial rites to demand, under penalty of economic pressure, that any citizen who may be called upon for jury duty find Pearlie guilty. He makes this demand before the first piece of evidence is presented, before the first witness is heard, before the opening arguments are made.

"I say no, a thousand times no, to this demand. I say to all our citizens, and especially to whoever may be selected to serve upon this jury, that you remember your obligation to uphold the principles upon which our nation was founded, the rights for which, in the recent Civil War, so many brave young men, in the words of Abraham Lincoln, 'gave their last full measure of devotion.'

"Whether this young visitor to our town is found guilty or innocent, let it be by a fair trial, decided upon by men of honor and character. It is time for us to reclaim our rights, to lay possession to the civil liberties that are granted to all men by the grace of a just and merciful God, and preserved by the noble efforts of men. Let us walk the streets of Santa Clara with our heads held high and proclaim to one and all that we are Americans!"

When Murchison finished the article, someone in the galley started clapping. Soon another joined, and another still, until the entire gallery was applauding.

Judge McCabe was so taken aback by this sudden and unexpected event that for a moment he sat there in shocked silence. Then he picked up the gavel and banged it, calling for order in the court until the applause subsided.

"I—I will not allow another demonstration like this," he said.

Murchison noticed as he sat down, however, that the judge's words, though chastising, were not harsh. It was as if he understood the natural outpouring of emotion the citizens of the town had at hearing the last words ever written by the editor of their newspaper.

Chapter Twenty-two

Gilmore had three witnesses for the prosecution, all of whom worked for Pogue Quentin, and all of whom claimed that Pearlie started the fight by hitting Billy Ray over the head. Jerry Kelly claimed that when Billy Ray came in through the door carrying the shotgun, Pearlie shot at him first.

Murchison countered with half a dozen witnesses. Doc Patterson testified that it was Billy Ray who got angry first and drew his gun on Pearlie.

"Pearlie could have shot him right then if he had wanted to," Doc said. "But instead of shooting him, he hit him over the head and took away his pistol."

Deckert substantiated Doc's account, then went on to say that Billy Ray had charged back into the saloon brandishing a shotgun.

"Billy Ray saw Pearlie standing at the bar and he just opened up on him without so much as a by-your-leave. I swear to you, I don't know how Pearlie managed to escape getting killed," Deckert said.

The testimonies of Evans, Lenny, and Mary Lou concurred with Deckert's account. All said that Pearlie did not shoot back until it was obvious that Billy Ray was about to shoot the other barrel.

"And he wouldn't have missed this time," Lenny said.

Gilmore's questioning of Doc, Deckert, Evans, and Lenny was perfunctory. It wasn't until Mary Lou took the stand that his questions became more intense.

"Miss Culpepper, do you expect the court to believe that you were in the saloon at the time of the shooting?" Gilmore asked during his cross examination.

"Yes, I expect the court to believe I was there because I was," Mary Lou replied.

"But you are a woman, Miss Culpepper. What on earth would you be doing in the saloon? The New York Saloon is not a place normally habituated by women, is it?"

"I was working in the saloon," Mary Lou said. "I was serving drinks."

"You were serving drinks?"

"Yes, sir."

"What else did you do?"

"I don't understand."

"Oh, I'm sure you do understand."

"No, I don't."

"Isn't it true, Miss Culpepper, that you are a whore?"

"Objection, Your Honor, the question is irrelevant," Murchison called out.

"Your Honor, goes to character," Gilmore replied. "If this woman is a whore, then her entire character can be questioned. For example, can she be trusted to tell the truth?"

"Witness will answer the question."

"Are you a whore?"

"*Am* I a whore?"

"That's my question."

Mary Lou stared directly into Gilmore's eyes before she answered.

"No," she said resolutely.

Gilmore had turned toward the jury, but hearing her answer, he spun back toward her. "You are under oath, Miss Culpepper. Now, I will ask you again. *Are* you a whore?"

"No."

"Miss Culpepper," Gilmore started, but he was interrupted by Murchison.

"Objection, Your Honor, question was asked and answered."

"Sustained. Get on with your cross-examination, Counselor," McCabe said.

"Miss Culpepper, there is a scar on your nose and though it has nearly cleared up, it is obvious that both of your eyes were recently blackened. How did you get those injuries?"

"Billy Ray hit me."

"Why did he hit you?"

Mary Lou didn't answer.

"Your Honor, please instruct the witness to respond."

"Answer the question, Miss Culpepper," McCabe said.

"He hit me because I wouldn't go upstairs with him."

"Did he have a reasonable expectation that you would go upstairs with him? My question is, did you sometimes go upstairs with others?"

"Sometimes I went upstairs with others," Mary Lou replied.

"So you are a whore?"

"No, I am not a whore."

"Objection, Your Honor, your ruling has already closed this line of questioning."

"Sustained."

Gilmore was obviously frustrated, but he went on. "You did not care much for Billy Ray Quentin, did you?"

"No. He was mean and brutal."

"So, if someone killed Billy Ray, you wouldn't mind seeing him get off, would you?"

"Objection, Your Honor."

"Sustained."

"No further questions, Your Honor."

"Redirect?"

"Yes, your honor. Miss Culpepper, the prosecutor asked you several times if you are a whore. Now the operative word here is 'are.' Is that correct?"

"Yes, sir."

"Have you ever been a—I think the more genteel term is—'soiled dove'?"

"I was, yes."

"But no more?"

"No more."

"What do you do now?"

"I work for Mrs. York."

"Thank you. No further questions, Your Honor."

Closing arguments were short. Murchison pointed out that Doc Patterson and Deckert concurred in their testimony as to how the fight started, with Billy Ray attempting to draw his gun on Pearlie. He also reminded the jury that Deckert, Evans, Lenny, and Mary Lou gave nearly identical accounts as to how Billy Ray came bursting back into the saloon, firing his shotgun without warning.

"The burden of proof is with the prosecution. That means that normally the guiding principle in a trial like this is that you cannot find a defendant guilty unless you are convinced, beyond a shadow of a doubt, that he is guilty, and in his charge to the jury, the judge will, no doubt, so instruct you. But in this case, I believe that even if that standard were reversed, if the burden of proof, beyond a shadow of a doubt, was with the defense, you would still have no recourse but to find Pearlie innocent of this charge," Murchison said in his closing.

In his closing remarks, Gilmore again reminded the jury that Pearlie was a stranger, an itinerant wanderer who came into town and while there, for no reason other than his own innate evil, gunned down a local man.

"Billy Ray walked and talked with us, he laughed with us, he participated in the town's celebration of the Fourth of July with us, he played cards with us. That in itself is enough to require that we demand justice be meted out to his murderer, but Billy Ray wasn't just any local man. He was the son of the leading citizen of our town, a man to whom more than half of our citizens are beholden for their livelihood. And now, Billy Ray's bones lie in the cemetery, at the edge of town."

Gilmore pointed in the direction of the cemetery; then he put his hand to his ear. "Listen," he said. "Listen closely, because if you do, you can hear in the very wind, the cry of the mournful soul of one of us—our friend—our brother, calling to us from his grave, demanding that we give him justice."

The jury had only been out fourteen minutes when they came tramping back into the saloon turned courtroom and took their seats.

"Have you selected a foreman?" Judge McCabe asked.

"We have, Your Honor. My name is Greg Paul."

"Mr. Paul, has the jury reached a verdict?"

"We have."

"Would you publish the verdict, please?"

"We find the defendant, Pearlie, not guilty."

"No!" Quentin shouted angrily. He stood up so quickly that the chair tumbled over behind him, and he pointed at Pearlie, who was already receiving a congratulatory hug from Sally.

"You son of a bitch, you'll pay for this!"

Judge McCabe slammed his gavel down. "Marshal Dawson, escort that man out of this courtroom!" he demanded.

"Come on, Pogue," Dawson said. "Let's get out of here."

Pogue glared a moment longer toward Pearlie and the others; then he, Marshal Dawson, and Snake Cates left the saloon.

The townspeople gathered around Pearlie, congratulating him, and several offered to buy him a drink as soon as the bar reopened.

"I just wish Mr. Brandon could have been here for this," Lenny said.

"He was here," Doc said. "At least his words were. Mr. Murchison, thanks for reading them. You read the words beautifully, and he would have been very proud."

"Mrs. York," Mary Lou said.

"Mary Lou, dear, please, call me Kathleen."

"Kathleen, if you don't mind, I think I would like to go over to the kitchen and make an apple pie. We can have it later in celebration."

"Can you bake an apple pie?" Lenny asked. "That's my favorite."

Mary Lou smiled. "Mine, too," she said. "It's a recipe my mama taught me."

"Well, of course you can, dear," Kathleen said. "Do you need my help?"

For the next several minutes, Smoke, Sally, Pearlie, and the others engaged the townspeople in conversation. Many in the town had heard of Smoke, and they were taking this opportunity to get close to someone who was already famous.

"Mr. Jensen?" someone said.

Looking up, Smoke saw a big bearded man with a wandering eye.

"Yes?"

"I'm Cole Mathers," the man said.

"What do you want, Mathers?" Doc asked in a tone of voice that wasn't too friendly. "Mathers is Quentin's foreman," he said to the others.

"I ain't his foreman anymore," Cole said.

"Did he fire you?" Doc asked.

"No, sir, he didn't fire me. I quit. I couldn't go along with what he's plannin' now."

"What is he planning now?"

"Well, for one thing, he's got the whore," Cole said.

"What?" Lenny asked.

"The whore," Cole said. "He's got her and he says he's goin' to kill her if Pearlie don't come out and face his man, Snake Cates."

"I need a gun," Pearlie said.

"No, wait," Smoke said. "We've just got you through one trial. There's no sense in getting you mixed up in another one. I'll go out."

Mathers nodded. "That's what Quentin figured you

would do," he said. "Truth is, I think he wants you dead as much or more than he wants Pearlie."

"Where is Mary Lou?" Lenny asked.

"Deputy Wilson and a couple others are holdin' her down at the Quentin's Freight Warehouse."

"Pearlie, you and Cal go down to the depot and get Mary Lou."

"I'm going, too," Lenny said.

"All right, you can go as well."

"My pistol is down at the jailhouse," Pearlie said.

"I've got one behind the bar you can use, Pearlie," Evans said.

"Mr. Evans, I'll borrow the shotgun if you don't mind," Lenny said.

"Hold on a minute," another voice called and looking around, Smoke saw that Judge McCabe had been listening in on the conversation. "You men can't go out there like this."

"Judge, they have the girl," Smoke said.

McCabe lifted his hand. "You can't go out like this until I deputize you," he said. "Raise your hands, all of you."

Smoke, Pearlie, Cal, and Lennie lifted their hands.

"By the power vested in me by the state of Colorado, I hereby vacate the law-enforcement responsibilities of Dawson and Wilson, and grant temporary deputy status to each of you."

Smoke smiled. "Thanks, Judge," he said. "And here, I thought you were called the Hanging Judge."

"I will hang them if they are guilty and need hanging," McCabe said.

"There's nothing wrong with that," Smoke said.

"Mr. Jensen," Mathers called as they were starting toward the door. Smoke turned back toward him. "I just thought you ought to know. If Cates doesn't kill you, Quentin and Dawson plan to do it themselves."

"Thanks," Smoke said.

The street was empty when Smoke stepped out onto the boardwalk in front of the New York Saloon. The street was empty, but it wasn't unobserved, because word had already spread throughout the town that there was going to be a showdown between two of the fastest guns in the West.

Smoke eased his pistol from his holster, turned the cylinder to check the loads, then slipped his pistol back into the holster. He stepped out into the street and started walking toward Cates.

"Is Quentin paying you for this, Cates?" Smoke asked.

Cates's tongue flicked out of his mouth a couple of times before he answered.

"Yeah," Cates hissed. His lips spread into what might have been a smile. "Quentin paid me to kill the newspaper man, too. Don't you be tellin' him now, but this killin' I would have done for free."

"Really? And why is that?"

"You got 'ny idea how much money I'm goin' to be able to charge for my services once I kill the great Smoke Jensen?"

"Doesn't matter," Smoke said.

Cates tongue flicked out a couple more times. "What do you mean, it doesn't matter?"

"It doesn't matter, because you aren't going to get off this street alive."

"I wouldn't be so sure about that," he said. "You're a lot bigger target than I am." Again, he smiled.

"My target will be the same size, no matter how big you are."

"What do you mean by that?"

"I mean, Cates, that I'm going to shoot you right between the eyes," Smoke said, his voice as calm as if he had just ordered a cup of coffee.

Suddenly, Cates went for his gun, but Smoke was ready for him, and his own pistol was out and booming before Cates could even bring his gun level. A black hole appeared between Cates's eyes and he fell backward, sending up a puff of dust as he hit the street. His arms flopped out to either side, the unfired gun dangling from a crooked, but stilled, finger. It had all happened so quickly that many of those who had been watching through windows, or from around corners of the buildings, missed it.

Smoke stood there for a moment longer, the gun still in his hand, smoke curling up from the end of the barrel. He looked at Cates's still form, lying on the dirt street. Already, flies from a nearby horse apple were drawn to the bloody hole between his open, but sightless, obsidian eyes.

"Shoot him! Shoot the son of a bitch!" Quentin shouted.

The voice came from the hayloft of the livery and when Smoke looked up, he saw the flash of two guns being fired. The bullets hit the ground close by, then ricocheted away with a loud whine. Smoke fired back, shooting twice into the dark maw of the hayloft. He ran to the water trough nearest the livery, and dived behind it as Quentin and Dawson fired again. Both bullets hit the trough with a loud thock.

Smoke left his position behind the water trough, and ran toward the door of the livery. He could hear the water gurgling through the bullet holes behind him. When he reached the big, open, double doors of the livery, he ran on through to the inside.

"Where'd he go? Dawson, do you see him? Where did the son of a bitch go?"

"He come through the doors," Dawson replied. "He's in here somewhere. Keep your eyes peeled."

Smoke fired again into the hayloft, and the barn rang with the sound of his shot.

"He's inside," Quentin shouted. "He's right below us!"

"Quentin, Cates told me you paid him to kill Elmer Brandon. That makes you as guilty of murder as he was, and I'm putting you under arrest," Smoke called up.

"Ha!" Dawson said. "You are putting someone under arrest? Maybe you forgot, Jensen, but I'm the law here."

"Not anymore, you aren't," Smoke replied. "Judge McCabe just removed you and Wilson from office and made me the law. Come to think of it, Dawson, I'm putting you under arrest, too."

Dawson's laugh was forced. "You ain't arrestin' nobody," he said.

"Dawson!" Quentin called again. "Who are you talking to? Do you see him?"

"No," Dawson answered.

With his pistol pointed up toward the loft above him, Smoke moved quietly through the barn itself, looking up at the hayloft just overhead. Suddenly, he felt little pieces of hay falling on him and he stopped, because he realized that someone had to be right over him. Then he heard it, a quiet shuffling of feet. Smoke fired twice, straight up. Then he heard a groan and a loud thump.

"Dawson! Dawson, are you hit?" Quentin called.

Smoke realized then that he had expended every shot,

so he opened the gate and started poking the empty shell casings from the cylinder chambers of his pistol.

"Well, now, look here," a calm voice said. Smoke glanced over to his left to see Quentin standing in the open, on the edge of the loft. He was holding a pistol pointed at Smoke, and from this range, it would be very hard for him to miss.

"You're out of bullets, aren't you, you son of a bitch." He voice was confident, almost triumphant.

Smoke heard the pistol shot, then saw the expression on Quentin's face change from triumph, to shock, then to pain. Quentin dropped his pistol, grabbed the hole in his chest, then pitched forward, turning over once on the way down to land on his back.

Looking toward the open doors, Smoke saw Sally standing there, holding a smoking pistol.

"What took you so long?" Smoke asked.

Sally smiled. "You know how we women are, Smoke. I didn't want to come outside until I knew my hair looked all right."

Smoke chuckled. "Your hair is beautiful," he said.

When Smoke and Sally went back out into the street, they saw Cal running toward them.

"Where's Pearlie?" Smoke asked.

"He and Lenny are down there at the freight warehouse. They have Wilson and a couple of cowboys from the Tumbling Q holed up inside with Mary Lou."

"Is Mary Lou all right?" Sally asked anxiously.

"Yes, ma'am, I think she is. It's just that they say that if we try and come in after 'em, they'll kill her."

"Let's go get her out," Smoke said.

By now, nearly the entire town was out in the street, many of them gathered around Snake Cates's body, others beginning to come into the livery to see the bodies there.

When Smoke, Sally, and Cal walked down to the other end of town to the warehouse, most of the town followed, until there was a crowd gathered just outside the warehouse.

"Wilson," Smoke called into the warehouse.

"What do you want?" Wilson called back, his voice muffled.

"Do you have Mary Lou in there?"

"Yeah, we've got her."

"Why?" Smoke asked.

"What? What do you mean, why?"

"I mean, what good is it going to do you?" Smoke asked. "Quentin is dead. Dawson is dead. Cates is dead. That leaves you boys all by yourselves. You've got two choices now. Let the girl go and live—or keep her and die."

"I don't believe they are dead," Wilson said.

"Take a look out here. Do you see all these people? You think they would be standing out here in the street if Quentin or Dawson or Cates were still alive?"

"Kelly, Reeves, Jensen is telling the truth. Quentin is dead," Cole Mathers shouted. He was standing out in the street with others from the town.

"Cole, what are you doing here?" Wilson asked.

"Trying to talk some sense into you," Cole replied.

"Son of a bitch, Wilson, look out there!" another voice from inside called out. "What are we holdin' this girl for now? Quentin's dead. Who is it we are workin' for? I'm goin' out."

"No, you ain't, Reeves. You're stayin' right here with Kelly an' me."

"If you stay, you'll be stayin' by yourself," Kelly said. "I don't plan on gettin' killed for Quentin, especially when Quentin is dead his ownself."

"That leaves just you, Wilson," Smoke said. "Make up your mind. You can die or you can live."

There was a long moment of silence from inside the warehouse. Then, Mary Lou appeared in the door.

"Mary Lou!" Lenny shouted.

Mary Lou ran toward him and they kissed and embraced.

"We're comin' out now," Wilson said.

A moment later all three came out, holding their hands in the air.

One year later
Sugarloaf Ranch

"All right, Juan, hold her, here she comes!" Smoke shouted to his old Mexican hand. Juan was helping a cow give birth.

The heifer bawled, and shuddered; then the calf popped out.

"Look there, it's a male!" Cal said.

Sally came into the barn then and stood for a moment looking at Smoke, Pearlie, and Cal as they looked down at the new calf. Juan started cleaning it up.

"Un fino niño ternero, señor," Juan said. "A fine boy calf."

"What do you think, Miss Sally?" Pearlie asked excitedly. "This is number twenty-one from Prince Henry."

"Look over there at Prince Henry," Sally said. "He knows this is his calf and he is strutting around just as proud as a peacock."

Cal laughed. "Miss Sally, do you remember when

Smoke said that all we needed from Prince Henry was that he have an eye for the ladies?"

"I remember," Sally said. "But it turns out, Prince Henry isn't the only one with an eye for the ladies."

"What do you mean?"

Smiling, Sally held up a letter. "When I went in to town today, I picked up our mail. We got a letter from Lenny. He and Mary Lou have just had a baby."

"Oh, wow, that's great!" Pearlie said.

"What did they name it?" Cal asked.

"Elmer Brandon York," Sally said. "They named it after the newspaper editor."

"They couldn't have chosen a better name," Smoke said.

"Just think of Lenny with a young'un of his own," Cal said.

The calf, clean now, got up on wobbly feet, then walked over to nudge up against Cal.

"Look at the way that calf is taking to Cal," Pearlie said. "Looks to me like Lenny isn't the only one with a young'un of his own."

The others laughed.

TURN THE PAGE
FOR AN EXCITING PREVIEW OF

MATT JENSEN, THE LAST MOUNTAIN MAN:
SNAKE RIVER SLAUGHTER

by William W. Johnstone
with J. A. Johnstone

Coming in February 2010

Available wherever Pinnacle Books are sold!

Chapter One

Sweetwater County, Wyoming

The Baker brothers, Harry and Arnold, were outside by the barn when they saw Jules Pratt and his wife come out of the house. Scott and Lucy McDonald walked out onto the porch to tell the Pratts good-bye.

"You have been most generous," Jules said as he climbed up into the surrey. "Speaking on behalf of the laity of the church, I can tell you that every time we hear the beautiful music of the new organ, we will be thinking of and thanking you."

"It was our pleasure," Scott said. "The church means a great deal to us, more than we can say. And we are more than happy to do anything we can to help out."

"We'll see you Sunday," Jules said, slapping the reins against the back of the team.

Lucy McDonald went back into the house, but before Scott went back inside, he looked over toward the barn at two brothers.

"How are you two boys comin' on the wagon?" Scott called toward them.

"We're workin' on it," Harry called back.

"I'm goin' to be needin' it pretty soon now, so you let me know if you run into any trouble with it," McDonald replied, just as he went back inside.

Harry and Arnold Baker were not permanent employees of the MacDonalds. They had been hired the day before for the specific purpose of making repairs to the freight wagon.

"Did you see that money box?" Harry asked.

"You mean when he give that other fella a donation for the organ? Yeah, I seen it," Arnold replied.

"There has to be two, maybe three hunnert dollars in that box," Harry said.

"How long would it take us to make that kind of money?" Arnold asked.

"Hell, it would take the better part of a year for us to make that much money, even if we was to put our earnings together," Harry said.

"Yeah, that's what I thought," Arnold said. "Harry, you want to know what I'm thinkin'?"

"If you're thinkin' the same thing I'm thinkin', I know what it is," Harry replied.

"Let's go in there and get that money."

"He ain't goin' to give up and just give it to us," Harry said.

"He will if we threaten to kill 'im."

Harry shook his head. "Just threatenin' him ain't goin' enough," he said. "We're goin' to have to do it. Otherwise, he'll set the sheriff on us."

"What about the others? His wife and kids?"

"You want the two boys to grow up and come after us?"

"No, I guess not."

"If we are goin' to do this thing, Arnold, there's only one way to do it," Harry insisted.

"All right. Let's do it."

Pulling their guns and checking their loads, the two brothers put their pistols back in their holsters, then crossed the distance between the barn and the house. They pushed the door open and went inside without so much as a warning knock.

"Oh!" Lucy said, startled by the sudden appearance of the two men in the kitchen.

"Get your husband," Arnold said, his voice little more than a growl.

Lucy left the kitchen, then returned a moment later with Scott. Scott wasn't wearing his gun, which was going to make this even easier than they had planned.

"Lucy said you two boys just walked into the house without so much as a fare-thee-well," Scott said, his voice reflecting his irritation. "You know better than to do that. What do you want?"

"The money," Harry said.

"The money? You mean you have finished the wagon? Well, good, good. Let me take a look at it, and if I'm satisfied, I'll give you your ten dollars," Scott said.

Harry shook his head. "No, not ten dollars," he said. "All of it."

"I beg your pardon?"

Harry drew his pistol, and when he did, Arnold drew his as well.

"The money box," Harry said. "Get it down. We want all the money."

"Scott!" Lucy said in a choked voice.

"It's all right, Lucy, we are goin' to give them what they

ask for. Then they'll go away and leave us alone. Get the box down and hand it to them."

"You're a smart man, McDonald," Arnold said.

"You'll never get away with stealing our money," Lucy said as she retrieved the box from the top of the cupboard, then handed it over to Harry.

"Oh, yeah, we're goin' to get away with it," Harry said as he took the money from the box. Folding the money over, he stuck it in his pocket. Then, without another word, he pulled the trigger. Lucy got a surprised look on her face as the bullet buried into her chest, but she went down, dead before she hit the floor.

"You son of a bitch!" Scott shouted as he leaped toward Harry.

Harry was surprised by the quickness and the furiousness of the attack. He was knocked down by Scott, but he managed to hold onto his gun and even as he was under Scott on the floor, he stuck the barrel of gun into Scott's stomach and pulled the trigger.

"Get him off of me!" Harry shouted. "Get him off of me."

"Mama, Papa, what is it?" a young voice called, and the two children came running into the kitchen. Arnold shot both of them, then rolled Scott off Harry and helped his brother back on his feet.

"Are you all right?" Arnold asked.

"Yeah," Harry answered. "I've got the money. Come on, let's get out of here."

The next day

Matt Jensen dismounted in front of the Gold Strike Saloon. Brushing some of the trail dust away, he tied his horse off at the hitching rail, then began looking at the other horses that were there, lifting the left hind foot of each animal in turn.

His action seemed a little peculiar, and some of pedestrians stopped to look over at him. What they saw was a man who was just a bit over six feet tall with broad shoulders and narrow waist. He was young in years, but his pale blue eyes bespoke experiences that most would not see in three lifetimes. He was a lone wolf who had worn a deputy's badge in Abilene, ridden shotgun for a stagecoach out of Lordsburg, scouted for the army in the McDowell Mountains of Arizona, and panned for gold in Idaho. A banker's daughter in Cheyenne once thought she could make him settle down—a soiled dove in the Territories knew that she couldn't, but took what he offered.

Matt was a wanderer, always wondering what was beyond the next line of hills, just over the horizon. He traveled light, with a bowie knife, a .44 double-action Colt, a Winchester .44-40 rifle, a rain slicker, an overcoat, two blankets, a spare shirt, and spare socks, trousers, and underwear.

He called Colorado his home, though he had actually started life in Kansas. Colorado was home only because it was where he had reached his maturity, and Smoke Jensen, the closest thing he had to a family, lived there. In truth, though, he spent no more time in Colorado than he did in Wyoming, Utah, New Mexico, or Arizona.

At the moment, Matt was on the trail of Harry and Arnold Baker for the murder of Scott McDonald, his wife, Lucy, and their two young sons, Toby and Tyler. Before he died, Scott McDonald managed to live long enough to scrawl the letters B-A-K on the floor, using his finger as a pen and his own blood as the ink. McDonald had hired the Baker brothers, not because he needed the help, but because he thought they were down on their luck and needed the job.

Matt had known the McDonalds well. He had been a guest in their house many times, and had even attended the baptism of one of their children. When the McDonalds were killed, Matt took it very personally, and had himself temporarily deputized so he could hunt down the Baker brothers and bring them to justice.

One of the Baker brothers was riding a horse that left a distinctive hoofprint and that had enabled Matt to track them to Burnt Fork. That brought him to the front of the Gold Strike Saloon, where he was checking the shoes of the horses that were tied off at the hitching rail. On the fourth horse that he examined, he found what he was looking for. The shoe on the horse's left rear foot had a V-shaped niche on the inside of the right arm of the shoe.

Loosening his pistol in the holster, Matt went into the saloon.

A loud burst of laughter greeted him as he stepped inside, and sitting at a table in the middle of the saloon were two men. Each of the men had a girl sitting on his lap and the table had a nearly empty whiskey bottle, indicating they had been drinking heavily.

Matt had never seen the Baker brothers, so he could not identify them by sight, but the two men resembled each other enough to be brothers, and they did match the description he had been given of them.

"Hey, Harry, let's see which one of these girls has the best titties," one of the men said. He grabbed the top of the dress of the girl who was sitting on his lap and jerked it down, exposing her breasts.

"Stop that!" the girl called out in anger and fright. She

jumped up from his lap and began pulling the top of her dress back up.

"Ha! Arnold, you done got that girl all mad at you."

They had called each other Harry and Arnold. That was all the verification Matt needed. Turning back toward the bar, he signaled the bartender.

"Yes, sir, what can I do for you?" he asked.

"I need you to get the women away from those two men," Matt said, quietly.

"Mister, as long as those men are paying, the girls can stay."

"I'm about to arrest those two men for murder," Matt said. "If they resist arrest, then I intend to kill them. I wouldn't want the women to be in the way."

"Oh!" the bartender said. "Oh, uh, yes, I see what you mean. But . . . I don't know how to get them away without tellin' what's about to happen."

"Go down to the other end of the bar and take out a new bottle of whiskey. Tell the men it's on the house, you're giving it to them for being good customers. Then call the women over to get it."

"Yeah," the bartender said. "Yeah, that's a good idea."

Matt remained there with his back to the men while the bartender walked down to the other end of the bar. He put a bottle of whiskey up on the bar.

"Jane, Ellie Mae," he called. "Come up here for a moment."

"Hey, bartender, you leave these girls with us. They're enjoyin' our company," one of the men said. This was Arnold.

"We are enjoying your company, too, sir," the bartender said. "You've spent a lot of money with us and you been such good customers and all, we're pleased to offer you a bottle of whiskey on the house. That is, if you'll let the girls come up to get it."

"Well, hell, you two girls go on up there and get the bottle," Harry said. "And if you are good to us, why, we'll let you have a few drinks. Right, Arnold?"

"Right, Harry," Arnold answered.

From his position in the saloon, Matt watched in the mirror as the two girls left the table and started toward the bartender. Not until he was sure they were absolutely clear did he turn around.

"Hello, Harry. Hello, Arnold," he said.

"What?" Harry replied, surprised at being addressed by name. "Do you know us?"

"No, but I know who you are. I was a good friend of the McDonalds," Matt said.

"We don't know anyone named McDonald," Harry said.

"Sure you do," Matt said. "You murdered them."

The two men leaped up then, jumping up so quickly that the chairs fell over behind them. Both of them started toward their guns, but when they saw how quickly Matt had his own pistol out, they stopped, then raised their hands.

"We ain't drawin', mister. We ain't drawin'!" Arnold said.

When Matt returned to Green River, Harry and Arnold were riding in front of him. Each man had his hands in iron shackles, and there was a rope stretching from Harry's neck to Arnold's neck, then from Arnold's nect to the saddle horn of Matt's saddle. This was to discourage either, or both, from trying to bolt away during the return journey.

Chapter Two

Within a week of their capture, the two brothers were put on trial in the Sweetwater County Courthouse. Although seats were hard to come by, Sheriff Foley had held a place for Matt so he was able to move through the crowd of people who were searching for their own places to sit. Rather than being resentful of him, however, those in the crowd applauded when Matt came in. They were aware of the role Matt had played in bringing the Baker brothers to trial.

Matt had been in his seat for little more than a minute when the bailiff came through a little door at the front of the courtroom. Clearing his voice, the bailiff addressed the gallery.

"Oyez, oyez, oyez, this court of Sweetwater County, Green River City, Wyoming, will now come to order, the Honorable Judge Daniel Norton presiding. All rise."

As Judge Norton came into the courtroom and stepped up to the bench, Matt Jensen stood with the others.

"Be seated," Judge Norton said. "Bailiff, call the first case."

"There's only one case, Your Honor. There come now before this court Harry G. Baker and Arnold S. Baker, both men having been indicted for the crime of murder in the first degree."

"Thank you, Bailiff. Are the defendants represented by counsel?"

The defense attorney stood. "I am Robert Dempster, Your Honor, duly certified before the bar and appointed by the court to defend the Misters Baker."

"Is prosecution present?"

The prosecutor stood. "I am Edmund Gleason, Your Honor, duly certified before the bar and appointed by the court to prosecute."

"Let the record show that the people are represented by a duly certified prosecutor and the defendants are represented by a duly certified counsel," Judge Norton said.

"Your Honor, if it please the court," Dempster said, standing quickly.

"Yes, Mr. Dempster, what is it?"

"Your Honor, I object to the fact that we are trying both defendants at the same time, and I request separate trials."

"Mr. Dempster, both men are being accused of the same crime, which was committed at the same time. It seems only practical to try them both at the same time. Request denied."

Dempster sat down without further protest.

"Mr. Prosecutor, are you ready to proceed?"

"I am ready, Your Honor."

"Very good. Then, please make your case," Judge Norton said.

"Thank you, Your Honor," Gleason said as he stood to make his opening remarks.

Gleason pointed out that the letters B-A-K, written in

the murder victim's own blood, were damning enough testimony alone to convict. But he also promised to call witnesses, which he did after the opening remarks. He called Mr. Jules Pratt.

"Mr. Pratt, were you present at the McDonald Ranch on the day of the murder?" Gleason asked.

"Yes," Jules replied. "My wife and I were both there."

"Why were you there?"

"We went to see the McDonalds to solicit a donation for the church organ."

"Did they donate?"

"Yes, they did. Very generously."

"By bank draft, or by cash?"

"By cash."

"Where did they get the cash?"

"From a cash box they kept in the house."

"Was there any money remaining in the cash box after the donation?"

"Yes, a considerable amount."

"How much would you guess?"

"Two, maybe three hundred dollars."

"Was anyone else present at the time?"

"Yes."

"Who?"

Jules pointed. "Those two men were present. They were doing some work for Scott."

"Let the record show that the witness pointed to Harry and Arnold Baker. Was it your observation, Mr. Pratt, that the two defendants saw the cash box and the amount of money remaining?"

"Yes, sir, I know they did."

"How do you know?"

"Because that one . . ." He pointed.

"The witness has pointed to Arnold Baker," Gleason said.

"That one said to Scott, 'That's a lot of money to keep in the house.'"

"Thank you, Mr. Pratt, no further questions."

Gleason also called Pastor Martin, who, with four of his parishioners, testified as to how they had discovered the bodies when they visited the ranch later the same day. Then, less than one half hour after court was called to order, the prosecution rested its case.

The defense had a witness as well, a man named Jerome Kelly, who claimed that he had come by the McDonald ranch just before noon, and that when he left, the Bakers left with him.

"And, when you left, what was the condition of the McDonald family?" the defense attorney asked.

"They was all still alive. Fac' is, Miz McDonald was bakin' a pie," Kelly said.

"Thank you," Dempster said. "Your witness, Counselor."

"Mrs. McDonald was baking a pie, you say?" Gleason asked in his cross examination.

"Yeah. An apple pie."

"Had Mrs. McDonald actually started baking it?"

"Yeah, 'cause we could all smell it."

"What time was that, Mr. Kelly?"

"Oh, I'd say it was about eleven o'clock. Maybe even a little closer on toward noon."

"Thank you. I have no further questions of this witness." The prosecutor turned toward the bench. "Your Honor, prosecution would like to recall Pastor Martin to the stand."

Pastor Martin, the resident pastor of the First Methodist Church of Green River City, Wyoming, who had earlier testified for the prosecution, retook the stand. He was a tall, thin man, dressed in black, with a black string tie.

"The court reminds the witness that he is still under oath," the judge said. Then to Gleason he said, "You may begin the redirect."

"Pastor Martin, you discovered the bodies, did you not?" Gleason asked.

"I did."

"What time did you arrive?"

"It was just after noon. We didn't want to arrive right at noon, because Mrs. McDonald, kind-hearted soul she was, would have thought she had to feed us."

"You testified earlier that you and four other parishioners had gone to thank the McDonalds for their generous donation to the organ fund?"

"Yes."

"And that all five of you saw the bodies?"

Pastor Martin pinched the bridge of his nose and was quiet for a moment before he responded. "May their souls rest with God," he said. "Yes, all five of us saw the bodies."

"You have already testified as to the condition of the bodies when you found them, so I won't have you go through all that again. But I am going to ask you a simple question. You just heard the witness testify that Mrs. McDonald was baking a pie when they left, just before noon. Did you see any evidence of that pie?"

Pastor Martin shook his head. "There was no pie," he said. "In fact, the oven had not been used that day. It was cold, and there were no coals."

"Thank you. No further questions."

"Witness may step down," the judge said.

In his closing argument to the jury, the defense attorney

suggested that the letters B-A-K were not, in themselves, conclusive.

"They could have referred to Mrs. McDonald's intention to bake an apple pie. After all, the letters B-A-K are the first three letters of the word bake. Perhaps it was a warning that the oven needed to be checked, lest there be a fire," he said. "Don't forget, we have a witness who testified that the Bakers left the McDonald Ranch with him on the very day the McDonalds were killed. And, according to Mr. Kelly, the McDonalds were still alive at the time that they left. The burden of proof is on the prosecution. That means that, according to the law, in order to find Harry and Arnold Baker guilty, you are going to have to be convinced, beyond a shadow of a doubt, that they did it. Prosecution has offered no evidence or testimony that would take this case beyond the shadow of a doubt."

During Gleason's closing, he pointed out that Kelly was not a very reliable witness, whereas the two witnesses who had seen the Baker brothers at the ranch on the morning of the murder were known citizens of good character. He also reminded the jury that the witness said that the donation had come directly from a cash box and that Arnold Baker had commented on the money.

"Mr. Pratt said he believed there was at least three hundred dollars left in the box, and maybe a little more. An affidavit from the bartender in Burnt Fork says that the two men spent lavishly while they were in the saloon, and Matt Jensen, acting as a duly sworn deputy, found two hundred sixty-eight dollars on them when he made the arrest."

In addition, the prosecuting attorney pointed out that, according to Pastor Martin, whose testimony was also unimpeachable, there was no evidence of any apple pie having been baked, which cast further doubt on Kelly's story.

"With his own blood, as he lay dying, Scott McDonald scrawled the letters B-A-K. B-A-K for Baker. He hardly had time to actually leave us a note, so he did what he could to see to it that those who murdered him, and his family, would pay for their act. We owe it to this good man to make certain that his heroic action is rewarded by returning a verdict of guilty of murder in the first degree for Harry and Arnold Baker."

Less than one hour after the court had been called to order, the jury returned from their five-minute deliberation.

"Gentleman of the jury, have you selected a foreman and have you reached a verdict?" Judge Norton asked.

"We have, Your Honor. I am the foreman," a tall, gray-haired man said.

"Would you publish the verdict, please?"

"We find the defendants, Harry and Arnold Baker, guilty of murder in the first degree."

There was an outbreak of applause from those in the gallery, but Judge Norton used his gavel to restore order. "I will not have any demonstrations in my court," he said sternly. The judge looked around the court room. "Bailiff, where is the witness Jerome Kelly?"

"He's not present, Your Honor."

"Sheriff Foley?"

"Yes, Your Honor?" the sheriff said, standing.

"I'm putting out a bench warrant on Jerome Kelly for giving false testimony. Please find him and take him into custody."

"Yes, Your Honor."

"Now, Bailiff, if you would, bring the convicted before the bench."

The two men were brought to stand before the judge.

"Harry Baker and Arnold Baker, I have presided over thousands of cases in my twenty-six years on the bench. But never in my career have I encountered anyone with less redemptive tissue than the two of you. Your crime in murdering an entire family, a family that had taken you into their bosom, is particularly heinous.

"You have been tried, and found guilty by a jury of your peers. Therefore, it is my sentence that, one week hence, the sheriff of Sweetwater County will lead the two of you to the gallows at ten of the clock in the morning. Once upon the gallows, ropes will be placed around your necks, all support will be withdrawn from under your feet, and you shall be dropped a distance sufficient to break your necks. And there, Harry Baker and Arnold Baker, you shall continue to hang until it is obvious that all life has left your miserable bodies. May God have mercy on your souls, for I have none."

Chapter Three

One week later

The gallows stood in the middle of Center Street, well constructed but terrible in the gruesomeness of its function. A professionally painted sign was placed on an easel in front of the gallows.

On this gallows
At *ten o'clock* on Thursday morning
Will be hung
The murderers Harry and Arnold Baker.

☛All are invited.

Attendance is Free.

The idea of a double hanging had drawn visitors from miles around, not only because of the morbid curiosity such a spectacle generated, but also because the McDonald family had been very well liked and the murders the two condemned had committed, including even the murder of Scott McDonald's wife and children, were particularly shocking.

The street was full of spectators, and the crowd was growing even larger as they all jostled for position. Matt glanced over toward the tower clock in front of the courthouse to check the time. It was five minutes after ten.

The judge had said they would be hanged at ten o'clock, which meant that the prisoners should have been brought out by now. Some in the crowd were growing impatient, and more than one person wondered aloud what was holding up the proceedings.

Matt began to have the strange feeling that something was wrong, so he slipped away from the crowd and walked around into the alley behind the jail. He was going to look in through the back window, but he didn't have to. The moment he stepped into the alley, he saw the Baker brothers and the man who had given false testimony on their behalf, Jerome Kelly, coming through the back door.

"Hold it!" Matt called out.

"It's Jensen!" Harry Baker shouted, firing his pistol at the same time.

The bullet hit the wall beside Matt, sending little brick chips into his face. Matt returned fire and Harry went down. By now, both Arnold Baker and Kelly were shooting as well, and Matt dived to the ground, then rolled over and shot again. Arnold clutched his chest and went down.

Kelly, now seeing that both Bakers were down, dropped his gun and threw up his hands. At that moment, Sheriff Foley came out of the jail, holding his pistol in one hand, while holding his other hand to a bleeding wound on his head.

"Jensen, are you all right?" the sheriff called.

"Yes, I'm not hit. How about you?"

"They killed my deputy, and I've got a knot on my head where this son of a bitch hit me," Foley said. The sheriff looked at Harry and Arnold Baker, then chuckled. "I wonder if you saved the county the cost of the execution, or if we will have to pay the hangman anyway. Or maybe we can just go ahead and have the hanging, only it'll be Kelly instead of the Baker brothers."

From the Boise, Idaho, *Statesman:*

Deadly Shootout in Wyoming !

MURDERERS KILLED WHILE TRYING TO ESCAPE.

Last month the brothers Harry and Arnold Baker committed one of the most heinous crimes in recent memory when they murdered Scott McDonald, his wife, Lucy, and their two young sons, Toby and Tyler. The crime, which happened in Sweetwater County, Wyoming, raised the ire of all decent citizens who knew Scott McDonald as a man of enterprise, magnanimity, and Christian faith.

The murderers were tracked down and arrested by Matt Jensen, who had himself deputized just for that purpose. Jensen brought the brothers back to Green River City for a quick and fair trial, resulting in a guilty verdict for both parties. They were sentenced to be hanged, but moments before they were to be hanged, Deputy Sheriff Goodwin was killed, and Sheriff Fred Foley knocked unconscious, resulting in the prisoners being broken out of jail. All this was accomplished by Jerome Kelly, a cousin of the Baker brothers. Jerome Kelly was himself wanted for having provided false testimony at the trial of Harold and Arnold Baker.

Had Matt Jensen not discovered the escape in progress, the two brothers would have made good their getaway. In the ensuing shootout, Matt Jensen dispatched both murderers with his deadly accurate shooting. The accomplice, seeing that further resistance was futile, threw down his gun and surrendered. A quick trial found him guilty and he is to be hanged for murdering Deputy Goodwin.

Some readers may recognize the name Matt Jensen, as he has become a genuine hero of the West, a man about whom books and ballads have been written. Those who know him personally have naught but good things to say of him. Despite his many accomplishments, he is modest, a friend of all who are right, and a foe to those who would visit their evil deeds upon innocent people.

The *Boise Statesman,* being published in the territorial capital, was the largest newspaper in Idaho. And though only five thousand copies were printed, it was circulated by railroad and stagecoach throughout the territory so that a significant number of the thirty-two thousand people who lived in Idaho were aware of, and often read, the newspaper.

Sawtooth Mountains, Idaho Territory

Colonel Clay Sherman was a tall man with broad shoulders and narrow hips. He had steel gray eyes, and he wore a neatly trimmed mustache, which now, like his hair, was dusted with gray. He was the commanding officer of the Idaho Auxiliary Peace Officers' Posse. The posse consisted of two officers and thirty-two men, all duly sworn as functioning, though unpaid, deputies to the Idaho Territorial Task Force. Clay Sherman had received his commission from the assistant deputy attorney general of the territory of Idaho, and as such, was duly authorized to deputize those who joined the posse. Sherman and his Auxiliary Peace Officers wore deputies' badges, but because they were not paid by the territorial government, the posse supported itself, and supported itself very well, by acting as a private police force. Most of the posse's income was generated when it was hired by the disgruntled to get justice where they felt justice had been denied.

So far, the posse had managed to avoid any trouble with territorial or federal law agencies, because they managed to find loopholes to allow them to operate. But their operations always walked a very narrow line between legality and illegality, and had either the territorial or federal government taken the trouble to conduct a thorough investigation, it would have discovered that, in fact, the posse often did cross over that line.

There were many citizens, and a few quite a few lawmakers, who felt that the posse was little more than a band of outlaws, hired assassins who hid behind the dubious authority of deputies' badges. It was also pointed out by these detractors that very few of the wanted men they went after were ever brought back alive, including even some who were being pursued for the simple purpose of being served a subpoena to appear in civil court. The *Statesman* and other newspapers had written editorials critical of the Idaho Auxiliary Peace Officers' Posse, pointing out that, despite its name, it had nothing to do with "peace." Some of those newspapers had paid for their critical observations by having their offices vandalized by "irate citizens who supported the posse," or so it was claimed.

At this moment, Sherman and a few members of the posse were engaged in one of the many private police force operations by which it managed to earn its keep. They were operating in the Sawtooth Mountains, and Colonel Sherman stepped up on a rock and looked down toward a little cabin that was nestled against base of the sheer side of Snowy Peak. The posse had trailed Louis Blackburn to this cabin, and now their quarry was trapped. The beauty of it was that Blackburn had no idea he was trapped. He thought he was quite secure in the cabin.

Part of the reason for Louis Blackburn's complacency was due to the fact that he didn't even know he was being trailed. Two weeks earlier, Louis Blackburn had been tried for the murder of James Dixon. At least three witnesses testified that Dixon not only started the fight, he had also drawn first. The jury believed the witnesses, and found Blackburn not guilty by reason of self-defense. The judge released him from custody, and Blackburn went on his way, a free man.

The problem with the court finding was that not everyone agreed with the verdict, and principal among those who disagreed was Augustus Dixon, James Dixon's father. And because the senior Dixon had made a fortune in gold and was now one of wealthiest and most powerful men in Idaho, he was able to use both his money and influence to find an alternate path to justice, or at least the justice he sought.

Dixon managed to convince a cooperative judge to hold a civil trial. It was Augustus Dixon's intention to sue Louis Blackburn for depriving him of his son. No official law agency of the territory of Idaho would serve a subpoena for the civil trial, but then, Dixon didn't want any official law officer involved in the process. Dixon hired Clay Sherman and his Idaho Auxiliary Peace Officers' Posse to run Blackburn down and bring him back for civil trial.

Sherman had eight men with him and as he looked back at them, he saw that everyone had found a place with a good view and a clear line of fire toward the cabin.

"Lieutenant," Sherman said to Poke Terrell, his second in command.

"Yes, Colonel?"

"It is my belief, based upon our conversation with Mr. Dixon, that he doesn't particularly want us to bring Blackburn back alive."

"Yes, sir, that is my belief as well," Poke replied.

"You know what that means then, don't you?"

"Yes, sir," Poke said. "We have to get him to take a shot at us."

"You know what to do," Sherman said.

Poke nodded, then cupped his hand around his mouth. "Blackburn!" he called. "Louis Blackburn! Come out!"

"What?" Blackburn called back, his voice thin and muffled from inside the cabin. "Who's calling me?"

"This is Lieutenant Poke Terrell of the Idaho Auxiliary Peace Officers' Posse. I am ordering you to come out of that cabin with your hands up!"

"What do you mean, come out with my hands up? Why should I do that? What do you want?"

"I have a summons to take you back for the murder of James Dixon!" Terrell shouted loudly.

"You're crazy! I've already been tried, and found innocent."

"You're being tried again."

"My lawyer said I can't be tried again."

"You're lawyer lied. And if you don't come out of your cabin now, I'm going to open fire," Poke called.

"Go away! You ain't got no right to take me back."

"You are going back, whether it's dead or alive," Poke said.

As Sherman and Poke expected, a pistol shot rang out from inside the cabin. The pistol shot wasn't aimed, and was fired more as a warning than any act of hostile intent.

"All right, boys, he shot at us!" Sherman called.

"Beg your pardon, Colonel, but I think he wasn't actual aimin' at us. I think he was just tryin' to scare us off," one of the men said.

"That's where you are wrong, Scraggs," Sherman said. "He clearly shot at us. I could feel the breeze of the bullet as it passed my ear." Smiling, Sherman turned to the rest of his men. "That's all we needed, boys. He shot at us, so now if we kill him, it is self-defense. Open fire," he ordered.

For the next several minutes, the sound of gunfire echoed back from the sheer wall of Snowy Peak as Sherman, Poke, and the other men with them fired shot after shot into the cabin. All the windows were shot out and splinters began flying from the walls of the little clapboard structure. Finally, Sherman ordered a cease-fire.

"Lieutenant Terrell, you and Scraggs go down there to have a look," Sherman ordered.

With a nod of acceptance, Poke and Scraggs left the relative safety of the rocks, then climbed down the hill to approach the cabin. Not one shot was fired from the cabin. Finally, the two men disappeared around behind the cabin, and a moment later, the front door of the cabin opened and Poke stepped outside, then waved his hand.

"He's dead!" Poke called up.

"Dead—dead—dead!" The words echoed back from the cliff wall.

"Gentlemen, we've done a good day's work here today," Sherman said with a satisfied smile on his face.

Boise City

For a time during the gold rush, Boise had prospered and boomed. After the gold rush, Boise began declining in population, and had shrunk to less than one thousand people in 1870. But now, with both the territorial prison and the territorial capital in Boise (some wags suggested that there was very little difference in character between the prisoners and politicians), there had been a rather substantial rebirth and, once again, Boise was a booming community.

Clay Sherman had an office in Boise, boldly placing it right next door to the Territorial Capitol Building. He had no reservations about advertising his location, and a sign, hanging from the front of the office, read:

IDAHO AUXILIARY PEACE OFFICERS' POSSE
Colonel Clay Sherman, Commanding
PRIVATE POLICE SERVICE

At the moment, Sherman was meeting with Poke Terrell, his second in command. Poke had brought him a proposal for a job down on the Snake River in Owyhee County.

"What do you think, Colonel? Should we take the job?" his first lieutenant asked.

"I don't know," Sherman answered. "It's not the kind of thing we normally do."

"No, but he's offerin' fifteen hunnert dollars, and the job don't seem all that hard to do. I just don't think we should walk away from it."

"Who is it that's wantin' to hire us?"

"His name is Marcus Kincaid. He's a rancher down in Owyhee County."

Sherman, who had once been an Arizona Ranger, stroked his jaw for a moment as he contemplated the suggestion his second in command had made.

"If you ask me, I think we should do it," Poke said. "I mean, we don't need ever'one. I could prob'ly take care of it myself."

"All right, I'll tell you what," Sherman said. "How about you go down there and meet with this fella? If it looks like something you can handle, go ahead and do it."

"By myself?"

"Why not? You just said you could probably handle it by yourself."

"Well, yeah, I think I can. But maybe I should take a few of the men with me?"

"No. Because of the type operation it is, I want to keep as much separation as I can between that job and the posse," Sherman said. "In fact, I think you should quit the organization."

"What? No, now wait, I didn't have nothin' like that in mind," Poke said. "I was just suggestin' that it might be a good way to make some money."

Sherman held up his hand to halt the protest. "Don't worry, you won't really be quitting," he said. "We'll just make everyone think you have quit. In fact, we can let it out that I fired you."

"Oh. All right, whatever you say. As long as you ain't kickin' me out, I mean."

"Now why would I want to kick you out, Poke?" Sherman asked. "You are one of the best I've ever ridden with. I told you, you leavin' us would be just for show, just to keep anyone from tracing your operation back to us."

"What if I need help?"

"If after you get down there, you decide that you need help, hire some locals. If the job is really worthwhile, you should be able to afford it."

"Oh, the job will be worthwhile, all right," Poke said. "I don't see how it can miss."

THE MOUNTAIN MAN SERIES BY
WILLIAM W. JOHNSTONE